DARK HEART RISING

DARK HEART RISING

LEE MONROE

h

**Hodder
Children's
Books**

A division of Hachette Children's Books

For Alexandra, Flora and Josh

PROLOGUE

Pressed back against the dark wood panelling, I felt his lips brush my cheek. No longer cold, but warm and full, gently touching my skin. I felt myself breathe out, not wanting to feel anything, but feeling everything all at once, my head resting on his chest. I could hear his heartbeat and mine, loud and fierce . . .

'I never thought I would feel this way about a mortal,' he whispered softly into my hair, and I felt the softness of his mouth as it tenderly kissed my neck. I shivered, hot suddenly, and instinctively my back arched.

'I don't want this,' I managed to say, my voice husky and strained. 'This isn't right.'

But as his arms moved to circle my waist I didn't push him away. Because, despite the words I had just spoken I did want this. I hated myself for wanting it, but it was consuming me. It was all there was. Right then, in that

1

moment, it was all I wanted.

Finally he drew back and took my face in his hands, his eyes glinting in the darkness, the sharp line of his cheekbones cutting a hard but beautiful shape. And his mouth, wide and perfect, moved closer to mine, taking my breath away.

He put one finger on my lips, and with his other hand he stroked my face.

'It's OK,' he said. 'It was a mistake, but I couldn't help myself.'

'I . . .' I struggled with relief, and intense disappointment.

'*Shhh.*' He pressed his finger more firmly against my mouth.

And then he was moving away from me, gently opening the door. He disappeared through it leaving me wide-eyed and disbelieving.

I was left alone, with the sound of my fiercely beating heart.

And the taste of betrayal in my mouth.

CHAPTER ONE

'Have you got everything?' My mother picked up a sweater, folded ready to pack in my suitcase. 'Passport? Underwear?' She refolded the sweater, and a shadow passed across her face. 'You will phone—'

'Mum.' I tried to keep the exasperation out of my voice. 'I'll phone.'

'Good.' She smiled. I could see the brave face she was putting on and my heart skipped at the thought of what I was about to do.

'Grandma Ellen's got the hotel booked in Paris,' she said. 'At least you'll have someone to look after you there.'

'It'll be fun spending time with her for a few days,' I said, smiling. 'I don't think I've really done that since I was little.'

'You need a break,' said Mum. 'After everything that's

happened this year . . .' She paused, watching my smile fade. 'It might help you forget.'

'Yeah . . .' I frowned. 'I don't know if I'll ever forget. It's not that easy.'

'I know,' she said softly, taking my hand. 'Believe me. I know.'

'And I don't know that I *want* to forget.' I felt my good mood finally evaporate.

'You're going to fall in love again,' she said. 'It may not feel like it now. But there are lots of people out there who you can be happy with.'

Mum was saying all the right things. And she was right. But I frowned anyway.

'Luca was special.' I swallowed. 'There won't be anyone else like him. There can't be.'

There was a silence, and I knew she was in agreement. But being a mother, she was supposed to be sensible.

'No. There won't be. That's true. But you're going to find out that being unique is not . . . unique.' She squeezed my hand. 'We all are . . . when you think about it.'

'Do you have a rational answer for everything?' I smiled wryly in spite of myself.

'Yep.' She placed the folded sweater neatly inside my case. 'Now you'd better get downstairs and say goodbye to your dad and Dot.'

I shifted off the bed and stood facing the window, taking in the treetops, the darkening sky and the sliver of moon just appearing.

I'll miss you, I whispered inside my head, my eyes pricking with tears. I promise I'll never forget.

'So,' said Grandma Ellen, adding sugar to her café au lait, 'How's your love life?'

I swallowed a mouthful of piping hot chocolate, feeling heat flood my cheeks. It was partly the boiling milk, partly Grandma's unexpected direct question.

'I don't have one.' I used the standard bullish teenager tone I used with my mother.

She nudged me gently with her elbow. 'I'm not going to go telling your mum, if that's what you're worried about.'

I shrugged, stirring the syrupy foam at the bottom of my cup. 'Really, Granny. I don't have a love life.'

'Hmm.' She drew in a breath and directed her gaze at the pelican crossing opposite our café. 'I'm surprised.'

'Why?'

She turned back to me, smiling. 'Have you looked in the mirror lately, Jane?'

I glanced down at my nondescript faded black T-shirt, lanky legs – encased as ever in boyish jeans – and scruffy baseball boots. Nothing special there.

'You're biased,' I told her smiling. 'And there aren't actually any boys in Bale. Not unless you count Eric and his cousin Zane.' I made a face. 'And they're . . . you know . . . young.'

Grandma looked amused. 'Well, what about college? You're starting soon. You're bound to meet new people. More mature people . . .' She smiled. 'When I was your age I liked the older boys, too. Boys my age seemed so . . . childish somehow.'

I crossed my arms over my chest. 'I'm giving boys a miss this year. I just want to concentrate on studying.'

'Right. Of course.' She raised an eyebrow then, seeing my serious expression, put down her cup. 'Your mother told me, dear – a little bit about that boy you broke up with in the spring.' She put one hand on my arm. 'I guess you're not over it yet.'

I sighed, but relaxed a little. 'I'm getting there,' I said, not sure whether I really was. 'I think I just need a bit more time. Luca . . . well, he's not someone you forget in a hurry.'

I stared into the middle distance. It all seemed such a weird, incredible dream. Last winter a boy I had literally been dreaming about for weeks, walked into my life. Not just any boy. In fact, if truth be told, not a boy. A wolf, who looks like a boy, who kisses like a boy, who loves like a boy. But it was so complicated. Luca lived . . . well, he lived in another world, one like Earth, but purer, more controlled, where all manner of supernatural creatures lived apparently in harmony. Nissilum. But it was a world where I couldn't live. And Luca was bound by the rules there. He wasn't allowed to love me. And it was all because of an angel called Gabriel, who had loved a mortal woman. No ordinary woman either; my mother, Anna. Gabriel was part of the Celestial family, the rulers of Nissilum. As a role model, Gabriel was supposed to be impervious to such weakness. The shame of what happened between him and my mum had been his downfall. Death on Nissilum is not like it is in the mortal world. The people of Nissilum just cease to be. No illness, just fading away until . . . they just disappear.

A chill went through me as I recalled the events of nearly a year before. When Gabriel's son Raphael had come to Earth, masquerading as a mortal boy called Evan, to avenge Gabriel's fate. Evan had drawn me in, fooled me into wanting him, making me confused about my feelings for Luca. But if it hadn't been for Luca, Evan would have killed my entire family. Luca and his sister Dalya had saved us all. Had I been naïve to think then that everything would be OK? That Luca and I could be together? When we had returned to Nissilum, I realised that nothing had changed. If anything Luca's family were more firmly resolved than ever. And Luca had chosen them over me.

Granny's hand stayed where it was, but her fingers gave me a little squeeze, bringing me out of my sad trance. 'You're sensitive. Just like your mother,' she said softly.

I frowned. Not really wanting to be anything like my mother at that particular moment. I loved Mum, of course. But I wasn't her.

'Right then,' Grandma said briskly, getting out her purse. 'Let's try and cheer you up a little.' She tucked a ten euro note underneath her cup and saucer. 'The Pompidou first, I think. Then some shopping down the Ille de la Cite.' She winked at me. 'And I know it's getting chilly, but we can't leave Paris without having one of the glorious ice creams on the Left Bank. Your grandfather asked me to marry him over a blackberry scoop in October 1963.'

I couldn't help smiling. 'That is actually quite romantic.'

'Come on.' Grandma wrapped her scarf round her neck. 'I can't promise romance, but let's go and have some fun.'

* * *

It was evening, and after a heavy day's shopping and sightseeing, we were inside Notre Dame, which was heaving with tourists. Grandma studied the little guide, while I stared at the hordes of German students crowding around the entrance to the chapel.

'I think I might go and light a candle . . .' Grandma said, frowning at the throng in front of us. 'I may be some time.' She gave me a wan smile and set off, waving her bag about imperiously. I grinned as the students parted to let the elegant older lady through. As she reached the entrance she turned to raise an eyebrow at me. 'I'll see you outside,' she mouthed.

In front of the church I settled myself on one side of the steps and, taking out my camera, looked through the photographs I'd taken over the last days. Lots of my grandmother: in a comical French beret, asleep after lunch the day we'd arrived, buying herself a Chanel handbag in the Galleries Lafayette. And there was me, in a café, smiling like the Mona Lisa, one hand tucked under my chin.

'You don't like the church?' A deep voice behind me made me jump.

I turned to see a tall, black-haired boy, dressed beatnik style in a close-fitting reefer jacket and striped T, skinny jeans and skinny legs. *Not fair that boys have thinner legs than girls*, I thought, while trying not to look as though I was looking at all.

The boy was obviously assessing whether I was simple. He bent down, crouching on his long thin legs, and spoke again.

'The church,' he said slowly, annunciating each syllable. 'You're not a believer?'

'I . . . I'm not sure,' I said, equally slowly. His eyes were the darkest brown I'd ever seen. Almost black. 'I think it's a beautiful church. I just needed some air.'

The boy moved seamlessly to sit next to me.

'I am Soren,' he said, holding out a pale hand.

'Jane.' I hesitated before doing the same. His skin felt smooth and marble cold. 'Are you French?' I couldn't quite place his accent.

He smiled, and it transformed his severe features. His teeth were perfect. His eyes deep set but almond shaped.

'I am from Hungary,' he said after a pause, looking intently at me. 'But I am studying here. Art.'

He smiled again and I felt the effect more this time. My insides contracted a little. He was attractive. If I had been interested I would have said stunning.

'And you?'

'Oh, I'm just here for a few days . . . with my

grandmother,' I said, feeling lame. I waited for Soren to decide he'd picked the wrong girl to talk to, but he didn't move – in fact he seemed to be smiling more.

'And you are English,' he said, nodding. 'I thought so. You have that air about you.'

I raised an eyebrow.

'I mean . . . English girls are always the most interesting.' Though his expression was assured I thought I saw his face colouring slightly. 'I am not saying this very well.' He shook his head. 'By interesting I mean—'

'It's OK. I'll take that as a compliment.' I smiled broadly. 'Really. Interesting is good.'

'It is!' He met my smile with real warmth. 'Clever girl for knowing that.'

I overlooked the somewhat patronising comment. 'So, art. That's pretty interesting. Where are you studying?'

'At the Sorbonne,' Soren said simply. 'I am very lucky. I have a great life in Paris. It is a wonderful city.' He studied my face. 'Full of creativity . . . and romance.' He grinned then, almost bashfully. 'But I am sometimes lonely. I have had to work hard at my English, and my French' – he waved a hand theatrically – 'it is getting there.'

'It's very good.' I found myself feeling shy under his gaze. 'I'm sure you've got lots of friends . . .'

Soren shrugged. 'Not so many. I am . . . what you'd

say . . . a "loner".' He smiled wryly. 'I am not good with the small talk.'

Well, that made two of us.

'Oh. Yeah.' I smiled down at my feet. 'Me neither.'

Heels clambering down the steps disturbed us.

'There you are.' Grandma Ellen was a little breathless. She looked curiously at Soren.

'Granny . . . this is Soren,' I said, glancing at him. 'Soren, this is my grandmother.' I saw her face turn thoughtful. 'Did you light a candle?' I asked her.

My grandmother lowered herself to sit on the step next to me. 'I did. For your grandfather.' She turned to look wistfully in front of her. 'He loved it here.'

I reached out and squeezed her arm. Beside me I felt Soren shift awkwardly.

'Well, it was great to meet you, Soren,' I said, turning to him. 'We'd better be going—'

'No need to go now,' Grandma cut in smoothly. 'Not you at any rate.' She beamed at Soren. 'I'm feeling a little tired . . . and could do with some time alone. Why don't the two of you stay here and I'll wander back to the hotel?'

'I'm sure Soren has better things to do,' I said, embarrassed.

Soren didn't hesitate. 'Nothing better, I assure you.'

I didn't look at him but I could feel his eyes on me.

'That's settled then.' My grandmother got to her feet. 'I'll see you in the morning, darling.' She nodded at Soren. 'I'm sure you'll see Jane back to her hotel, won't you, dear?'

'Grandma,' I said, through faintly gritted teeth, 'I can find my own way back to the hotel.'

'Of course.' Soren rose to stand, took Grandma's hand and expertly kissed it. 'It goes without saying.'

Grandma raised an eyebrow, and I could see she was impressed.

'Wonderful,' she murmured, kissing me warmly on the cheek. 'Goodnight, Jane.'

I watched her, sailing down the steps, and smiled in spite of myself. She was matchmaking. She'd totally misconstrued the situation, but her heart was in the right place. A hopeless romantic. She wasn't to know there was no room for Soren – or any other boy – in my heart. There was only one boy taking up that place.

Luca.

CHAPTER TWO

Luca pressed his soft lips to mine, his arms around me. We lay, basking in pure happiness. It was all going to be OK. I didn't know how, but I couldn't imagine that anyone would force us apart. Not now, not after everything.

Luca stroked my cheek. 'What are you thinking about?' he said.

'I'm trying not to think,' I said. 'I just want to savour this. I never want us to move from here.' I looked up at him. 'Can't we just stay here?'

He smiled, kissing my nose. 'I don't think we can. But we'll have many moments like this.'

I drew closer in to him, inhaling his familiar smell.

'Come on.' Luca gently pulled away. 'Once I explain to my parents . . . once they know how much we feel for each other . . . they will love you as much as I do. He stood and pulled me to my feet. 'Come on, let's walk.' He put one arm

around me and we began the journey to his parent's house.

As we approached, a sudden gust of wind seemed to slice through me. I hesitated, not really knowing why.

'Jane,' Luca whispered, his arm tightening around me, 'we have to do this.'

Inside the house was quiet. Eeerily quiet. Luca felt it too. He frowned.

'Luca,' came a strong female voice, 'where have you been?'

Luca glanced at me. 'Did Lowe not tell you?' he asked, cautiously.

'He told me.' Her voice was icy.

'Everything? He told you everything?' Luca sounded wary.

Lowe, I thought. I knew it had been too good to be true. That compliant act.

Luca led me through to the kitchen, where Henora sat at the table, her face a picture of hard disapproval.

'Henora.' Luca stood proudly in front of his mother, one hand gripping mine. 'Don't judge me. I can't pretend to be someone . . . the one you want me to be.' He paused and glanced to me at his side, his grip strengthening further. 'I love Jane. I don't want to be punished for loving someone.' He stopped speaking, a little breathless, and held Henora's gaze.

I wanted more than anything to run then. Just turn and not have to watch him go through this. When I found the courage to look at Henora, I expected anger, disappointment at least, in her expression. But what I saw now was a calm sort of smile and kindness in her eyes. She sighed.

'Luca.' She held out her hand and drew him closer to her. 'I . . . I understand. I even have sympathy, believe it or not. But it's too late.' And then she looked past him to me, standing quietly in the doorway. 'It is all decided now.'

Luca's head jerked. He turned and frowned at me, confused.

'What do you mean,' he said slowly, 'decided?'

Henora sighed again, more deeply. 'Lila . . . she is Hanni's daughter. I have talked of her, remember? From the east?'

Luca shrugged. 'What—?' he began.

'Ulfred and I have been in discussion with Hanni and Elsa,' she went on, determinedly not making eye contact with her son, 'about Lila's future.'

'Her future,' Luca murmured. 'I don't understand.'

'Hanni is bringing Lila to us in a week, Luca.' This time Henora stared hard at him, unblinking. 'To begin preparations for your wedding.'

For a few seconds, a heavy doom-laden silence hung between us all. I could hear Luca breathing deeply in and out in front of me, as though calming himself. After what seemed a lifetime, he spoke.

16

'I will not marry Lila,' he said quietly, but in a voice charged with anger.

'Oh you will.' Henora's tone was imperious and final. 'You will do exactly as you're told.'

Behind Luca, I saw my arm reaching out, my fingertips trying to grasp hold of his shirt, fumbling and missing. I felt a ball of pure frustrated misery coming up from my stomach.

'Luca!' I wailed, but heard no sound coming from my mouth. I felt him slipping away from me, his whole body tense.

And when he turned to me, all I saw was a kind of deadness in his eyes.

'It is decided,' he said bleakly. 'There is nothing I can do.'

I sat upright in bed, my T-shirt sticking to my back. In front of me, I saw a shaft of dull light through the gap in the curtains. I put my hand to my throat, nausea and pain surfacing.

I concentrated on breathing slowly. Trying to calm down. It was a dream. This time it was only a dream. But the memory of that awful moment made my insides curl up.

I got out of bed and walked robotically to the bathroom.

Turning on the shower, I pulled the damp T-shirt over my head and studied my flushed, puffy face in the mirror above the sink, my hair messy and tangled, as though I had been thrashing against my pillow all night.

I stood underneath the nearly scalding water until my fingers puckered and my skin began to sting. Finally I stepped out and dried myself, dressed and teased the tangles out of my hair. Glancing at the clock by my bed, I saw it was early. Eight o'clock. Grandma would still be asleep. Tying my hair in a messy bun, I collapsed back on the unmade bed, focussing on the light hanging from the ceiling.

The phone beside my bed rang out. Frowning, I rolled over and picked up the receiver. I hadn't ordered room service . . .

'Hello?' I said tentatively, my voice hoarse.

'It is Soren.' There was a pause. 'I am sorry it so early to call.'

I sat up. 'What do you want?'

'I would like to take you to breakfast,' he said in his deep, accented voice. 'On your last day . . . I thought this would be nice. To say goodbye.'

'I am spending the day with my grandmother . . . I'm sorry.'

'Oh. Just some breakfast?'

18

He sounded so plaintive. I shut my eyes.

'I don't know . . . my grandmother—'

'Of course, I asked her first,' he said. 'She seemed only too delighted.'

I puffed out my cheeks not sure whether to be annoyed or not.

'OK,' I said at last. 'Breakfast would be nice. But I need to get ready . . .'

'Take your time,' he said. 'I will make my way to your hotel and wait in the lobby.'

I pulled on my tights, a short grey skirt and a long-sleeved T-shirt, and began lacing up my boots, still trying to push away the horrible homesickness I was feeling. Soren was sweet, but I really didn't feel like making conversation with a virtual stranger this morning. I wanted to lie around in my room and stare at the ceiling.

But, eventually, I made my way down to the lobby and found Soren, engrossed in a newspaper, sitting in one of the posh Chesterfield armchairs facing reception.

He lowered his paper at the sound of my heavy boots, regarding me carefully.

'Good morning,' he said. I had forgotten how dark his eyes were. His black hair was pushed off his face, and he wore a checked scarf and a battered leather jacket.

'Morning.' I was relieved to hear my voice back to its

normal pitch. Not exactly full of the joys of spring, but not as depressed as I was feeling inside.

I buttoned up my denim jacket as Soren stood, and I realised that he was much taller than I remembered. He loomed over me.

'Jane.' He smiled. 'A little English rose.'

I half snorted. 'You make me sound like a delicate flower,' I said, looking down at my boots self-consciously. 'Which I'm not.'

Looking up again, I caught the amusement on Soren's face. His mouth twitched before opening into a wide, handsome grin.

'Well I know that now,' he said deferentially, 'if I didn't before.'

'Good.' I lifted my chin. 'Now, where are we going for breakfast?'

'So, Jane.' Soren tore a hunk off his croissant and spread a liberal amount of jam on to it. 'What is waiting for you at home? You are continuing your studies?' He put the croissant into his mouth, chewing while watching me.

'I'm starting college in a few weeks. I am taking A-levels in English Lit, History and Art.' I blew on my hot coffee. 'But other than that, nothing much is waiting for me at home.'

I must have sounded a little too despondent because Soren's eyes narrowed in curiosity. He threw his napkin neatly on his plate.

'Do I detect a sad story?' he said, looking serious. 'A tale of a broken heart?'

He said it without pity, as though he was just a little bit interested, nothing more, and this made me more inclined to answer him truthfully.

'Something like that,' I began. 'But it doesn't matter any more.'

'No?' Soren seemed confused. 'Perhaps you should tell your face this?'

He waited as I stared at him for a second before understanding, and shook my head with a small smile.

'Guess I'm not very good at hiding my feelings,' I said, shrugging. 'Sorry about that.'

'Please. Don't apologise.' Soren leaned back in his seat. 'If there is a subject I know very well, it is love.' His eyes drifted absent-mindedly around him, as though recalling some sweet, sad memory of his own. 'I too, am suffering in this way.'

For some reason, hearing this made me properly relax. Soren was only interested in being my friend. Friends I could deal with. Friends I needed.

I leaned forward, eager to concentrate on someone

else's troubles for a change. 'Who was she?' I said as gently as I could. 'Is she French?'

'*Non.*' A wry smile crossed his face. 'She is from far away. And now she is even further away, metaphorically speaking. She is in love with someone else.'

'Oh.' I struggled for the right words.

'We have known each other since children,' went on Soren. 'I have cared for her for a long time . . . and I thought – I assumed – that we would always be together.' He paused to take in a breath, and for a moment I thought I saw his eyes grow misty, but in a flash he had pulled himself together, adding only, 'I was wrong.'

'I'm sorry,' I said. 'When did this happen?'

'Not long ago. Not long enough,' he said. 'I have been trying to keep myself busy with my studies. I even rented a studio. I hoped to spend all day, every day in there, shutting out the world, shutting her out . . .'

'But you didn't,' I said.

'No.' Soren studied my face, before clearing his throat. 'I was all ready to do that . . . But then I saw you.'

So I'd been wrong about the friends thing. I hid irritation.

'Oh?'

'Yes. You looked so at peace with your own

22

company. So calm. I was drawn to you . . .' He frowned. 'I mean . . . I don't wish to be unflattering . . . but in a platonic way. I felt as though we could be friends.'

I smiled again. 'Well we can be. I need a friend,' I said, firmly. 'I certainly don't need a boyfriend.'

'Because your heart is still with him,' said Soren. 'Even though he betrayed you.'

I jerked slightly, taken aback by the accuracy of this statement.

'How do you know he betrayed me?' I said suspiciously.

Soren's eyes widened. 'Because all lovers betray each other. It is one of the few certainties in life.' He stared hard at me, before dropping his eyes and reaching for his wallet from his coat.

'Enough of this melancholy,' he then said lightly. 'I have taken the liberty of agreeing with your grandmother that we shall spend the day together . . . I would like to show you my studio.'

'I don't know,' I said, worrying that I had hardly spent enough time with Granny as it was.

'Come on.' Soren took my arm and gave it a little shake. 'We both need to have some fun for a change. Forget about the broken hearts.' He smiled impishly at me. 'Agreed?'

I opened my mouth but found no good defence. Luca wasn't coming back to me. I'd lost him for ever. There was nothing either of us could do this time.

I took a deep breath. 'Agreed,' I told Soren, linking my arm through his.

'You see this one?'

Soren pointed to a canvas, an unfinished painting done in oils. I made out wavy hair, and a soft face in profile. Soren moved and stood beside me.

'This one I am having trouble completing,' he said, reaching out and pressing his fingertip into the canvas. Drawing his hand away, I saw a spot of rich blue. He sighed, and picked up a paint-spattered cloth from a nearby table and carefully wiped off the paint. 'I just lose enthusiasm.' He shook his head.

'It's good,' I said, for want of something to say. I had no idea whether it was good or not, it was jagged and messy. Kind of like that guy Jackson Pollock's art, but with people rather than paint splatters. I made a good show of looking with interest at the canvas.

'It's OK,' he said. 'Don't pretend you like it.' He sniffed. 'You are not supposed to like it.'

'Hmm.' I stepped back and my eyes travelled around the room. There were several other canvases the same:

messy and . . . angry.

'Maybe this is therapeutic,' I said awkwardly, 'this kind of art.'

'You think?' Soren's eyes narrowed. 'I am just an angry young man with no talent at all!'

His tone startled me. 'I didn't mean that,' I went on nervously. 'Of course you're talented.' I moved away from him and towards a painting that caught my eye. This one had a pure black background and an imposing woman in a tight red dress. She had long hair pulled back in a single ponytail, draped over her shoulder. I frowned as I moved closer. She was beautiful, a little dangerous-looking. But something about her mouth was familiar. In fact a flutter went through my heart as I studied her face.

'Who is this?' I asked, more sharply than I wanted to. 'This woman?'

Soren didn't answer.

'Soren?' I turned, but he was staring out of the window. A large art deco window which looked down on a quiet Parisian mews. Eventually he looked back at me.

'Just someone I used to know,' he said calmly. 'Nobody important.'

'Oh . . .' I glanced back at the painting. The woman's eyes seemed to be staring right back at me. I shuddered.

'I have always wanted this,' Soren said quietly. 'To

study here, at the Sorbonne. And now that I am here, I realise I am not talented at all. I paint girls I used to know . . .' He chewed his lip. 'All in an effort not to paint the one girl I love.'

Soren seemed to shrink then, become more vulnerable. It was corny but I felt his pain. I too was trying to think of anything, anyone else but the boy I loved. It wasn't working out too well for me either.

'Hey,' I said, giving him the brightest smile I could muster, 'I thought I was the Debbie Downer round here. Weren't you supposed to be cheering me up?'

Though his eyes were still sad, Soren's lips twitched.

'Misery likes company,' he said. 'Isn't that what they say?'

'Soren.' I sighed. 'Let's make a pact. Here and now.'

He raised a dark eyebrow. 'Go on.'

'No more broken hearts.' I gestured at his paintings. 'You've been in a bad place. No wonder your paintings are . . . reflecting that. It will pass. Feelings pass.' I stared hard at him, hoping to convince myself of this as much as him. 'We can move on.'

Soren looked blank; except for the furrowed brow, his eyes were trained, unblinking on me. Then he started to relax and I saw the tension evaporate.

'I'm sorry,' he said at last. 'This is your last day, and I

have acted like the' – he stopped, searching for the rest of the sentence – 'like an asshole.' He smiled. 'Let me take you to my favourite bar . . . It is near here, on the Left Bank. It is charming. Very traditional – no tourists.'

I crossed my arms over my chest. 'And we won't talk about sad stuff?'

'Absolutely not. No sad stuff.' Soren looked me up and down. 'Are you sure you're warm enough in that little jacket?' he said. 'Here, borrow mine.' He unzipped his leather jacket and held it out to me.

'I think I could live in Paris.' I looked around at the cosy interior of the tiny restaurant, hidden down an alley near the left bank. The place was full of old men, huddled over beer and wine, and the walls, painted rich reds and pinks, were covered in old posters of Parisian icons, tube stations – or Metro stations. Jazz played quietly in the background and a white-aproned waitress flitted skilfully between tables, taking orders and carrying tray-loads of food with just one hand. I sighed, properly contented, and wriggled out of my denim jacket.

'You like it?' Soren grinned. 'This is my favourite place. I came across it, quite by accident, when I first arrived. 'It is a little secret. It is the kind of place you can sit for hours on your own with just a glass of wine and some saucisson.'

At the mention of saucisson I realised I was starving again.

'I'll have the lamb cutlets,' I said. 'And a glass of mint tea.'

Soren grimaced. 'I forgot, you English. You can't go anywhere without your tea.' He patted his stomach. 'I will have a beer, I think. I am not hungry.' He smiled apologetically. 'But you eat. Please. It will make me happy.'

'Really?' I frowned.

'You need a good meal. You are thin.' He sat back regarding me as I took a piece of bread.

'I'm not thin,' I said, reaching for the butter. 'But I'm starving.'

Soren beckoned to the waitress and ordered, then turned to the mirror at his side and smoothed his hair back off his face.

He was vain. Not that I blamed him, with a face like that. I waited, amused, until he'd finished his inspection and turned his attention back to me.

'So, Jane. I'm thinking,' he said, clasping his hands together. 'On your last day here in Paris, we must celebrate.' He raised an eyebrow. 'A glass of champagne . . . just one.'

I picked up the wine list. 'Eighteen Euros?' I wedged it back between the breadbasket and the salt mill. 'It's too much.'

'No, no, no.' Soren shook his head in a melodramatic, slow fashion. 'Don't worry about the money. It is my gift to you.'

'Really,' I protested. 'The tea is enough—'

'Ridiculous.' He slapped a palm on the table. 'Just one glass of champagne. Don't you think you deserve a treat, after—'

'Soren,' I warned, 'we said no sad stuff.'

'Exactly.' He smiled triumphantly as the waitress bought over my tea. As she put it down in front of me, Soren waved a hand dismissively at it. 'This. This is sad.'

I flared my nostrils, staring at the tiny pot. 'Well . . . maybe you have a point. OK.' I set my shoulders. 'I'll have a glass of champagne. Thank you.'

'Thank *you*.' He caught the waitress's eye. 'Two glasses of the Dom Perignon,' he said delightedly.

I glanced at the big clock above the doorway to the restaurant. Half past four. I touched my forehead, feeling hot and a little woozy. In front of me, Soren's eyes were sleepy, too. A lock of his black hair fell on to his face and he looked in a dreamlike state. The place had emptied out; deserted tables with napkins and half-finished glasses of red wine left behind. The waitress moved about with her tray, picking up the debris. As she passed our table she gave me a small secretive smile and disappeared back into the kitchen.

That left the two of us to be serenaded by the music – Ella Fitzgerald . . . something like that. For the first time in a long time I stopped thinking about before. About him. I closed my eyes, letting that deep lilting voice wash over me.

'I'm drunk,' I said with my eyes still shut. 'On a glass of champagne.' I tasted something a little bitter in my mouth and decided that alcohol was over-rated. Now I knew how my dad felt when he'd been out for the evening with his drinking buddies.

'See.' Soren's voice cut through my thoughts. 'It makes everything go away, doesn't it?'

My eyes snapped open. 'Why would anyone want that?'

Soren was smiling at me. 'Well, you did,' he said, in a sing-song voice. 'Little Miss No-sad-stuff.'

'I know . . . I know I said that.' I sat forward and put my head in my hands. 'But I didn't exactly mean it.'

'You didn't?' Soren was alert now. He looked like a fox. Angular, keen.

'No. Because it's not real, is it . . . ?' I felt my thoughts blurring. 'It's just a trick.'

Then Soren started saying something. I lifted my eyes and saw his mouth opening and closing, but I couldn't make out any of the words. I put my palms on the table and pushed my chair back – the sound of the chair-legs scraping against the wooden floor was piercing. My head thumped. With an enormous effort, I rose from my seat.

'I'm just going to the ladies' room . . .' I murmured. 'Don't go away . . .'

As if in slow motion I turned, saw the waitress looking bemused, her hands on her hips, and then the floor moved and my feet struggled to follow it.

'Jane?' I heard someone say. 'Jane, are you OK?'

I nodded, and my head seemed to weigh a tonne. It felt horrible. My limbs started to feel disconnected. How could I possibly be so drunk on just one glass of champagne?

And then the lights dimmed. The last thing I saw before darkness fell was long legs in dark jeans standing in front of me. And nothing there when I put my hands out for help.

CHAPTER THREE

The sun was scorching as I ran through the corn field. The heads rasping against my hands, stinging. But a rush of adrenaline kept away any stinging, any pain. I saw it in the distance. Pretty rose bowers framing the gate. I saw people inside. Familiar faces.

As I came closer, I saw long dark hair in a loose braid, and a grey tunic. She was playing ball up against the garden wall, but she heard me breathing and turned as I reached her.

'You?' Her eyes were wide with shock, but a smile caught her mouth.

'Dalya!' I knew I sounded weird. Hysterical, maybe. I was just so happy to see her.

She took a step towards me, her face brightening, her hands outstretched, but as I reached out to take them a shadow fell across her face.

'You shouldn't have come here,' she said sadly. 'There are people—'

'Shhh.' I put my finger to my lips.

Dalya picked up her ball, turning it over in her hands. 'Let's go to the Water Path,' she said. 'It's nice there. Peaceful. Remember?'

'Dalya,' I said quietly, 'it's all right. You don't have to protect me.'

'I'm so sorry,' she said. 'There is nothing I can do.'

I shook my head. 'It will be fine. Luca would never leave me. Not after everything. He wouldn't do that.'

'You don't understand. You mortals never really do.' Dalya sank on to the grass, plucking an ear of corn and stroking the rough spiky hub with her fingertip. 'Luca is promised to her. Once the decision has been made. He will abide by it. He will make the best of it.'

'Oh.' I dropped to my knees, feeling a wave of pain come over me. 'He is so honourable.'

'I wish it wasn't so,' she whispered.

'Dalya!' Henora's voice rang through the hubbub the other side of the garden wall. 'Where are you, child?'

Dalya tossed the corn on the ground and lifted her head. Her eyes, big and dark, searched mine.

'I must say goodbye now.' Her voice caught and I thought I saw the hint of tears in her eyes. She took my hand and gripped *it in her own smooth pale one.*

'Dalya!' This time the voice was male. Dalya and I locked eyes in panic, but it was too late.

Footsteps advanced to where we were sitting. I swallowed. Half of me triumphant, the other half frightened.

Now that I was here. I felt so insignificant.

'Dalya, go back inside. Henora is nagging about you to anyone who'll listen.'

Not looking at me, Dalya got to her feet and walked stiffly back through the garden gate.

Leaving us alone together.

'Why did you come back?' My heart contracted at the dull tone to his voice. He wasn't pleased to see me. He sounded . . . annoyed.

I looked up at him, standing so familiar: willowy, strong, lean. His floppy brown hair cut short, his green eyes a little lifeless.

'I came back for you,' I said. My voice sounded weak and distant. 'I thought—'

'You thought I would change my mind. That I could pretend I don't have to do this.'

Have to do this. A little hope stirred inside me. He doesn't want to, he has to, I thought.

'I don't know. I suppose I didn't think . . .' I stood now, remembering how tall he was. Wanting so badly to press myself

against him, bury my head into his chest and feel his strong hands stroking my back.

For a moment I saw him waiver. I saw a tremble in his cheek and his eyes flickered. His wide soft mouth seemed to be struggling to stay set, stern.

'Luca?' I moved cautiously closer, my heart pounding.

'Dearest, don't disappear. You can't leave me alone with all these strangers.'

The garden gate creaked open and behind Luca I glimpsed a full-skirted kind of cocktail dress, a low bodice, smooth honey skin, and silky blonde hair in a pretty chignon.

Even from this distance I saw her green eyes — green like his.

Luca's own eyes shut, as though he were in pain, then snapped open again quickly. The light had gone out of them again, I noticed.

'I'm coming, Lila,' he told her, turning and smiling. 'This young woman has lost her way.' He kept his head turned. He didn't see the hurt in my face.

Somehow my pride took control of the situation.

'Yes,' I said briskly, 'thank you for your help . . . I'll be on my way.'

I moved quickly, before my brain caught up with what had just happened, before the horrible finality of Luca's behaviour bored a hole into my heart.

'You'll be OK.' Luca's voice betrayed a tiny note of regret, and he had stated a fact rather than asked a question.

'Yes,' I said as brightly as I could, 'of course.'

In front of me stretched the muted yellow of the corn field, and beyond that a patch of tall green trees. I focussed on them, picking up speed bit by bit until I was running, forcing through the heavy corn, ignoring the tears forging uncontrollably down my face.

'Jane!' I felt a rush of breath coming up through my throat and my eyes flashed open. 'Are you all right?' Soren's hand took hold of my wrist. He pulled me up. Confused, I looked around me. His canvasses leaning up against walls, a cold draught coming through the windows. I seemed to be lying on an ancient sofa. A chaise longue. I leaned back on my elbows.

Soren held out a glass of water. 'Drink,' he ordered.

I took the water and swallowed the whole lot in one go. I felt a bit more human at least.

'What day is it?' I asked, taking in Soren's bright almost-black eyes. With a sharp pain I remembered the field, and running, miserably, away from Luca.

Soren sighed. He shrugged off his jacket and tried to put his arm around me.

'You got a little . . . drunk,' he said. 'I apologise. I didn't think a little champagne would have such an effect.' He tucked my hair behind my hair.

'I had a dream,' I said. 'But it didn't feel like a dream. It was so clear. I can remember everything.'

'Mmm.' Soren studied my face. 'A dream.'

'I've had champagne before,' I said. 'I had it last Christmas. It was fine. I was fine. I don't understand.'

Soren chewed his lip and his eyes flickered away from me. All of a sudden his face looked so pale against the black of his hair, his cheekbones more angular.

I felt a cold feeling run through me. I couldn't explain it. I shut my eyes. I had had this feeling before, the last time I was with Evan . . . I had not realised then how dangerous he was until it was nearly too late. Maybe I had trust issues, but Soren was hiding something.

'I have to get back. My grandmother will be so worried.' I looked around, flustered, for my bag.

'I called your hotel,' Soren said calmly. 'I explained you would be a little late back.'

'But I want to go back now,' I said. I wanted to see Granny. She was safety.

'Of course.' Soren stood, running his hands through his hair. 'I will take you back in a taxi.'

'I don't mean to be rude,' I said, more apologetically. 'It was fun. I think.'

At this Soren laughed out loud.

'I like you, Jane,' he said. 'You're funny.'

'Well, I'm glad you think this is amusing, Soren. I am never drinking alcohol again. It's evil.'

And then he sighed again, deeply, and lifted his eyes to the ceiling. I watched him, wondering what was going on.

'OK,' he said, addressing the ceiling light, 'it is time for me to tell you the truth.'

The chill returned. As if on cue, a gust of wind seemed to blow in, through what I saw now was a broken window.

'What?' My voice quavered and I crossed my arms around me, hugging myself.

'I took you back,' he said. 'I took you back to find him . . . I'm sorry.'

'Sorry?' I frowned.

'Come on,' he said, a half-smile on his face. 'You know what I'm talking about.'

'I . . .'

'To Nissilum,' he went on. 'To your beloved Luca.' He paused. 'It didn't go quite as I thought. I guess I underestimated the boy.'

My heart felt like a butterfly in my chest.

'I knew there was something off about you,' I breathed.

'You're telling me you're one of them . . . What do you want from me?' I knew my voice sounded panicky and scared. 'Are you a werewolf?'

Soren said nothing, simply looked at me.

I put my hands to my face. 'I really was there. It wasn't just a horrible dream. It actually happened.' I glared at him. 'How could you play with me like that!'

And in the moment of silence that followed, another tonne of questions rolled through my head.

'Answer me then? Who are you?'

Soren's smile was calm, infuriating me further.

'Stop it!' I said angrily. 'Stop scaring me. I thought you were—'

'You thought what?' Soren's voice was more gentle now. He moved closer to me. 'OK. You need not be frightened. You are not in danger. I came to find you here . . . in Paris, because I thought we could help each other.' He paused before continuing. 'Luca is about to marry the girl I have loved my whole life.'

I sank down on to the chaise longue.

'Lila,' I breathed. 'She's the one?'

He nodded sadly. 'So. You see. This really is not about you. You have no reason to fear me. I am on your side. I thought that together we could reclaim what is meant for us.' He paused. 'I need you. Without your remaining link to Nissilum through Luca, I cannot get back there.'

I looked up at him questioningly.

'I have friends on Nissilum, who told me about you . . . I too can communicate through my dreams.'

'Which friends?' I narrowed my eyes, but he shook his head.

'Just people I am still in contact with. I needed to find the link on Earth to get back to Lila. You are that link.'

'Using me.' I sighed.

'Don't you see? Your link with Luca is still strong,' he said eagerly. 'It means that Luca hasn't let you go yet . . . If he had, I would never have been able to take you back . . . So whatever my motivation, this is a mutually beneficial arrangement.'

My eyes lingered on him for a while. I still had a link with Luca. Luca hadn't forgotten me. It was a glimmer of pathetic hope. I took a deep breath. 'Well it hasn't worked out so well so far, has it? Your clever little plan – it's just made everything worse.'

'There's still time,' Soren said slowly. 'The wedding is not for a while yet.'

'They don't want me there. He doesn't want me there.'

'Who cares?' Soren gave a short bark of a laugh. 'They cannot stop you going . . . any more than they can stop me.' He dropped his head, as though regretting speaking out, but I was still caught up in my own thoughts.

I gazed down at the floor for a few seconds, my mind whirring, then lifted my head to look Soren in the eye.

'You and I against the force of Henora's will . . .' I smiled sadly. 'The force of family unity – I don't see how we can possibly win.'

Soren dropped to his knees in front of me. 'Luca and Lila are not meant to be . . . whatever the highers intend. It will be a lifetime of regret and unhappiness.'

I thought of Gabriel, tortured by his weakness, by his disloyalty to his own kind.

'Maybe not.' I lifted my head. 'Maybe his family duty means more to Luca than me . . . in the end.'

Soren's lips curled in a gesture of disappointment.

'I thought you were stronger than that,' he said wearily. 'I thought you would fight for him. Not just let him destroy his life.'

'Well.' I sniffed, a mass of conflicting feelings tumbling inside me. 'You were wrong about that, I guess.'

There was a silence and Soren got to his feet. I stayed looking down at the floor, unable to meet his eye.

'I won't give up,' he said softly. 'I will leave you to think about it.'

'Wait,' I said. 'All this stuff – studying at the Sorbonne . . . your childhood in Hungary . . . is it all a lie?'

'It's complicated,' said Soren. 'Let's just say it is partly true. I belong to this world as well as to Nissilum.'

I lifted my head then. 'So, you're not a wolf? You're mortal? I don't understand.'

Soren hesitated, putting his long pale hands in his jeans pockets. 'I am whoever I choose to be,' he said. 'I came from there . . . but I am able to pass from this world to Nissilum, as long as I have a link. I can move from place to place.'

'You're an outcast,' I guessed. 'They threw you out of Nissilum.'

He shrugged. 'I suppose I am not quite "loyal" enough. I just couldn't face a world where all my natural desires . . . all my dreams . . . are forbidden to me.'

'So how would it ever work with you and Lila,' I said, 'if you can't live with her?'

'Lila wanted the same as me . . .' he said, 'until family got in the way.'

I frowned, not really understanding what he meant by that. A figure of speech, I guessed.

'Does it really matter what she wanted before?' I asked. 'She wants Luca now.'

42

As I said the words, I felt the injustice of it all. It was cruel. A burst of anger shook me. I clasped my hands together, trying not show it.

'Hmm.' Soren paced the floorboards slowly. 'I underestimated you, I think, also.' He swung back to me. 'Luca is a foolish boy. To give you up. You are strong after all.' He gave a dry laugh, then spoke more gently. 'To let the one you love go.'

My eyes pricked with tears. Right then I didn't feel strong. I wanted to scream at the top of my voice. But I knew there was no point in fighting . . . How could I win over Luca's family, his obligations, his traditions?

I bit my lip, not daring to speak.

'If you change your mind,' said Soren, 'you only have to say my name and I will be with you.'

I stared at him. Part of me wanted to do it. To go along with his plan. The other part felt it was too hopeless. This was beyond my power.

Or was it?

'I had an interesting time,' I said, 'meeting you. But now I just want to forget. I need to forget. Don't you understand?'

Soren looked at the clock above the studio door.

'I'd better get you back to your grandmother,' he said. He picked up his jacket and put it round my shoulders. 'I am glad to have met you too.' He gave me a wan smile. 'I don't feel as alone somehow.'

'No,' I took his hand. 'Me neither.'

CHAPTER FOUR

'How are you feeling about college?' Mum put a chicken in the oven and moved towards the kettle.

'OK.' I shrugged, leaning closer to the radio.

Mum filled the kettle and switched it on. 'Good to see you're feeling better. Must be your grandmother's magic touch.' She smiled, glancing through the doorway then pulling out a chair to sit opposite me.

I could tell she was trying to get me to talk, but I didn't feel like it. I closed my eyes and hummed along to the track playing.

Eventually I opened them again. My mother was staring at me, affectionately. It bugged me for some reason.

'What?' I said, trying to keep the annoyance out of my voice.

'Nothing.' She gave a light little shrug. 'I'm just glad all that stuff is over.' She lowered her voice. 'I hate to say this, because I know how strongly you felt for Luca . . . but it would never have worked. Not in the conventional way.'

'Well, maybe I'm not conventional,' I snapped.

'OK!' Mum held her palms out, defensively. 'No need to bite my head off.'

'Sorry.' I sighed. 'I'm just feeling a bit . . . you know . . .'

'Yes. I do know. But you're on the brink of such an exciting time. You're going to meet so many new people. New boys . . .' She reached out and took hold of my fingertips. 'Boys who live in this world.'

I sniffed. 'Yeah. I know that . . .'

'You're a special girl. You're right. Not conventional in the least. But, believe me, there are plenty of unconventional men out there. Flesh and blood, non shape-shifting, Earthly boys . . . Your father is one of them.'

I laughed. 'Dad?'

'Yeah, your dad.' Mum scratched at the vinyl tablecloth. 'He's uniquely reliable, and patient, and good. He'll never let us down. He would never leave us.' She paused. 'I just know.'

'Even if he found out about you and Gabriel?'

She didn't flinch. 'He just wouldn't understand . . . it would be too much. And none of that matters any more.'

46

'But it means he doesn't properly know you,' I said. I knew I was being unfair to her but it was true.

'Sweetheart. I'll let you into a little secret. Sometimes it's better that your husband doesn't know everything about you. Sometimes, you need to keep some things to yourself. Things that have no bearing on your relationship.'

I wrinkled my nose. 'Sounds like dishonesty to me.'

She got up, properly ruffled now. 'You're young, you're an idealist. And you're a romantic.'

'I'm not!' I was horrified at the idea.

'Yes, you are. And that's wonderful. As long as you're realistic too. There are some things you're better off not knowing about a person, and vice versa.' She picked up the boiled kettle, poured the water into a pan and put it on the hob.

'Maybe you're right.' I switched off the radio. 'I certainly didn't like what I found out about Evan . . . Or Luca. But I still would rather have known than not known.'

Mum came over and put her hands on my shoulders. 'I know,' she said softly. 'And that was awful. Really awful. But Evan was a psychopath and Luca . . . Luca has just proved what I told you.'

'I know. That the laws of Nissilum are beyond mortal understanding.'

Behind me, I knew she was nodding. Her fingers gave me a small squeeze.

'So, you see. Better to stick to mortal boys from now on. Infuriating they might be, but at least they're vaguely . . . human.'

'Can we stop talking about this now?' I said with a heavy sigh.

'Gladly. I want to hear all about Paris,' she said. 'You still haven't told me what you got up to. Your grandmother told me you made a friend.'

'Not really.'

'A nice, responsible art student,' she wittered on. 'If that isn't a contradiction in terms.'

'Ha. Funny.' I fake-smiled at her. 'He was just a boy I bumped into outside the Notre Dame.'

'Well that sounds great,' she said. 'What's he like? Are you two going to stay friends?'

'I doubt it.'

My mother emptied scrubbed potatoes into the pan of bubbling water.

'OK, well. Nice to meet someone interesting, I suppose . . .' She bent to turn the gas down.

'He wasn't that interesting. In fact he was quite annoying . . . in the end.'

She gave me an odd look, which I ignored. I dragged

this month's *Timber World* towards me and pretended to be absorbed in it. Taking the hint, Mum checked the chicken and then the clock.

'Well, dinner will be ready in about an hour. If you're going to be a grouch, you can go to your bedroom and take that magazine you're feigning interest in.'

'Fine.' I stood, leaving the magazine open on the table, and moved into the hall. Instead of climbing the stairs to my room I opened the back door.

'Where's the dog?' I called.

'Oh . . . your father took him in the truck when he went to get Dot.'

Great, just when I needed a dog to walk.

'Oh, Jane,' Mum yelled from the kitchen, 'we got you a present while you were in Paris.'

I stood where I was outside the back door. I felt ungrateful, but I couldn't imagine any present my parents picked out would be that exciting.

My mother appeared next to me. She held out a plastic bag. I took it. Inside was a box.

'Finally,' I said, impressed. 'The last teenager in the world to get a mobile phone.'

'You're the one who refused to get one,' said Mum, smiling. 'I just thought, with you going to college and everything you might change your mind . . .' She nodded at the box. 'Go on. Open it.'

It was actually quite a cool smartphone.

'Thanks, Mum.' Forgetting to be stroppy for a second, I turned it on.

'We fully charged it already,' Mum said, craning over my shoulder to take a look. 'So you can use it straight away.'

'Right, because I have so many friends to call,' I said, wondering for a bizarre moment what Luca would think. He and I had a mutual dislike of mobile phones. I swallowed the sad feeling. Who cared what he thought.

'Thanks, Mum, it's great,' I told her. 'Really, it's kind of you and Dad.'

'You're welcome.' She beamed. 'Oh, look, you have two messages already!'

I stared down at the screen. The first was a welcome message from the network provider. The other was from an actual telephone number. I clicked on it.

LET'S MEET AGAIN. BEFORE IT'S TOO LATE. SX

I clicked out of the message, shocked.

'Who was that?' Mum leaned in closer.

'Just the phone people . . . Welcome messages,' I mumbled, putting the phone in my pocket.

'Right . . . Well, I'll leave you to play with it,' she said, and disappeared inside.

I remained outside the back door for a few minutes, trying and failing to work out how on earth Soren had got my phone number. It was just too weird. I squinted into the late summer sun. On the way home from Paris I'd had time to go over what had happened. As hideous as it was to think of Luca with someone else, I didn't trust Soren, with his nearly-black eyes and his dry, amoral attitude. I'd decided to just forget him. Get on with my life. And here he was reminding me that he wasn't going anywhere.

'Just leave me alone,' I whispered, staring at the trees, longing for another boy.

As if on cue, my phone beeped again. I fished it out of my pocket.

'If I ignore you enough, will you go away?' I muttered, opening a new text message.

HOPE YOU LIKE YOUR PRESENT DARLING, DAD X

I smiled, relieved.

It started to rain, great drops turning torrential. The back door creaked as the wind picked up, and I shivered, turning to go back inside.

CHAPTER FIVE

'It is good to see you so well.' Celeste, great-mother of the Celestial family, stroked Raphael's hair away from his face. 'I must be honest, Raffy, I didn't know whether you would ever get well.'

He smiled, picking up her hand and kissing it. 'I am so ashamed,' he said quietly, 'for everything I did. I lost my mind . . .'

'It's in the past.' She drew away her hand and held her back straight, picking up her porcelain cup and drinking some tea. 'The important thing is that you are better now and ready to start taking your place as part of this family.' Her eyes were grave as she replaced her cup on its delicate saucer. 'You have many responsibilities ahead of you.'

'I know.' Raphael kept his head down as he stirred his tea. 'And I am happy to take them on.'

'Good.' Her face regained its usual radiance.

A serving girl entered the room, carrying fresh coffee.

'Not for me, Rosa,' Celeste told her. 'I must see to Cadmium, he is not well.' As she pushed back her chair, Raphael rose too.

'I will see you at dinner, Raffy,' she said, nodding at Rosa as the maid swept past her. 'I trust you will find a useful way to occupy yourself, Raphael,' she called back over her shoulder.

Rosa followed her and the door shut behind them. Raphael sank back into his chair, his demeanour already altered. He grasped his cup and emptied the contents noisily down his throat.

Then he sat, staring out of the window at the figures working on the gardens in front of him. As he watched, his eyes narrowed and his hands fiddled restlessly with the cup in front of him. One of his headaches was coming; he could already feel the dull throb, so familiar over the past few months. They'd begun when he was first locked away in the palace basements on his return from Earth – the mortal world. Some nights they were so bad he had cried out in pain. The guards, taking it as another sign of his madness, had ignored him. So, Raphael had borne the pain, while slowly a plan hatched inside him.

Soon, Celeste's face had turned from anxious to hopeful as she made her nightly visits. Eventually she had dismissed the guards hovering outside Raphael's room and had sat comfortably talking to her great-son for as long as an hour at a time.

Slowly, surely, Raphael had convinced his great-mother – Queen of the Seraphim – that he was completely cured. A model of rational remorse. He had shed so many tears in front of her – tears that had him wincing in self-loathing as soon as the door had shut behind her. Celeste was now assured of his rehabilitation. She so wanted to believe it, and Raphael had made it so much easier. He had always been her favourite. There was nothing she wanted more than to restore him to his rightful place. The eventual heir to the whole of the Celestial Kingdom.

Raphael rose from the breakfast table and stood looking down on the palace gardens. In the field just beyond the garden wall, a couple caught his eye. The boy was tall and graceful, his brown hair blowing messily in the breeze, the girl handsome, with honey-coloured hair in a neat French plait, dressed in loose trousers and a light T-shirt.

Raphael rubbed his temple. Luca, the one who had saved him from committing a terrible act. He had hated the boy at one time. Or had it been jealousy? For all that Luca and his family symbolised the ethos of Nissilum – the great 'sacrifice' that Raphael despised – he had to admit he almost felt a little sorry for him now. Luca was soon to be married to a girl he barely knew and couldn't possibly love. Not so long ago Luca had nearly followed the same path as Gabriel – falling in love with the mortal girl, Jane. Even Raphael had been swayed by the intensity of their feelings for each other in the end. But of course, it couldn't be allowed. Not if Luca's mother had anything to do with it. Under pressure from Celeste, who had a soft spot for the wolf-boy, Raphael was obliged to host the marriage, though it would sicken him to do it. He looked coldly at the pair as they walked arm in arm through the field. Luca was insufferably good. So ready to be compliant in the suffocating future his family had laid out for him. And now Jane was dismissed. Raphael shook his head. Not so hard-hearted that he couldn't see the injustice in that.

Raphael turned from the window. His headache was getting worse; he screwed up his eyes and put his hands to his head, pushing back his thick blond curls – it would soon be agonising.

Slowly, the boy made his way up the back staircase to his bedroom, and collapsed on to his bed. He just had to wait it out and then start gathering his trusted few, begin preparations for the final act of rebellion.

* * *

'And so Hanni will arrive in the half moon,' Lila said, leading Luca to a public seat nestled against the palace wall. She smiled at him, small pretty dimples appearing in her cheeks. 'Our two families will make a fine union . . . Your mother has been in discussion with my parents for a long time.'

'Yes.' Luca returned her smile, hoping it didn't betray his lack of enthusiasm. 'It will make our families very happy.' He dropped his head and focussed on a blade of grass on the ground in front of them.

'You don't say much.' Lila leaned playfully into him. 'Hanni always tells me to be wary of a man too fond of the sound of his voice, but still . . . I wonder you don't just find me dull.'

Luca lifted his head to look at his fiancée. 'Please don't take my silence as anything sinister, Lila,' he told her. 'Perhaps your mother is a wise woman.'

'She is.' She put her hands in her lap, before turning away a little coyly. 'But some boys might be proud of a girl who chatters. I will make a good hostess.'

Luca struggled with how to respond. He had a sudden, painful longing for the awkward sincerity of the girl he could not think about any more, for the dark-grey eyes he could have looked into for ever.

Eventually he put his hand over Lila's. 'And I like

your chatter,' he said, feeling bad for her. 'And proud to be with you.' He stopped short of saying he was proud to be marrying her. That, he couldn't manufacture. Not yet, maybe not ever.

The two of them fell quiet, Luca reflecting on how seamlessly Lila had taken Jane's place in the eyes of his family – how popular she already was with anyone who met her. No one, not his parents or his siblings, nor any of the Royal family, had spoken of what had happened, or of the girl he brought to the Great Ball – it seemed like a lifetime ago now. It was as though Jane had been erased from everyone's memory.

Not mine, though, Luca thought. *Nobody can make me forget her, even if I never speak of her again.*

'Look.' Lila spoke, sitting up and turning in the direction of the palace garden gate. 'There is your brother.'

Lowe lolloped towards them, that familiar insouciant expression on his face. For a change, Luca was relieved to see him. At least Lowe, with all his insensitivity, would break the intense atmosphere.

'Lila.' Lowe nodded, giving her the full benefit of his superficial charm. 'What a pretty picture you are. Let's hope some of your radiance will infect your husband-to-be.' He smiled maddeningly at his brother.

'What are you you up to, Lowe?' Luca asked, refusing to rise to the bait.

Lowe drew himself up grandly. 'I am on my way to the stables,' he said. 'Raphael and I are going riding today with a few of the palace boys.' He paused, his chest puffing out slightly. 'He particularly asked for me as a companion . . .' Lowe left a deliberate pointed pause.

'Well, go carefully with him,' Luca replied gravely. 'We cannot be sure he isn't still fragile.'

'He is such an old man.' Lowe addressed Lila. 'Be warned, Lila, Luca is against fun on principle. You may have to make your own entertainment once you are married.'

Lila frowned briefly before coming to Luca's defence. 'I admire his reticence,' she said seriously. 'He will make a thoughtful husband. And it is kind of him to be so concerned with Celeste's great-son.'

'Well, then.' Lowe kicked at the ground beneath his feet. 'I will leave the two of you to sit in joyless silence.' As Luca turned to him, he caught the cruel mischief in his brother's eyes. Lowe was clearly enjoying the sacrifice Luca was enduring.

Why has he grown to despise me? he wondered. Lowe's very existence cast doubt on the notion of family love. He was quite sure his brother didn't love or care for him. Not any longer.

Lowe leaned forward to kiss Lila on both cheeks, and gave Luca a curt nod. 'Have fun!'

CHAPTER SIX

'This is a day for you to familiarise yourself with the college campus,' said Mr Farrelly, the college principal. 'And to meet your tutors.' He paused, looking around the hall at the throng of new students. 'I hope you'll take a minute to get to know each other,' he added. 'This is a time not just for learning, but to broaden your social horizons, too.' He smiled at us. 'Now, does anyone have any questions?'

As hands shot up in the air, I took the opportunity to look at my fellow students. It was a while since I'd been in this situation, and I was relieved to find that it was bearable. In fact, it was actually liberating. A chance to reinvent myself. The last time I had sat in a classroom, I had been fourteen and the subject of one girl's constant bullying. Sarah Emmerson had made my life hell every day, all because I didn't look or act like her or her

Barbie clique. In the end my parents had taken me away and home-schooled me. It was early days, but it seemed like here nobody looked at me like I was a freak. Maybe I could now be the confident sociable Jane I had never been before?

An Asian girl called Tammi introduced herself to me. She was studying the sciences. She seemed sweet, though we wouldn't have any classes together. A red-haired bespectacled boy told me his name was Tom. He was studying Art, English and History, like me – though he was taking Maths too. He seemed OK, if a bit nerdy.

Then there were the twins, Ashley and Emma, wearing tiny little dresses and heels – who looked me up and down and, clearly deciding I was absolutely no threat whatsoever, dragged me to the cafeteria to get some hot chocolate before we all went to meet our tutors.

'Everyone calls us A&E,' said, Ashley, giggling. 'You know . . . like Accident and Emergency? Because we're always getting into trouble. And we're pretty clumsy . . .'

I genuinely smiled then. At least they weren't arrogant.

Sitting in the canteen, I listened to A&E's chatter, wondering how long it took them to get dressed and make themselves up every morning. My jeans and V–neck wool sweater seemed woefully understated. Everyone, I realised, was making some kind of fashion statement here. Everyone but me.

'You have such pretty hair,' said Ashley, attempting to draw me into the conversation. 'Do you tong?'

I shook my head, self-conscious, and made a mental note to do a drastic wardrobe makeover. Looking like you'd been to a fashion camp was clearly the way to fit in here.

Finally a bell rang, telling us to make our way to our respective subject classrooms and tutors. Saying goodbye to A&E, I walked with Tom, who talked so quickly that I could hardly keep up with what he was saying. Something about taking his Maths A-level early . . . Every so often he'd glance at me and go a little red, then apologise for talking too much. I wished I was the kind of socially-gifted person who could have made him feel at ease. But years of being a hermit had taken their toll.

Needless to say, Tom and I were both relieved when we arrived in the Art room and scurried off to find empty seats some way from each other.

Flopping down at my desk, I opened my bag and started riffling through it to find a pen and a notebook.

Around me, the chatter of students was a novelty. I hadn't yet decided whether I was enjoying it or not.

I bent over my bag, scrabbling around trying to locate my pen.

The room fell quiet. The teacher had arrived and was clearing his throat.

'Good morning, everyone.' I processed a familiar voice, but was still focussed on the contents of my bag. 'Your assigned tutor has, I'm afraid, been taken seriously ill over the summer holiday and I will now be teaching you over the next college year.'

I finally found my pen and looked up to the front of the class. When my eyes rested on the young man standing addressing the room, my breath froze in my throat.

'My name is Mr Balzac,' he continued. 'But please feel free to call me by my first name. Soren.'

Black eyes found mine and a slow smile crept over his handsome angular face before he turned his attention elsewhere.

'Let's begin by going round the room and introducing ourselves,' he went on. He pointed at Tom, sitting in the far corner. 'Let's start with you . . .'

The Art orientation class lasted a very long forty-five minutes, during which I tried hard to focus on what I was there for and not cast dagger-like looks at Soren Balzac. I had to admit he seemed to know his stuff, he sounded convincing enough, so that part of his story was true. As to the rest of it, I didn't care whether it was true or not. Now that I had got through most of this day and actually not disliked it, I decided I had no choice but to stop moping after the past. I tapped my pen on the desk as Soren wound up his coursework itinerary, every so often nudging studious-looking black-framed glasses further up his nose. My eyes rolled in a bored fashion.

'So,' he concluded, 'does anyone have a question they would like to ask? Has there been any confusion in what I have been telling you this afternoon?' He looked casually around the room. I waited for his gaze to arrive and settle on me, which it did.

'You.' He pointed at me, then bent and pretended to study the list in front of him. 'Jane . . . Jonas? You look a little confused . . . Is there something of concern to you?'

Stupid question, I thought, my eyes narrowing in response. I gave a barely perceptible shake of the head, as though dismissing him.

'Nothing?' His mouth widened into a broad grin. 'I was mistaken then.' His eyes lingered infuriatingly on me before he checked his watch.

'So . . . I look forward to seeing you all again in a few weeks' time,' Soren said to the room. 'Please now make your way back to the school noticeboard, where your next orientation class will be listed.' He removed his glasses, placing them in a case, and started packing books inside a leather bag. The rest of the class trailed out, and I waited until the last student had left the room before I stood, slung my bag over my shoulder and walked slowly to his desk.

'What do you think you're doing?' I hissed as he put on his corduroy jacket. Looking at it, I gave a short derisory laugh. 'Just because you've got the geeky jacket and glasses, Soren, you're not going to fool anyone you're an actual teacher. You're nineteen, for heaven's sake.'

Soren merely looked amused. 'Ah, that,' he said. 'Well, I am actually any age I choose to be . . . Didn't I tell you?'

'No. You didn't tell me.' I sighed. 'But why I am surprised? It's not like you're a human being.'

Soren pouted. 'You're cruel,' he said. 'I can assure you my emotions are very human indeed.'

'Whatever,' I said. 'The point is, I want you to leave me alone.'

'You don't really mean that,' he said. 'I know, it looks strange, but really . . . I don't think you will be happy until you have resolved your situation.' He paused. 'I know I won't. At the very least I want some . . . closure.'

'Does that exist?' I said. ' I mean . . .'

He stared at me for a minute and then his mouth

twitched. 'I like you, Jane,' he said, smiling. 'You're impossible, but you have a little fire inside you.'

I shrugged, though I couldn't help feeling quite pleased by the remark.

'Which is why . . .' he went on, more intently '. . . I know you will regret not doing everything you can to save what you love so much.'

'I'll meet someone else,' I said, with a bravado I didn't feel.

'But don't you see? Luca believes he has an obligation . . . This is not what he wants.' Soren put his hands on my shoulders.

'And what about Lila?' I said. 'She doesn't seem to see it as an obligation.'

Soren bit his lip. 'Maybe not. But at least now I have a chance to win her back.'

I crossed my arms over my chest. 'So you need me more than I need you?'

'We need each other,' he said calmly. 'Without me you can never return to Nissilum.'

He left me to think about that prospect, which was indeed hideous.

I leaned against the desk behind me, defeated. 'Well, you're certainly persistent. I mean how on earth did you find out my new phone number?'

'Oh that sort of stuff is easy,' Soren said dismissively. 'But impressive, I suppose. I thought it would be nice to keep in touch.'

I stopped myself from smiling.

'OK,' I said at last. 'I will come with you once, but that's it. I have no wish to be humiliated like that again. He was so . . . He doesn't want me any more.'

'And how did that make you feel?' said Soren.

'Terrible. It felt like my heart was being ripped out.'

'See . . . you remember that strength of feeling. I know somewhere underneath his sense of responsibility, Luca feels exactly the same.'

'He can't.' I felt my eyes welling up. 'You should have seen his—'

'Jane. Boys do that. They make a decision and it is as though an iron shield comes down between their heart and their head,' said Luca. 'If you were more experienced, you would know this.'

Soren's plan seemed like such a long shot, but it was my only hope. If it didn't work then . . . I couldn't bear to think of it not working.

'I'm about to start college,' I said. 'Luca is getting married in a matter of months. That's all the time we have.'

Soren nodded and picked up his leather bag. 'I

know . . . And don't be afraid. You are doing the right thing.' He suddenly looked more genuine than I'd ever seen him. 'I'll be in touch.'

As the door swung shut behind him I realised how fast my heart was beating.

Was I being incredibly stupid? Would this hurt me more in the end?

I didn't know, but I was sure now that I would only regret it if I didn't try.

CHAPTER SEVEN

Henora held a swatch of grey silk up to Luca's face.

'The colour is good,' she said. 'But you have grown in the past few months I see. You are broader.' She smiled. 'You look like your father.'

Luca, embarrassed by her scrutiny, made a dismissive gesture with his hand. 'I want a plain suit,' he told her. 'Nothing ostentatious.'

She shook her head. 'It is important that you dress in the manner in which you wish to conduct your marriage,' she told him. 'With exuberance.'

Luca sighed, allowing himself to be turned by Henora, who brandished a tape measure. 'Yes,' she went on, 'your back is at least two inches wider than it was.'

She took hold of his sleeve.

'Lila will be back with her family, now,' she mused, bringing her tape measure to Luca's arm. 'I miss her about the place. She is a very mature girl.' She sniffed. 'Dalya could learn a thing or two from her indeed. That young lady is showing signs of rebellion too . . .'

She paused, pointedly.

Luca rolled his eyes above her bent head. 'Dalya is a good girl,' he said loyally.

'Well . . . you would think that,' she said archly. 'Right, I think I have the measure of you now.' A small smile played about her lips.

'Good. Can I go now?' Luca felt ten years old again. 'He disliked being fussed over. It would help if he could muster some enthusiasm for his forthcoming nuptials, but as the wedding date loomed, the reality of his future was weighing heavy on him.

'Luca.' Henora's voice was quiet but authoritative. 'You will not let me down again. I am relying on you . . .' She sighed. 'Lowe and Dalya are relying on you.' Her eyes swept over his face. 'I am proud of you for what you did for Raphael. Truly . . . But that other matter . . . that girl. You have to tell yourself she doesn't exist. Never existed. It can be done. It is down to your will. As a family we have built a reputation on our mental strength. Our ability to resist fickle temptation. It is the true test of character not to indulge selfish desire.' She drew her shoulders back. 'Do you understand me, Luca?'

In that moment Luca came close to hating his mother, but he hid his feelings, and instead nodded, looking away from her immediately.

'Good.' Her demeanour softened. 'And Lila is such an appropriate companion for you.'

Appropriate. Luca realised what a tedious word that was. How joyless and cold.

'Yes, Henora,' he said. 'May I now leave?'

'Of course,' she said, shooing him away. 'Go and find your brother. He needs to be measured too.'

Luca walked out through the gardens, whistling for his horse, Indigo, who cantered happily over to him. Mounting, he set off for the palace, where he was certain he would find his brother.

As he circled the field he deliberately didn't look at the distant patch of trees across the acres of corn. He hadn't been back to the Water Path since that day he had lain with Jane in his arms, both of them convinced that their struggles were over. How happy, how blissfully unaware they had been of what was waiting for them back at his home.

Luca dug his heels into Indigo's flanks, urging her to speed up. He was trapped and there wasn't a thing he could do about it. In time, he would learn to live without her . . . But she would always be there at the back of his mind, just as she had been before he had even met her. He needed to be a man for his mother, he couldn't betray his family.

As he raced towards the Palace's back entrance, he allowed a single tear to roll. He would cry once, and then never again.

When Luca finally found his brother, Lowe was combing Raphael's horse . . . Raphael himself was laughing at something, trying to remove his riding boots. Luca slowed Indigo down to a trot, wishing to observe the two of them for a while before they noticed he was there.

Raphael looked almost back to his old self. His streaky blond curls framing his now handsome, honey-brown face. Luca was glad to see it – despite what the boy had done to Jane and her family. It hadn't been the real Raphael, he had been possessed by something quite evil.

But as Luca watched the boys together he felt uneasy at his brother's recent closeness with Raphael. Lowe was suggestible at the best of times.

'Brother!' Lowe turned to see Luca approaching them. 'Enjoying your last weeks of freedom?'

Luca ignored him, dismounting and nodding at Raphael in greeting.

'Henora is anxious for you to be fitted for your suit,' he told Lowe, a little breathlessly. 'She is in a determined mood today . . . Don't anger her.'

'When do I ever?' Lowe said, accurately enough. 'That's *your* role, Luca . . .' He paused. 'Except now you are putting in such a good show with her. I am impressed. Bravo.'

The dullness in his tone betrayed his contempt for his older brother, and wasn't missed by either Luca or Raphael.

'Hold your tongue, Lowe,' said Raphael, calmly. 'You are a troublemaker.' But his expression was thoughtful. He continued to stare at Lowe as though mulling something over.

'Luca is used to me,' said Lowe, grinning now. 'He knows I am always watching . . . waiting.'

'Perhaps you need to find yourself a girl?' Luca said a little wearily. 'Something to distract you from my business . . .'

'A girl like Lila,' Lowe replied, a dreamy expression now on his face. 'She would do me very nicely. Those smooth alabaster breasts—'

Instinctively Luca's fingers snapped forward to give Lowe's cheek an admonishing pinch. 'Enough,' he said sharply. 'Do not disrespect her.'

'Sweet,' cooed Lowe. 'I should wrestle you for that, but I find your defence of your fiancée heartening. Perhaps now you will see what a plain nobody that mortal girl really is.'

He stared at Luca, daring him to react, but Luca just breathed deeply, two pink spots appearing in his cheeks from the effort of not retaliating to his brother.

'Take Indigo,' he told him, when he felt calm enough to speak. 'I will walk back.'

Lowe rolled his eyes, pushing past Luca and grabbing hold of Indigo's reins. The horse skittered back nervously as he attempted to mount her, and she stared mournfully at Luca.

'Good girl.' Luca stroked her nose then patted her side to see her on her way.

With Lowe gone, Luca turned his attention to Raphael.

'How are you?' he asked awkwardly.

'Never better,' said Raphael, pushing his hair from his face and buttoning his shirt. 'Fully restored to good mental health and ready for duty!' He gave a comedy salute at Luca, who laughed a little nervously, wary of the boy.

Raphael stopped laughing and gave him a long look. 'You are ready to be married then?'

Luca kept his expression calm, answering in a stilted

tone. 'Lila is a worthy bride. I'm lucky she has been chosen for me.'

Raphael chewed his lip, thoughtfully. 'But she is not the one you would have chosen for yourself?'

Luca cleared his throat. 'You more than anyone understand what is expected of us here.'

'Expected, yes . . .' Raphael was about to continue his tack, but appeared to change his mind, straightening his shoulders. 'It is the mark of adulthood. Duty . . . Selflessness.' He smiled a little too brightly at Luca. 'Celeste says it is a privilege and we should all be thankful.'

The boys locked eyes in what seemed to be an understanding.

'She is pretty enough.' Raphael kicked lightly at the ground.

Pretty, yes, thought Luca; *a sweet, harmless, pretty girl.*

'Great beauty is dangerous, Luca,' said Raphael, as though he had read his thoughts. 'Be glad that Lila doesn't stir jealousy in you. You can be safe in the knowledge that she will be devoted.'

The moment was intensely awkward, and heavily tinged with the memory of Jane. Raphael's manner unsettled Luca. He seemed a little emotional. Luca reminded himself that the boy was still recovering from his . . . breakdown. He was anxious to change the subject.

But Raphael pushed further, daringly. 'You believe that the way of your elders is the right way?' He kept his eyes trained on Luca's. 'That all this is for a greater cause.'

Luca was careful not to betray his true feelings. 'I believe that we live here without conflict . . . That breaking the fundamental rules of Nissilum – those laid out by your family – means we abuse that protection.'

'Ah. Protection.' A small tic appeared in Raphael's cheek. 'One thing I learned from the mortal world is that they live without that security . . . In fact, they see the lack of protection as vital to building strength.'

Luca saw clearly the truth in his words, yet the thought of turning his back on all that his parents had given him, albeit in their own austere way, was too much.

'One thing,' Raphael added. 'Mortals live with lack of certainty – except for death. They live with the knowledge that love may not last for ever.'

'No.' Somehow this fortified Luca. Gave value to what he was preparing to do. Jane may love him now . . . if she still did. But he could not be sure that she always would. What then would he do, if he betrayed Henora and Ulfred – and the Royal Seraphim? He would be alone, outcast. His act of rebellion for nothing.

'I feel that there is reward in not giving in to the

sliver of weakness that exists in us all here. The reward is satisfaction in being selfless – the knowledge that you have given to others . . . self-sacrifice,' Luca said, after a pause.

'And life here goes on for ever and ever . . .' Raphael murmured, in a miserable tone. 'That sacrifice never ends.'

Luca frowned.

'Ignore my melancholic ramblings,' Raphael said, recovering himself. 'I am questioning everything. It is no doubt connected to the weight of dubious responsibility I will have soon.'

Luca's head was too full of profound discussion to pick up on the odd meaning in Raphael's words. He planned to walk off the conversation, never to return to it.

'I had better get home,' he said.

'Of course,' said Raphael, turning away. Already Luca was dimissed from his thoughts.

Luca started to walk away but something made him hesitate. He turned back to Raphael, who was staring after him, a strange intense look on his face.

Raphael couldn't see him, Luca realised. He was looking straight through him. As Luca watched, Raphael shut his eyes, wincing as though he was in pain. Even from this distance his face was tense.

CHAPTER EIGHT

'Where are we?' I whispered, struggling to see in the dark. 'It's like the middle of the night.'

'Hmm.' Soren squinted, crouching on his knees, looking over the low stone wall we had appeared in front of. 'My timing was not perfect. It does seem to be late.' He put both hands on the wall and leaned out into the pitch black.

I shivered, pulling my jacket closer around me. 'Is it winter here?'

'No,' he sighed. 'It's late. The temperature drops at night.'

I ignored the patronising tone to his voice. 'Well, what good is it arriving when everyone is asleep?'

'We wait,' he said calmly, 'until the morning.'

'Excuse me, but I have a really nice, warm bed back home,' I grumbled, 'which I could be making good use of right now.'

'Stop whining,' said Soren, but with a half-smile. 'I thought you were the tough mountain girl?'

'Soren,' I said, careful to keep the whinge out of my voice, 'do you have a plan? Somewhere civilised we can go?'

'I am thinking,' he said. 'Please be patient.'

I slumped against the wall, pulling my socks further up my legs. 'Well, let me know when you have thought,' I replied dryly.

Finally Soren dropped down again, rubbing his hands together.

'OK, I have friends here. Of course, it is impossible for me to go back east – where I was born. But I do have some . . . acquaintances here. Fortunately they don't sleep at night . . . In fact, this is when they are most awake.'

I stared at him. 'Please say that again but in a way that makes sense.'

'Well,' he said carefully, 'I don't want you to be alarmed. I am sure you have been told many exaggerated stories about my friends. But they are decent, really . . . And they have always been good to me—'

'Soren,' I cut in, 'please get to the point before I die of cold.'

'The Borgias,' he said. 'Vanya Borgia and her—'

I gaped at him. 'Vanya? You can't be serious? She's a vampire!'

'She would never hurt you. For one thing she would respect any friend of mine. For another, this is Nissilum. There is no danger here.'

'I know what Vanya's capable of!' I hissed, before an uneasy thought occurred to me. 'You haven't been lying to me, have you?'

Soren frowned. Even in the darkness I saw his black eyes flash.

'Of course not,' he said emphatically. 'Honestly, Vanya and Valdar are old friends of mine.'

'Well, they're not my friends,' I said. 'She tried to . . . well, she knows I am mortal.'

'Yes, yes.' Soren waved a hand dismissively. 'She knows who you are. She knows I am bringing you here.'

'Soren,' I said, agitated, 'I don't like the sound of this. Vampires and werewolves don't get on . . . Vanya hates Luca. Will you stop being so flippant!'

'She doesn't hate Luca.' Soren sighed. 'Or you. Vanya was overwhelmed by you when she met you. She has lived here for so long . . . Been abstinent for all that time. It was a temporary lapse.'

I shook my head, recalling the last time I'd seen Vanya.

How she'd very nearly seduced me.

'I don't trust her. And I don't trust you either.' I was beginning to shake now. 'I've changed my mind.' I stared at him, wondering already if it was too late.

'Please,' he said, softly now, 'I understand why you might be afraid. I apologise. I didn't think.' His black eyes looked dewy as he stared imploringly at me. 'The Borgias took care of me one year when I made the journey here for the Great Ball. Years ago. I was alone and nervous and they took me in.'

I said nothing. I thought of Luca and me dancing, the night of the Great Ball; his soft green eyes, the feel of his arms around my waist.

'I think they see me as a little brother of sorts . . .' Soren went on.

'But—'

'But no one will hurt you when I am around. I would not let that happen.'

He gently took hold of my hand. 'I will take you home now. I can see I have not been sensitive.'

Above us the sky was growing lighter. I thought for a moment.

'No.' I sighed. 'I said I would come back with you once. And now I'm here.'

The rustle of an animal nearby made us both tense.

'Come.' Soren took my hand, lacing his fingers through mine. 'Let's go.'

'Please.' Vanya held out a bottle of something dark and dubious-looking. 'More juice.'

Soren and I had arrived at her grand house and been greeted as long-lost friends – as though Soren was part of her family. We were sitting in a dimly lit, stone-walled kitchen at a vast wooden table.

I shook my head, avoiding eye contact. 'Thanks, but I'm fine.'

She smirked at Soren. 'She's no fun. I told you, didn't I?'

Soren half smiled, but his eyes flickered reassuringly towards me. 'Jane is wary of you, Vanya,' he said. 'I must say I don't blame her.'

'Oh, darling.' Vanya pouted. 'Not you too.' She rolled her eyes, putting the bottle noisily on the table in front of him. 'I have so little fun in my life. I at least thought you would join me.'

Soren picked up the bottle and poured himself a drink. 'There,' he said. 'Happy now?'

Vanya settled herself on the trestle bench by the table. 'So,' she said, with a sigh. 'That boy of yours has turned his back on you. I should have warned you about that.'

I shrugged. 'I should have known.'

'These wolves . . .' she said, considering her words. 'They're a stubborn breed.' She patted me on the shoulder and her hand felt cold through my clothes. I edged subtly away from her.

Soren cleared his throat. 'Jane needs assurance from you that she is not in danger,' he prompted.

Vanya sighed, pressing her palms together. 'My weakness is my strength,' she murmured. 'But, of course, Soren. Jane is safe.'

She smiled broadly at me. 'I pity you, dear. Luca has embroiled you in all sorts of strange goings on . . . and now he has deserted you.'

I kept my expression steady, but her words brought back a painful reminder.

'But together we can see if something can be done,' she went on thoughtfully. 'For both of you.'

Soren dropped his head, drawing his beaker towards him.

'Soren has been banished from this place,' she told me. 'He has to sneak about from this world and yours. But here, with Valdar and myself, he will always be welcome.' Her hand stole out and took hold of Soren's. 'As will his friends.'

I smiled tightly. Something didn't feel quite right, but then I was tired. Vanya seemed harmless enough tonight, but I was beginning to feel hopeless about Soren's plan. I didn't want Luca through subterfuge. I wanted him to be with me because he wanted to be. As horrible as it was to think of losing him for good, I wasn't sure I had it in me to steal him away from Lila.

'Well, I do have some news.' Vanya spoke. 'That fiancée of Luca's has gone back to her family. She will return in a few weeks for the wedding.'

Soren looked hopeful. 'She is East?'

'Now, darling,' Vanya purred, 'don't go getting any ideas about going after her. You'll only make her more determined to marry him. I hear she is besotted . . .'

I looked sympathetically at Soren, but he seemed to be taking that bit of news quite stoically. His eyes slid over to Vanya and locked with hers. The look that passed between them seemed loaded. But within seconds he turned his attention to me.

'Lila is a complex girl,' he told me. 'And a slave to her family's code of honour. It doesn't surprise me that she has convinced herself that she is in love with Luca.'

Why wouldn't she be? I thought to myself. Luca was everything I wanted. Why wouldn't Lila feel the same?

Mindful of hurting Soren's feelings, I gave

him a weak smile.

'Yeah,' I said lamely, feeling more despondent than ever.

Vanya cleared her throat.

'Now listen. It may well be that the girl is attracted to Luca. But that doesn't matter. Attraction can be fleeting . . .' She stroked her chin. 'It is very possible that she will transfer her attentions back to her childhood sweetheart. She just needs the right incentive.'

'Such as?' Soren said archly.

Vanya ignored his tone. 'Darling, surely you know the answer to that.'

I looked at them. There seemed to be a subtext here that I wasn't getting.

'I suggest we form a plan of our own,' Vanya went on thoughtfully. 'We need to be clever.'

Soren smiled sadly at me. 'Don't worry,' he said, touching my fingertips with his. 'It will be OK.'

His black eyes drew me in and the curve of his mouth sent a ripple of something through me. I kept my hand where it was, though I looked away from him, uncomfortably aware that his eyes were still on me.

'You have heard that the boy is back?' Vanya directed her words at Soren, though glanced quickly at me.

'Raphael?' Soren nodded. 'I heard, yes.' Was it my

imagination or was he carefully not looking at me. 'Ready to take on the mantle of king one day.'

Vanya's nostrils flared. 'We'll see. Personally I have long felt that kid was odd. Ever since he was a child.' She pulled her glossy black hair into a loose bun at her neck. 'He killed a fox once, all because it broke into the palace grounds?'

Soren shuddered. 'I remember you telling me. Celeste hushed it all up, blamed it on a servant.'

'But I saw,' said Vanya. 'I saw him do it. It was the early hours of the morning, not yet light. He was so intent. His expression . . .' She quivered theatrically. 'Pure ice.'

'People kill foxes all the time on Earth,' I said, frowning. 'It's actually a sport.'

Soren and Vanya turned, eyebrows raised.

'You mortals are a violent lot,' Soren said, with a hint of teasing. 'Indeed, it should be us that is afraid of you, little Miss Innocent.'

'Well I don't hunt foxes . . .' I protested. 'And I admit, it's barbaric.'

Vanya shook her head. 'The point is, Raphael is a bad seed. I would admire him if I weren't rather fond of his great-mother.' She sniffed. 'His mother is useless, of course.'

'Dorcas?' I was interested. 'Where is she?'

'Away with the fairies . . . literally.' Vanya's tone was dry. 'She has begun an odd sort of relationship with a gathering of beings in the Old Forest. Nobody talks about it because it is frankly embarrassing, but that's where she spends her time. Half mad with grief over Gabriel's death, or something like that.'

'So Raphael is more or less an orphan?' I said. 'Kind of alone in the world.' I must have looked pitying because I caught her scornful expression.

'Alone!' Vanya laughed. 'He is surrounded by love and devotion at the palace. Celeste dotes on him. Utterly blind to his true nature.' Her eyes widened at me. 'And I don't know why you're defending him. That boy tried to kill you, didn't he?'

'Yes. I know,' I said firmly, remembering with a shudder. 'And I'll never forget it. But I guess he went a bit mad. You'd have to be, to do something like he did.'

'You can say that again,' Vanya shrieked. 'Stark raving mad!'

'Vanya,' Soren said warningly, 'we're veering rather off topic here.'

'Yes, yes.' Vanya poured herself some more juice. She watched us for a moment before gracefully getting up from the table. 'I must go to my husband now,' she told us. 'Soren, you and Jane are welcome to stay here . . .

Though Valdar and I will spend much of tomorrow in our chamber.' She lit a candle, placed it in an elaborate silver candle-holder and swept out of the room.

'So, now you know. Vanya is not a threat.' Soren said softly, edging closer to me. 'Do you feel better?'

I shook my head. 'Not better. I'm not sure this is going to work, Soren. I—'

'*Shhh.*' He placed a finger on my lips. 'You're tired. I'll escort you home. Once you have slept properly, perhaps we can talk further.'

I nodded, wearily.

'This is your last chance, Jane,' Soren told me as he chivalrously helped me on with my jacket. 'Think carefully before you throw it away.'

CHAPTER NINE

Soren held my sketch up to get a closer look. 'Not bad,' he said. 'But watch that your lines are not too heavy . . .' He handed it back to me and moved on to the desk in front of me. I couldn't help notice the slink of his hips as he walked. There was nothing I could do about my Art teacher but put up with his constant criticism of my work, but did he have to be so good at acting?

'Now.' Soren was back at the front of the class. 'Time is nearly running out for today. There is just time to remind all of you of your individual assignments for this term. This is a chance for you to discover your natural mediums.' His eyes swept the room, alighting briefly on me, just as the bell rang.

'Thank you for your hard work,' he said solemnly. 'Ms Jonas, could you stay behind, please?'

I sat putting my pencils back in my bag, pausing to

check my phone. A message from my mother.

LATE HOME TONIGHT AT DOT'S PARENTS' EVENING.

FOOD IN THE FRIDGE. MUM.

Snapping the phone shut, I picked up my bag and slung it over my shoulder, making my way slowly to Soren.

'Do you have to be so critical?' I said, crossing my arms over my chest. 'It's not good for my confidence.'

He flashed a handsome smile. 'I'm sorry, Ms Jonas, I was trying to avoid preferential treatment. I wouldn't want to embarrass you.'

I shrugged, though for some reason I could feel myself getting hot in the face. 'There's preferential treatment and there's picking on a person,' I said sniffily.

'Oh, I'm sorry.' Soren shoved a notebook into his bag and took off his glasses. 'Perhaps I am overdoing it.'

'Do you even need glasses?' I asked, as he put them in an ancient-looking leather case.

'Nope.' Soren grinned. 'But I look good in them, yes?'

I rolled my eyes, colour creeping back into my cheeks.

'So.' He put on his jacket, also ancient leather. 'Now, you've done the hard part. Are you ready?'

'I don't know,' I sighed. 'It all seems too much. I mean,

90

I don't think I'm up to taking on the mighty Hunters. Henora is one scary lady.'

'A puppy.' Soren slung his bag over his shoulder. 'Vanya could eat her up for breakfast.'

'I'm sure,' I murmured. 'But I'm not Vanya. It's me who needs to convince Luca. And if he needs convincing then I don't think it's going to work.'

'Where's your fighting spirit?' Soren eyed me sternly. 'Think of what you have been through already. You simply need to hold your nerve.'

'Game playing.' I shook my head. 'I'm not into that.'

'Nonsense. Everyone plays a little game . . .' He hesitated. 'What's courtship if isn't a carefully balanced game of push and pull?'

'I . . .' I thought about it. 'I suppose so. But it's horrible.'

'Exciting, though.' Soren's eyes flashed darkly. 'Life is a dreary continuum, made bearable by those moments of excitement. It's called feeling alive.' He studied me. 'And for you mortals, that life is so short . . . You owe it to yourselves to feel alive . . . at the very least.'

I laughed. 'That's one spin on it, I suppose. But what about safety, stability and all that?'

'Pah. That is for when you are old.' He grinned. 'Youth should be full of adventure and experience.'

I thought about the months, years stretched ahead of me. I couldn't imagine meeting another Luca. And I wanted that feeling back. The feeling I had when he put his arms around me and I felt his breathing as he pressed his face against mine. The tiny sparks that flew around inside me when he kissed me.

I stared at Soren. 'You're right,' I said. 'I wish I didn't have to do this . . . It's all so complicated. But I don't want any regrets.'

'That's my girl.' Soren held out his arm and, without thinking about it, I let him pull me towards him.

'I have to tell you, Jane,' he said, leading me through the Art room door. 'I have had such a heavy heart since Lila has been promised to Luca, and have been so intent on getting her back' – he paused, as though wondering whether to go on or not – 'my intention was to use you. Convince you to help me, with no real thought of helping you in return. But meeting you . . . getting to know you, I find I care very much that you get what you want. It is no longer just about me now . . . It is about the two of us.'

He didn't look at me and, though I had been on the verge of outrage, his honesty knocked the anger out of me.

'Thanks for telling the truth,' I told him.

Soren turned to me then, his black eyes sweeping my face. I couldn't read his expression properly, but he looked sad.

It was dark outside college. Soren got out his car keys.

'Let me drive you home,' he said, pointing his keys at a beaten-up-looking vehicle in the car park.

'I've got my bike,' I said, remembering I had no helmet today. I'd been in such a rush to get to college that morning, I'd left it hanging on its hook in the hall at home.

'No helmet.' He raised an eyebrow. 'And so too dangerous.'

'I'll call my dad,' I said, flustered. 'It's fine.'

'Jane.' Soren's tone was exasperated. 'Stop being so . . . proud.'

I stood, tensely for a few seconds.

'OK, then.' But just to the mountain road.' I thought of bringing yet another strange boy back home to meet my parents.

'Fine.' He nodded. 'Get in.'

As he drove through the dark, Soren stared straight ahead of him, while I concentrated on not remembering another car, another boy. A boy who'd wanted to kill me.

'It must have been frightening for you,' Soren said after a while.

'What?' I turned to him. It was as though he'd been reading my mind.

'Raphael.' He was still looking straight ahead.

I tucked my hands between my knees. 'I don't really want to talk about it.'

'OK.' He returned to looking out at the road.

'I mean . . . It just reminds me of that time . . .' I shut my eyes. 'I thought it was all over. I thought everything was going to be OK.'

'It will be.'

'How do you know that?' I looked defiantly at the side of his head. 'Everything has gone wrong.'

'I just have a feeling.' With a swift movement his hand closed over mine. 'And I am here to help you.'

I pushed his hand away. 'Not you too,' I said, contemptuously. 'All these boys tripping over themselves to help me.'

Soren laughed then, tilting his head back. I saw the flash of his perfect teeth, his perfect cheekbones.

'I can see what it looks like,' he said, smiling. 'But I really am here to help you.' He tapped the steering wheel. 'And you will help me.'

This did make us more even, I had to admit. I sighed heavily.

'It's just up here,' I said, as we came up to the bottom

of the hill. Soren pulled up against the verge and stopped the engine.

'We don't have too much time,' he said gently. 'If you want a future with Luca, we have to go back . . .'

'I know.' I clasped my hands together. 'When?'

'It's the weekend tomorrow . . .' He studied my face. 'You need to tell your parents something . . . anything.'

'I can't.' I shook my head. 'It's impossible, Soren . . . What am I going to say?'

Soren shrugged. 'A college field trip . . . I don't know.'

I opened the car door, hesitating.

'Jane . . .' Soren's voice was serious now. 'This is our chance . . . It could be our last chance.'

'I know.' I hugged my bag to me, my hand hovering on the door-handle. 'I'll be here.'

CHAPTER TEN

'Luca is riding with us tomorrow.' Lowe eyed Raphael. 'He is keen to make amends with you.'

'Is he?' Raphael's expression was impassive.

'You don't seem enthusiastic.' Lowe slumped against the stable door.

Raphael plucked a blade of grass and ran his finger down the stem.

'Clearly it is not ever going to be a straightforward relationship.' He dropped the grass on to the ground. 'But he'll be a strong and reliable influence here one day.'

'Hmm.' Lowe narrowed his eyes. 'Apparently he is.'

'It makes my great-mother happy to see us at peace with one another. If I am to ascend to the throne I need people like Luca around me. Supporting me.'

'That's a nice speech.'

'It is, isn't it?'

'But you don't want strong and reliable people in your life . . .' Lowe stared hard at him. 'Isn't that the truth?'

'Not strictly.' Raphael got to his feet. 'I certainly need strength. And reliability, come to that.'

'I don't understand. What else would you require?'

'I require some backbone. Bravery.'

'Yes . . .' Lowe said nervously. 'Raphael . . . are you completely cured?'

'Indeed I am.' Raphael began pacing, lightly kicking the brick of the stable wall. 'But not exactly as I was before.'

'Meaning . . . ?'

Raphael seemed to be considering for a moment, pushing thoughts around his head. Eventually he turned to Lowe.

'Do you . . . do you never resent being told what to do all the time?' he asked. 'Your destiny is boringly pre-determined by people who don't really know you. And your innate power is tightly controlled. It's not exactly natural, is it?'

Lowe frowned. 'It is the best way.'

'For whom?'

'Well . . . for us all. We just follow tradition and we will be safe.'

Raphael laughed then. 'Was I safe?'

Lowe looked startled. 'I . . . I don't know—'

'I mean. I wasn't safe. I was dangerous. To my family . . . to myself.' He gave a short laugh. 'To mortals.'

'Yes, but—'

'So none of us is ever safe, Lowe. Nobody can prevent "madness".'

The way he pronounced the word 'madness' caused Lowe to step closer, intrigued.

'But you are better now. The madness is gone.'

'It wasn't madness!' Raphael almost spat the words out. 'That is simply a convenient term for Celeste – and your parents – and every other automaton here to use. I simply had other ideas, that's all.'

He held the boy's gaze.

Lowe tried to look away but found himself transfixed. 'They are not cowards,' he managed to say. 'They want the best for us all.'

'They have built this world on a false notion. The notion that a life without risk is a better life. A safer life. When all it is is a life suppressed.'

'Maybe it is. But people are happier here.'

'My father wasn't.'

'Wait a moment!' Lowe said angrily. 'You were angry about your father. You tried to kill that mortal girl's family.'

'I know.' Raphael dropped his eyes to the ground. 'I was wrong. I was very angry. Angry that he had gone. I needed to blame someone. Jane's mother seemed to be the one . . . that one I could pin all my anger on. But really . . . he is gone because of this world, all its suffocating expectations. Its refusal to allow any human weakness.'

'But we are not human,' Lowe said proudly. 'We are better than that.'

'Are you sure?' Raphael kicked a stone at his feet. 'I don't know that we are. We just *think* we are superior.'

Lowe shook his head. 'My mother says that sacrifice is the ultimate challenge.'

'What does that mean?'

'That by giving up indulgent pleasure we are made stronger.'

'Or perhaps,' Raphael replied, putting his hands in his pockets. 'She is just afraid of feeling.'

The sound of horses' hooves made the boys turn to see a black stallion cantering towards them.

'Perhaps you should talk to my brother about sacrifice,' Lowe said, recognising Luca astride the horse. 'The two of you can compare notes.'

Raphael ignored him, straightening up and fixing a welcoming smile on his face. He held his hand up in greeting.

Luca drew in his reins and brought the horse to a halt. Dismounting, he nodded at his brother.

'I didn't expect you until tomorrow,' said Raphael, running a hand through his blond curls.

'Henora is driving me to distraction,' replied Luca, catching his breath. 'I had to get out.'

Raphael cast a quick pointed glance at Lowe, before patting Luca on the shoulder.

'Your choice,' he said, lightly. 'You are not bound to this marriage . . . not yet, anyway.'

A flicker of annoyance passed over Luca's face.

'We are all bound to duty,' he said impassively. 'I don't want to have another discussion on the subject.'

Raphael shrugged. 'Fair enough. But you brought it up.'

Luca attempted a smile. 'I was struggling with my mother's determination . . . not the object of her determination.'

'I see. Well, good.' Raphael stretched and yawned. 'And how is Lila?'

'Good, as far as I know.' Luca avoided eye contact. 'I have not seen her for a while.'

'Lila is wonderful,' put in Lowe. 'She will make a good wife.'

'She will.' Luca looked about him, taking hold of his horse's rein. 'Are we riding today?'

'My horse is tired,' said Raphael. 'Lowe and I went for a long ride this morning – down to the Water Path. I had forgotten how peaceful it was there. I must spend more time by the river.'

Luca said nothing, but stroked the stallion's nose.

'The Water Path is my brother's favourite place,' said Lowe. 'It is where he does all his . . . thinking. He thinks it is his place . . . isn't that right?'

Luca looked sharply at him. 'Of course not, don't be ridiculous.'

'Well . . . anyway. It makes you think . . . or makes you forget,' said Raphael. 'A place to escape.'

There was a short silence. Lowe looked from Raphael to his brother, a glint of mischief in his eyes.

Putting one leg over his horse, Luca looked weary, exasperated. He nodded curtly at both boys before turning the mare round.

'Try and be happy,' Lowe called after him as he cantered away. 'No one wants a misery for a husband.'

The horse and rider sped up. As Lowe and Raphael watched, Luca thundered across the field, his back hunched, as though he couldn't get away fast enough.

CHAPTER ELEVEN

'You want more?' Mum hovered over me with a dish of apple crumble.

'No thanks, I'm full.' I pushed my bowl away from me, wondering how to tell my parents that I was disappearing off for a 'field trip' this weekend. Apart from Paris with Gran, I hadn't been anywhere by myself in years. Not with friends anyway. My mother was bound to smell a rat. And she'd want to know every detail.

'Er . . . Mum, I forgot to tell you. Completely forgot. I'm going on a college trip this weekend.'

Mum passed Dad the jug of custard.

'This weekend? Where? Why didn't you tell us before?' Her look was suspicious.

'I'm sorry. It just went right out of my mind. It's only till Sunday afternoon. To London.'

'Well, where are you staying? Who's taking you?'

She clasped her hands together anxiously.

'Mr Balzac – the Art teacher. He's taking us . . . to the Tate Modern, and the National Gallery . . . There's a Rothko exhibition on at the Tate. And we're seeing the old masters at the National.' I relaxed a little. Not bad, since it came off the top of my head.

'Right.' She glanced at my father, who was chewing on a mouthful of crumble. 'What do you think, Jack?'

He finished chewing and raised an eyebrow. 'I think it sounds fun,' he said, 'don't you?'

'Well. Yes . . . of course, it's just—'

'Anna. Jane will be fine. This teacher . . . Mr Balzac. He'll be supervising them. It'll be fine.'

'Well. OK.' Mum relaxed a little. 'I'm glad I got you that phone now, though.'

'Is your boyfriend going to be there?' Dot licked her spoon.

'What are you talking about?' I said wearily.

'You must have a boyfriend, right? At college?'

'Must I?' I glared at her.

'You don't?'

'No. I don't!' I got up from the table. 'And I'm not going to have a boyfriend for a long time. But when I do . . . you'll be the first to know about it.' I gave her a sugary smile.

She stuck her tongue out and dropped her spoon in her bowl.

Dad hid a smile, while Mum shook her head and started gathering up the bowls.

'What time are you leaving in the morning?' she asked. 'Dad can give you a lift.'

'Early . . . about eight.' I turned to Dad. 'But it's OK. Mr Balzac is picking me up at the bottom of the track.'

Mum flapped out a drying-up cloth. 'Well one of us will walk down with you. I want to make sure this Mr Balzac actually exists.'

'Mum,' I laughed, 'why would I lie?'

She narrowed her eyes. 'Why indeed?'

It was my turn to shake my head. 'It's a History of Art field trip—'

'Of course it is.' Dad whipped the cloth from my mother and pushed her towards the doorway. 'You and your sister can do the dishes while I pour your mother a nice calming glass of wine.'

'Jack . . . I'm perfectly calm,' said Mum. 'But I'll take the glass of wine. You' – she pointed at me – 'make sure you get enough sleep before tomorrow.'

'I will,' I said, knowing I would need more than a good night's sleep to get me through the next couple of days.

* * *

'It's freezing,' I said, walking up to Soren. 'Where's your car?'

'I hate to break it to you, but we can't actually get to Nissilum by car,' he said, zipping up his leather jacket.

'I know that,' I said annoyed. 'It's just that it's hardly even light yet. We have to go, now. My mother wanted to walk me down here . . . She doesn't believe I'm meeting my teacher.'

'Intelligent woman.' Soren put both hands on my arms. Strangely, I felt a few degrees warmer.

'Yeah, and she hasn't forgotten what happened six months ago,' I told him, 'with Luca. She's terrified I'll get myself caught up in the whole thing again.'

'Ah.' Soren pulled a face. 'Well, let's hope all ends well, then.'

I could hardly believe it would end well. I blinked at Soren, diverting my inevitable train of thought.

'Be strong. I will protect you,' Soren told me softly. He held out his arms.

I moved towards him, smelling the leather from his coat. He held on to me, firmly, and I willed myself not to compare his touch to Luca's. I emptied my mind of everything but the thought of Nissilum.

As a cuckoo called its early morning greeting, Soren pulled me closer to him and I let myself drift away.

Daylight hit me as I opened my eyes. I was lying on a bed, on the softest velvet bedspread, facing a large sash window, framed by dark brocade curtains. The floor was polished wood. On the wall either side of the window were two ancient-looking paintings: portraits of a man and a woman, both of whom looked familiar.

I turned over to stare up at the ceiling, remembering the sound of water, which had always been the first sound I heard in this place.

The door to the room opened and I jerked to face it.

'Good morning, my dear!' Vanya stood holding a cup of something steaming. 'I have brought you some of my special birch tea.'

She ignored my dazed expression and placed the cup on a small wooden table at the side of the bed.

'It's not poisonous, if that's what you're worried about,' she told me, and I could see she looked mildly offended.

'No . . . I'm just a bit sleepy is all.' I sat up and yawned, realising I was, actually, still sleepy.

Vanya pushed the curtains back and tied them.

'I hope you'll be comfortable with us. Feel free to come and go whenever you like.' She cocked her head and a slow, vaguely sinister smile crept across her face. 'Of course, Valdar and I are not out and about during the daytime so much . . .'

'Vanya,' I said, hugging my knees, 'what am I doing here?'

'Oh now, dear, don't be anxious,' she cooed. 'I'd forgotten how mortal women make themselves . . . such victims.'

'Harsh,' I said, raising an eyebrow.

'I tell it as I see it.' She perched on the side of the bed. 'Don't be so sensitive.'

'So, what would you do?'

Vanya drew a swathe of black hair away from her face.

'I would not let another woman have my man,' she said imperiously. 'No way.'

'At any cost?' I asked her, plucking at the bedspread.

There was a short pause, then Vanya sighed lavishly.

'Believe it or not, child, I am a romantic. A passionate woman. If anybody tried to take Valdar from me . . . well . . . let's just say there would be bloodshed. I believe you should fight for what you want. To the death.'

I started. 'Well, I'm not planning on killing anybody, Vanya—'

'No . . . of course you're not. You have the mortal code. The sanctity of life. The mortals are the originators of that theory, and occasionally I curse it.' She sighed, then leaned forward. 'I mean, it would be so much simpler if I made you . . . you know. Then that dreary spiel about committing murder you mortals crow on about would become meaningless.'

I leaned backwards, away from her.

'No chance,' I said. 'If Luca won't come to me through his free will, then that's it. I will forget him.'

She stared at me. 'Sweetness, you will never forget. He will sink to the bottom of your heart perhaps . . . like a forgotten shipwreck. But he will never go away.'

Her words sent a shiver down my spine. A cold, sad shiver. I knew she was right. I would never forget.

'As it happens, I have chosen to live on Nissilum because it offers respite from the scavenging vampires experience, which I never cared for. Too messy . . .' She tried to smile reassuringly at me, something that obviously didn't come easily to her. But the thought was there.

'Where's Soren?' I picked up the cup on the table beside me and peered into it.

'Sleeping . . . I think.' Vanya moved gracefully up off the bed. She took the cup out of my hands. 'Don't force yourself.' She smiled widely, her teeth, perfect like Soren's, seemed almost to blind me.

I suddenly noticed what I was wearing. An old-fashioned white nightdress. It was a little big for me and it looked really old. The delicate lace at the neck was on its last legs.

'You look so sweet, dear.' Vanya craned to look. 'Irresistible.'

I tugged the nightdress further up my neck in a protective, chaste gesture.

'Don't even think about it,' I told her.

She smiled, amused. 'If I were that boy of yours I wouldn't think twice,' she said. 'You really must realise your power.'

I stared open-mouthed at her graceful figure as she moved towards the door.

'Bedtime for me,' she said softly. 'I will see you at dinner.'

'First we will take a walk into the town,' said Soren, pushing up the arms of his white T-shirt. 'I can show you around.'

'What about Luca?' I hissed. 'What if he sees us?'

'That's the point, isn't it?' He took a gulp of water.

'But not yet,' I said. 'Don't we have to formulate a plan first?'

Soren's black eyes slid over to mine. 'Formulate a plan?'

he repeated. 'Well . . . no, I don't think so. No plan. Just act natural.'

'But—'

'You want Luca to want you again? You want him to look at you and feel an ache inside. Longing. Regret?'

I shifted uncomfortably. 'I guess, but—'

'So, you behave as though everything is normal.'

'Luca will know I am just trying to make him jealous. He'll see right through it.'

'You underestimate the allure of Soren Balzac,' he said seriously. Lifting his head, he gave me a long, undeniably alluring look.

I shook my head, embarrassed, trying to stop the now familiar colour creeping into my face.

'Besides, we won't see him.' Soren stood and stretched. 'He'll be busy helping his mother with the chores . . . or something like that. Not idling around the local shops.'

'You make him sound like such a square,' I said crossly. 'He's just good.'

'I know,' Soren said more gently, putting his hand on my back. 'I was simply trying to reassure you.'

Vanya's house was at a small distance from the main town. Strangely she lived in what Soren called the Celestial village – a cluster of grand houses where the leaders of various dynasties lived. A wide cobbled road ran down a slope to the main town, where more lowly families resided. It was the first time I had seen this side of Nissilum properly and the sight of people going about their daily business.

'It's like a posh village,' I said to Soren. 'A traditional country village.'

'Twee.' Soren sniffed. 'Not really my style. I would go insane cooped up in a place like this for ever.'

I glanced at him. I knew I would too. I felt a ripple of disloyalty to Luca.

'It is where they come to . . . retire,' he said.

'Who?'

'Vampires . . . werewolves . . .' He shrugged. 'It is where they have given up.'

I stared at him, seeing the faint tic in his cheek.

'You think of it as giving up?'

His mouth split into a broad smile then. 'It's a theory . . . And well, it's true. It doesn't mean I think it's wrong.'

'Everybody here is so . . . repressed.' I said. 'I mean . . . like they're acting unnaturally.'

Soren stopped. 'That's exactly what it is,' he said quietly. 'Unnatural . . . But they have made a choice not to be "natural" – not to exercise their powers. Just like we all do . . . We choose to love, we choose not to.'

'I don't think you can choose.' I shook my head.

'I think it takes you over.'

'Nonsense.' Soren started walking again. 'We do what we want, we make choices . . . Sometimes, knowing they're wrong. We could stop. But we don't. We just forge on ahead because desire takes over.'

'Hmm.' I sniffed. 'I'm not so sure about that.'

Soren took my arm, but I was arrested by someone unpleasantly familiar.

'Luca's brother,' I whispered. 'See . . . over by that store?'

We squinted at a cluster of boys standing outside a shop front. One of them detached from the group. Dark-haired, lanky.

'Lowe,' I said, trying to stop Soren from moving forward. 'He can't see me . . . We have to go back.'

'Just let me do the talking,' Soren said, squeezing my arm. 'Trust me. And perhaps it will do no harm for Luca to learn that you are back here . . . with a handsome stranger like myself.'

'Not a good time for jokes,' I said, glowering at him.

'But seriously. This is fortuitous when you think of it,' he said thoughtfully.

I knew it would be seconds before Lowe saw me, and my insides tensed. I wanted to run away, to forget the whole thing. But it was too late – he had seen me. I could see him, staring up at us as we approached.

Soren was half dragging me down the cobbled hill. I could feel my heart beginning to speed up.

Lowe was regarding Soren with deep suspicion. He stepped forwards, and I could see he had grown in the months since I'd seen him last. He looked just like Henora; haughty, authoratitive. Outraged

'You don't belong here,' he said angrily. 'I don't know who this is—' He pointed at Soren. 'But you need to go back – there is nothing for you here.'

I opened my mouth to speak but I couldn't find the right explanation.

Soren's hand tightened on mine.

'I would watch what you say,' he told Lowe, his voice suddenly like ice, 'if you have any sense.'

Lowe's expression was of familiar disdain. 'Really?' he drawled. 'I've never seen you before in my life. But her' – he glared at me – 'she has caused enough trouble for my family as it is. Yet here she is again . . . it's pathetic.'

'I am staying with some good friends of mine,' said Soren. 'And Jane is here as my guest.'

A flicker of confusion passed over Lowe's face. He was clearly trying to work out what the hell was going on. But he composed himself, always fearful of not having the upper hand.

'You do know she is mortal?' he told Soren.

Soren simply smiled, making a bit of a show of keeping hold of my hand. I remained silent, not daring to show my fear. Or my unhappiness that it had come to this.

'What's the matter, Jane? You can't speak for yourself?' Lowe glanced around at his friends, who gawped at us as though we were animals in the zoo.

'I am not here to cause trouble,' I said finding my voice. 'You needn't worry about that . . .'

Lowe had stepped closer to us, he was scrutinising Soren, perplexed.

'What are you?' he said. 'Are you wolf? How is it that you have friends on Nissilum?'

'I am whatever you want me to be,' replied Soren mysteriously. 'Does it matter?'

I looked sideways at him. He seemed perfectly relaxed, except for that tic in his cheek.

Lowe leaned forward wolfishly, his muscles tense, a low growling in his throat . . . Then slowly, recovering himself, he stepped back again. 'I'll find out,' he said, before turning to me. 'You'd better keep out of my family's way. Luca is happy. He is going to marry Lila. There's nothing you can do to stop it. He doesn't love you. Never has.'

'I . . .' I felt my eyes fill up with tears. Even though I

was used to Lowe's malice, his words stung. And deep inside I felt they could be true. If Luca had loved me, if he really felt the way he told me all those months ago . . . would he have just left me like this?

'The truth hurts, doesn't it?' Lowe added nastily. 'So, why don't you just scuttle off back to your own world? And take this interloper with you.'

I jerked forward angrily. But Soren quickly grabbed my arm.

'Rise above it,' he said quietly. 'The boy is an idiot.'

Lowe glowered at us as Soren gently guided me past him. His eyes followed us and even with my back to him I could feel them boring into me.

Soren didn't take his hand off my arm until we were safely at a distance from Lowe and his friends, and I could see the fields and trees beyond the town.

'So. Luca's brother,' he said, grimacing. 'Nasty bit of work, isn't he?'

'He's a little over-protective,' I said, not sure why I was defending Lowe. He certainly wouldn't do the same for me.

Soren chuckled. 'He's a brat. And somehow I doubt his motives are altruistic. I'd place a bet that the boy was born a troublemaker.'

I nodded. 'He and Luca don't get on. It's like Lowe just

wants to spoil everybody's fun.'

Ahead of us, the sun was now settled in the sky, beaming its rays out across the acres of green fields. I sighed, strangely content.

'It's so beautiful here, so perfect.' I breathed in the pure air.

'A little too perfect.' Soren made a face. 'Not my thing . . . probably why I left. I prefer my surroundings a little grimier, like the dark alleys of Paris at night . . . I never trust perfection. You shouldn't either.'

'Meaning?'

'Meaning that to truly love someone you have to see their flaws. See the dark side. The things you don't like.'

'I guess. I've certainly seen another side to Luca.' I remembered that day at his engagement party . . . his resolute coldness to me. I shuddered at the memory, but a part of me felt perversely relieved that he had the power to hurt me. It meant somehow that he was more human than I thought.

'Where are we going?' I said, coming out of my reverie.

'For a walk . . .' Soren lifted his chin. 'Nowhere special.'

At that moment the unmistakeable sound of horses' hooves thundered into our idyll. I glanced around me and there, through a large palatial-looking set of gates, were four riders.

At the sight of us the horses slowed, approaching cautiously, and as they came closer I recognised the blond curls, the arrogant demeanour of Raphael . . . Or Evan, as I had known him.

It was the first time I had seen Raphael since that awful rainy night in the abandoned air field back home. My insides tightened as I felt myself recoiling from this situation.

Next to Raphael were two boys I didn't recognise but who were identical. Twins. But the fourth rider was unmistakeable. Choppy dark hair, a long slender body.

Luca was riding with Raphael as though nothing had ever passed between them.

The horses came forward noisily and my breath caught in my throat. I instinctively moved to stand behind Soren, not wanting to be seen – but it was hopeless.

Raphael dismounted, then stood, gazing at the two of us. In front of me I felt Soren tense.

Finally, somebody spoke.

'What is your business here?' Raphael addressed Soren, and I stepped out so that I was in full view.

'And you?' Raphael raised an eyebrow. 'Jane?'

I couldn't bring myself to speak, I just stared, glad that I was not alone. Though he was unrecognisable as Evan

– the boy he had pretended to be to seduce me – there was a familiar hardness in his tone.

'It's all right,' Soren whispered, though still looking at the boy.

'Again, what are you doing here?' Raphael studied Soren from head to foot. 'I would surely remember seeing you before . . .'

Behind Raphael, I sensed that the others were as curious, though I didn't dare look to see Luca's face. I was already beginning to feel guilty about what I was doing here.

'I am visiting,' Soren replied calmly, 'with some . . . acquaintances of mine.'

'Not her,' Raphael said rudely, gesturing at me. 'She does not live here . . .'

Finally I allowed my eyes to drift beyond Raphael to Luca, astride his horse. From this distance I couldn't read his expression, couldn't see his green eyes. I swallowed nervously.

'I am visiting with the Borgias,' Soren said. 'And what business of it is yours, anyway?'

Raphael turned back to Luca, whose face registered shock at Soren's words and I distinctly saw his body jerk a little and seem to expand. Was that a flare of something in those eyes? I willed him to look at me but he wouldn't. Instead he dropped his head, his hands clutching the horse's reins tighter.

Raphael had turned back, his full attention on Soren now. I remembered the boy he had been – Evan. But that had been a different boy. Literally. And now Raphael was back, behaving as though he and I had never met. It didn't bother me. Not really. But it was all part of the strange power of, Nissilum. A place where crimes such as Raphael's could apparently be forgiven.

But then I noticed how pale he was. His handsome face gaunt, his eyes blank. Perhaps I was wrong.

'You are here to cause trouble?' Raphael asked Soren, and something about his tone was hopeful, I noticed. He looked perfectly composed, without emotion.

Soren shrugged. 'No. We are just going for a walk.'

Raphael's horse pawed the ground restlessly and he reached out to take its reins.

'Interesting,' he said, eyeing Soren. 'I sense . . . a renegade in our midst.'

'Takes one to know one,' Soren replied, provocatively.

There was a slight hesitation before Raphael's face cracked into a broad grin.

Soren was unruffled. 'Terrifying,' he murmured. If Raphael had heard, he didn't respond. For some reason I had the urge to laugh – at all this posturing. A gang of boys flexing their muscles. I guessed some things really were universal.

I smiled weakly, but my eyes were still trained on Luca, who had come a little closer and who returned my gaze. His mouth was set impassively. Not a smile, barely even a flicker of recognition. I stared, wanting to see him acknowledge me and, as I studied his face, I noticed his eyes. Sad, with a sheen of something that could have been tears. He blinked at me and I saw it. That familiar softness. But in a second it was gone, and he moved his face away to look at Soren. Now his expression was hard, though he made no move to dismount. No move to investigate.

Knowing I shouldn't, I took a tentative step forward.

'Luca,' I called, 'I didn't . . . this isn't . . .' I didn't know what to say. I hadn't prepared for this.

'We must be on our way.' Luca cut across me, speaking to Raphael. He pulled at at his horse's rein and turned back towards the gate.

I stepped back and felt Soren's hand on my back.

'Be patient,' he said softly. 'I expected this.'

I realised that Raphael hadn't moved and was watching the two of us – too far away to have heard Soren, I hoped.

Soren pulled me back protectively and cleared his throat.

'Good to meet you, Raphael,' he told the boy.

'Likewise.' Raphael nodded, before leading his horse closer so that he was almost nose to nose with Soren.

'I know you are here to cause trouble,' he whispered. 'And I am watching you.' His eyes flickered to me. 'Both of you.'

All I could think was how little this boy resembled Evan. He had even changed physically. Still blond and blue-eyed, but his features were different.

Raphael tugged at his horse and turned to follow the others. I watched the back of Luca, astride his horse, hoping he would turn around, but he kept riding resolutely ahead, straight-backed, proud.

Soren waited until they were at a safe distance before turning to me.

'Not so bad . . .' He raised an eyebrow.

'Did you see Luca,' I said miserably, 'how cold he was?'

Soren shook his head. 'Of course he was. He has a front to keep up.' He paused. 'I have to say, I admire him for it . . . in a way.'

'Me too.' I suddenly felt my eyes swimming with tears. 'Which makes it so much worse.'

'Jane . . .' Soren pulled me to him. 'Hush now. Luca cannot keep it up for ever.'

'But he will be married in a few weeks. As soon as

that happens, it really will be over.' I wiped my nose with my sleeve.

'A lot can happen in a few weeks.' Soren said soothingly. 'Just be patient.'

'The way he looked at me, like I was nothing . . . ' I stared into the distance, trying to pick out Luca from the four riders, but they were too far away. 'It was like I was a stranger.' I tried to keep the panic, the sob out of my voice.

Soren rubbed his hands together. 'I think now it is time for a plan.'

I looked at the side of his face: imperious, calculating. I wanted to feel the same way. If my feelings weren't in the way, I could see clearly, think straight. Soren seemed to find it easy.

'But don't you feel scared that Lila will reject you, too?' I asked him. 'That what we're doing will be for nothing?'

Soren smiled. 'Worrying doesn't change a situation . . . it will only make it worse.' He put an arm around me. 'This is our best bet.'

Somehow Soren had a way of making the impossible seem possible. I had to admit it was infectious.

'So. What next?' I asked him.

'We up the ante,' he said calmly. 'We give Luca something to throw him off balance.'

'Like?' I dug my hands in my pockets.

'Like jealousy,' Soren said quietly. He regarded me with his black eyes, a little softer now. 'And I know this is wrong . . . but I am going to enjoy making him jealous.'

I puffed out my cheeks. 'Well, it's going to be hell for me.'

'I'll try not to be insulted,' he said, drawing up his shoulders. 'I make a pretty good boyfriend when I put my mind to it.'

I tried to smile, but found myself wondering how Soren could be so chipper about what we were doing. He didn't seem to feel any anxiety or sadness about Lila. Maybe I was being too sensitive? It was just a boy thing: covering up their real feelings. Or was it because he couldn't care less about her, and I was somehow implicated in a warped plan that he and Vanya had cooked up between them? I didn't think so, but I still didn't completely trust Soren Balzac.

I couldn't afford to.

CHAPTER TWELVE

'Raphael was with them?' Vanya set her glass down on the table. 'He certainly seems to have ingratiated himself back with his old friends.' She pursed her lips, considering something. 'Clever boy, that one.'

I looked at her, not knowing what she meant.

'He seemed very friendly . . . as friendly as he would be in that kind of situation.' Soren leaned back in his chair.

'Angelic manners, you see,' Vanya replied with some distaste.

'Odd, though.' Soren narrowed his eyes. 'He was almost welcoming. I am a total stranger. Quite possibly a threat . . .'

'Well.' Vanya smiled tightly at me. 'Who knows what goes on in that boy's head?'

I smiled tightly back, then glanced subtly down at my

watch. It was half past four. Teatime. Who knew what time it was back home?

Vanya got up to get us some food, just as there was a loud hammering on the door. She stopped, glaring at the sound.

'Who the devil can that be?' she muttered. 'Nobody visits us. Nobody likes us.'

Valdar, who had been intent on reading his paper, raised his head calmly.

'Want me to get it, dear?' he said smoothly.

Vanya sighed heavily. 'Let's just ignore it. Whoever it is, they'll get the message.'

But the knocking grew louder and more persistent. Soren fidgeted in his seat.

'It could be important,' he told us. 'I'll deal with it.'

He moved quickly out of the room, to the now deafening sound coming from upstairs. Vanya got to her feet, gliding towards the doorway, craning her head up the stairs.

'A man,' she said quietly. 'It sounds like—'

But the door was slammed shut, heavily, and Soren was coming back down.

'Who was it?' Vanya said, almost excitedly.

'Just one of those boys . . .' Soren glanced quickly at me, before smiling at her. 'The ones that hang around in the town . . . some kind of prank.'

'But I heard you talking to someone . . .' Vanya frowned at him. 'I'm sure I—'

'I was shouting into thin air!' Soren gave a forced kind of chuckle. 'Whoever it was, they'd run off.'

I eyed him suspiciously. Something wasn't quite right here.

'Really,' Vanya huffed. 'How irritating.'

'Soren,' I said, getting to my feet, 'can I have a word? Alone?'

'What's going on?' I asked when we were safely alone upstairs. 'Who was that at the door?'

Soren opened his mouth, but hesitated before speaking. 'I told you . . . I didn't see anyone.'

I stared at him, and eventually saw his eyes soften, and then he shrugged.

'OK.' He sighed. 'It was Raphael.'

'What? What did he want?'

'I'm not really sure . . .' Soren got up from the bed, on which we were both sitting. 'He seems very interested in me.'

'You're a stranger. Maybe he is just doing what he thinks is his duty, checking you out?' Even as I said it I knew that sounded unlikely.

'Perhaps. There is something really quite odd about Raphael . . . I can't put my finger on it.' Soren looked thoughtful.

'Maybe he's still mad?' I shrugged. 'Or not completely over his . . . breakdown.'

'He has nobody.' Soren sounded so mournful that I almost laughed.

'Only the whole of the Celestial kingdom.' I rolled my eyes. 'He's really freaked you out, hasn't he?'

'It's just I am sure he is after something . . .' Soren shook his head. 'He lingered as though he wanted more than just to check I was staying here with Vanya . . .'

'Well he must have changed his mind,' I said. 'And to be honest Raphael is the last person I want to be thinking about right now. I had hoped I would never have to see him again.'

'No.' Soren smiled. 'I didn't think about that. Let's just forget it. It was nothing after all.' He ran his fingers through his inky hair. 'But perhaps we should keep out of his way from now on.'

I had never seen Soren so . . . down. But I couldn't fathom it. I decided to shrug it off.

'So. What next?' I asked, a sense of steeliness overtaking me.

CHAPTER THIRTEEN

'Raffy, dear.' Celeste entered the dining room, where her great-son was staring vacantly at his plate of food. She looked perturbed, her brow creased with worry.

The boy looked up, though still distracted.

'Good morning,' he said, rising from his chair out of courtesy.

'Everything all right?' She settled herself on a chair and poured some teas from the pot into a cup. 'You seem a little absent at the moment.'

'I *am* a little tired,' answered Raphael, smiling now. 'We went for a long ride yesterday.'

'We?' Celeste raised an eyebrow.

'Lowe, and a couple of the stable boys.' Raphael picked up a fork and poked at his food, now cold. 'It is good exercise, but I feel I am wasting my days . . . I should be engaged in something more productive.'

Celeste smiled approvingly. She sipped her tea elegantly, before putting her cup down.

'I am glad to hear you say that . . . And . . . as you know, the Celestial Parade is in a few days. I think it would be a good time for you to take up your place as a senior member of this family. I would like you to host the event.'

Raphael looked a little startled, but recovered himself quickly.

'Of course . . . it would be an honour.' He smiled, but with ambivalence. He had hoped to spend the next few days planning. The Celestial Parade was held twice a year, to celebrate the seasons of summer and winter. Marching bands, a military display – pomp and ceremony to show the people of Nissilum how mighty a place it was and how wonderful its traditions were. Afterwards, a selection of folk were invited back to the palace for a lavish banquet. It was this that Celeste meant him to host. He wondered if he was capable of pretending for that long.

'Wonderful.' Celeste beamed. 'Of course, the staff here will assist you in every way possible.'

'Yes.' Raphael nodded, hiding his irritation. 'Good.'

'I do worry about you still,' said his great-mother, her face softening with concern. 'You are still just a boy. But with your father gone—'

'Yes.' He cut her off and got to his feet. 'You need not worry. I am perfectly capable of stepping up to the mark.'

'I know that.' Celeste was taken aback. 'I simply meant—'

'I know. I must go . . . I need to inspect the cellar stores,' Raphael told her.

'Of course.' She nodded, waiting for his back to turn before giving vent to more anxiety in her expression.

Raphael made his way down to the palace basement. It was cold, dark, and his footsteps echoed on the stone steps. Reaching the bottom, he stopped outside a large wooden cupboard and opened it. Inside, dozens of keys hung on dozens of hooks. Reaching in, the boy ran his fingers almost tenderly across them before he plucked a bunch down and shut the door to the cupboard.

Advancing down the marble corridor, he made for a door at the end, next to the palace cells. The Armory. Inside he would find all the weapons the palace had at its disposal in the rare event of an attack. Raphael found the right key and opened the heavy door. Inside was an array of somewhat crude weaponry. Crossbows, swords. On the walls, assorted sizes of guns.

There wasn't much. But perhaps enough.

Raphael breathed in and out slowly, excitement was mounting inside him. He leaned back against the heavy door, his eyes running back and forth over what he could see inside this room. Then he slumped down to his knees, putting his hands to his temples. Pictures flashed through his mind. Today he felt as though he had seen a ghost. He had no idea where he came from, but the black-eyed boy residing at Vanya Borgia's house was significant. Almost as though he had arrived on Nissilum, just as Raphael was feeling such restlessness, by design. Raphael had somehow felt him to be a kindred spirit. But how he had come to know Jane . . . ? Raphael lifted his head, feeling fuzzy-headed. He must think clearly. He had much to do . . . and he needed all his wits about him.

CHAPTER FOURTEEN

'Here.' Soren tossed a stiff white card at me.

I had been lying in the bedroom, gazing out of the window, wondering what time it was back home. What day. It seemed like I had been gone for ever. I had to keep remembering that time here moved slowly. That in reality I had probably only been gone for a few hours.

The card landed beside me on the bed. As I focussed on what was written on it, I sat up blearily.

'The Celestial Parade,' I read out, then looked up at Soren. 'What is this?'

'Vanya got her special invitation today,' he said. 'It is a big occasion for all the heads of Nissilum's families. A time for spreading love and harmony amongst vampires, werewolves and witches . . .' He spoke in a facetious monotone.

'That's nice.' I handed him back the card. 'But it

has nothing to do with me, does it?'

He perched on the end of the bed. 'Why not?'

'Because I won't be going.' I laughed darkly. 'I mean, I can't see Henora greeting me with open arms, can you?'

'Well, no. But she needn't know you're there.'

I gave him a look.

'Listen. You want to see Luca, right?' Soren fixed me with a look of his own.

'Well, yes. But I don't think—'

Soren waved a hand dismissively. 'Think of it as fancy dress.'

I narrowed me eyes. 'Soren. What are you up to?'

'Vanya has a marvellous selection of disguises . . . Wigs, for example.' He cocked his head. 'Platinum blonde, perhaps?' He wrinkled his nose. 'No. Something dark to bring out your eyes and give you a vampirish edge.'

I flared my nostrils. 'No way.'

'For myself, I favour curls.' He turned to the mirror over the dressing table, and ruffled his hair theatrically. 'Chestnut curls.'

I fought a smile. 'Soren, you're actually enjoying this, aren't you?'

'Well, why not? If all else fails, think of the tale you will be able to tell your grandchildren.'

'I can't think that far ahead,' I sighed. 'And Luca won't even recognise me.'

'If he truly loves you . . .' Soren said, looking directly into my eyes. 'He will recognise you.'

Vanya threw open a white-painted door off the landing.

'Here,' she said, 'I have so many outfits to choose from!' She pushed me forward into a vast cupboard – the size of my bedroom at home. Two long rails stood end to end, packed with clothes. Below the rails, hundreds of pairs of shoes. Above, dozens of hats and wigs.

I fiddled with my hair. 'I don't know where to start.'

Vanya whirled round, flashing me a white smile. 'Luckily for you, I do.' She turned back and advanced towards one side of the room, riffling through some dresses. Sparkling, sombre, delicate and pale, dark and velvet.

'Now,' she said breathlessly, 'I think something dramatically different for you, darling.'

'I don't want to stand out,' I protested.

'No,' she said dryly, 'of course you don't.' She picked out a tight crimson velvet dress, strapless, with a bottom like a fish tail. Over the bust was a sprinkling of sequins, and a large velvet corsage, like a black rose, positioned where the shoulder should be.

I stepped forward, intrigued in spite of myself.

'You like?' Vanya's voice was syrupy and she beckoned me forward. 'Why don't you try it on?'

'I don't know.' I bit my lip. 'It looks a little . . .'

'A little *sexy*?' She sniffed. 'Honestly, you are infuriating. Why do you insist on hiding your body?' She looked me up and down. 'You really shouldn't . . . it could be your most valuable weapon.'

'You think?' I tried not to look down. Truth be told, I had never felt less sexy. It's funny what a little rejection can do for your confidence.

'Don't let it,' Vanya spoke softly, reading my mind. My eyes widened.

I took the dress from her. 'I'll try it.'

Vanya moved quickly to the shelf above the wheel, plucking a short black poker-straight bob from a doll's head. It was so glossy I could practically see my reflection in it.

'Absolutely not,' I said, shaking my head.

'Oh pleeeassse,' Vanya wheedled. 'Just try it?'

I grabbed it from her. 'OK. Now please leave.'

'OK,' she said meekly, picking up the hem of her dress. She had the tiniest waist imaginable I noticed. 'But I'll be just outside, dear. Let me know when you're ready.'

I waited for her to shut the door behind her before I

started taking off my jeans, T-shirt and cardigan. I pushed down my bra straps and stepped into the dress. It slipped up my body effortlessly. I looked down. I was long, and lean. My waist was tiny and the bust was the perfect size.

So far so good.

I looked at the wig, puffing out my cheeks, then gathered my long hair up and tied it as neatly as I could into a small bun. Luckily it was fine and, when I patted it down, didn't create too much of a bump. I pulled on the wig, tucking loose strands of hair underneath. It had a short blunt fringe and was cut geometrically, like a kind of sexy black helmet.

Finally, I turned to look in the mirror, shutting my eyes for a few minutes before opening them again.

I opened my mouth and almost gasped at my reflection. I was totally unrecognisable. The pitch black of my hair made my grey eyes look huge and vivid. The sharp bobbed style gave me cheekbones. My eyes travelled down to the dress. And the lusciousness of the crimson sent a subtle glow across my skin tone. I looked like a woman. Not a girl. I hadn't noticed my body changing that much, but it must have done. Because I went in and out in a way I had never done before.

'Jane!' Vanya trilled from outside. 'Everything all right

in there?'

I couldn't speak for a moment, too busy taking in the apparition in the mirror.

'Jane?' She rapped on the door. 'Please may I come in?'

'Yes,' I croaked, instinctively wanting to hide myself.

The door opened and she swept back in, stopping, her eyes sweeping like searchlights up and down my body.

'Well, well, well.' She put her hands on her hips. 'I knew it.'

'I'm really not sure about this,' I said quickly. 'It's just too . . . ostentatious.'

'Dear God in heaven,' she rolled her eyes. 'You really are the most pathetic, wheedling child . . .'

'What?' I said, outraged.

'You don't get it, do you darling.' She tapped her head. 'It's simply not sinking into that provincial, self-deprecating little head of yours.'

I set my mouth, furious, but on some level knowing she had a point.

'Listen,' she said wearily, 'you are never going to win this little game if you put yourself on the back foot all the time. If you refuse to dazzle.'

'Why should I need to dazzle?' I glared at her.

'Oh, sweetheart, you are so naïve.' She reached out and deftly adjusted the wig.

'This wig is itchy,' I said sulkily.

'We have to suffer to be beautiful,' she said. 'Get over it.'

I smirked, knowing she was too busy fiddling with my hair to see.

When she'd finished I turned back to the mirror myself.

'I guess, I do look . . .'

'Stunning,' came a voice from the open doorway. 'Absolutely stunning.'

Vanya and I turned to see Soren leaning up against the wall.

'Isn't she?' Vanya was almost maternal. Though a million miles away from the mother I knew.

Soren came forward.

'The time will come for us to shine, Jane,' he said, looking straight into my eyes. 'Don't you think?'

Colour was seeping up my body, heading for my cheeks. Something about the way Soren was looking at me, made me uncomfortable . . . coy even. Dragging my eyes away from his, I looked back down at my shape and stroked the pink velvet with my fingertips.

When I finally looked back, I met his gaze with new confidence.

CHAPTER FIFTEEN

The palace library was seldom visited these days. Gabriel had spent hours in there, much to the exasperation of his wife and Celeste. But Raphael had always loved seeing his father, seated at the large centre table, books open in front of him and his head bent in intent study. For a long time now the place had been chilly, underused and lonely. As Raphael turned the handle, a musty smell wafted out.

He pushed the door wide open, standing still for a moment, gazing at the hundreds of books shelved in glass cupboards.

Taking a deep breath, Raphael forced the memory of his father out of his head and advanced towards the glass cabinet beyond the centre table. He knew that somewhere in there he would find what he was looking for.

The cabinet rested on a large chest, housing several drawers. Raphael drew one out and found the key.

Unlocking the cabinet, he ran his finger along the books on the bottom shelf. Alphabetically ordered, with ageing leather spines. He crouched until his eyes settled on one near the end of the row.

Werewolf Dynasties: Nissilum 800 to 880.

As he slid the book out, Raphael was aware of how delicate it was, how fragile the case; the leaves within the book crackled. Holding it carefully in his hands, he seated himself at the table, and began slowly turning the pages. The book listed the family trees of all the first werewolf breeds that came to Nissilum. These breeds still existed, though they tended to stay in their original quarters: North, South, East and West. A small number of wolves had revolted, disobeyed the laws and been banished, or escaped. As a member of the Celestial family, Raphael was privy to more information than most on the exact individuals who had committed such acts of treachery, or insubordination. He had also listened at doorways as a child, heard his elders discussing cases; and on occasion had been allowed to sit in on state meetings where such matters had been analysed and punishments had been ordered. Some cases had stuck in his head. Others had been of little interest.

Raphael recalled the day that one young wolf was ruled as an outcast and a warrant issued for his imprisonment.

He had been particularly fascinated because the werewolf had been around his age. Born on the same day, the same month, the same year. Yet his crimes, his acts had been devastating to his family. *Pure evil*, had been the description in court. The cub had attacked his mother, his father, brother and one of his sisters. Another sister had curiously escaped attack . . . was found crouched in a wood in the Southern quarter, shivering and traumatised. She had been taken in, adopted by another family and everything about her previous life had been changed – even her name, it was said. Though after her errant brother had been destroyed, all of Nissilum had respectfully ceased their gossip, in the hope that she would live as normal a life as possible.

Raphael turned the pages, trying not to tear each one as he did so. Eventually he reached the page he was looking for and stopped. There, in type so tiny he had to squint to see it, was the report he wanted.

From this day forward the eldest cub of the Cage Wolves family will no longer be granted citizenship in Nissilum. With immediate effect he is to be transported to the Celestial Palace and imprisoned until such a method of punishment has been decided by the high court.

That punishment was banishment from Nissilum.

Raphael paused, staring hard at the cub's name: Saul.

It was very possible the cub boy had changed his name. After all, Raphael himself had lived in the guise of the mortal, Evan Forrest. Remembering this, Raphael caught his breath. The cub could be a shape-shifter. He didn't know how, since only the Royal family – the angels – of Nissilum where endowed with all supernatural powers. If this boy were truly a shape-shifter, then somebody within the Celestial family must have granted him this gift.

Raphael continued reading.

The cub's only living relative, his sister, Cina, will be rehabilitated with a neighbouring wolf family, whose name shall remain anonymous, but who will endeavour to rid the girl cub of all memory of her brother's evil massacre.

Raphael swallowed. If Saul was who he thought he was, then he was a grave danger to all here on Nissilum. And if it was he, then what was his true business here? The boy sat back in his chair, his mind racing. Could it be that he planned to kill again? Raphael had needed a second look at the stranger who had appeared out of nowhere with Jane Jonas. He had felt some kind of threatening force coming from him. At least he had felt something he couldn't explain. But Raphael wasn't officially privy to the Cage Wolves massacre case. He needed to keep an eye on the boy if he could. He couldn't just order him gone without proof.

Raphael carefully closed the book, stood and placed it back on the bottom shelf. As he closed the glass cabinet his own reflection stared back at him, muted and dark in the dim light of the library. His eyes, dark now, glowered piercingly, and though he knew he was just looking at himself, Raphael felt a ripple of fear at the sight.

'Dear, your great-father is not well,' Celeste said later that evening. She rubbed at the stem of her glass, a frown lining her normally smooth pale skin. 'It is most unusual. He appears to have some kind of fever . . .'

'A fever?' said Raphael in surprise. 'But—'

'Yes, I know.' Celeste shook her head. 'We do not get ill. We do not get feverish. Except . . . this appears to be some kind of delirium. He is muttering and writhing in his bed.'

'Well, what is he saying?' Raphael covered his plate with a napkin, his face set in concern.

'I can't make sense of most it. But he does seem to have a foreboding of some catastrophe . . . He keeps repeating the same words over and over again. "Protect your people."' She glanced bewildered at Raphael. 'I have no idea what he means by this.'

Raphael kept his expression calm. 'Cadmium has always been anxious,' he told her gently. 'I am sure it means nothing.' Seeing that the worry didn't disappear from Celeste's face, he reached out to take her hand. 'But I will ensure that the guards are extra vigilant . . . Perhaps we should call a meeting of the dynasties . . . If there is unrest, surely it will be spoken of then?'

At last she gave him a weak smile. 'Perhaps he is just overly cautious. His responsibilities have always weighed so heavily on him. He knows that you will become head of state one day . . . I think he finds it very difficult to let go.'

Raphael nodded silently, taking his hand away from his great-mother's.

'Do you recall the boy cub who was banished from Nissilum?' he said haltingly. 'The one who committed such terrible acts to his family?'

Celeste looked sharply at him. 'Saul,' she said quickly, a tiny visible shudder running through her. 'What a terrible tragedy.'

'Where did he go?' Raphael looked intently at her. 'Where was he banished to?'

Celeste looked down at her hands, then clasped them together.

'Nobody knows,' she said, after some hesitation. 'He was safely locked in the cellars beneath the palace, there was no possible way he could have escaped. But when the guards went down to check on him one morning, he was gone. Two of the bars on the tiny window down there had been pushed apart with what must have been considerable force and the cellar was empty.' She sighed heavily. 'And he was nowhere to be found on the whole of Nissilum. Everyone searched for him. Not a stone was left unturned. He just vanished.'

Raphael's eyes were wide. 'A wolf could not have done that,' he said quietly. 'There is no possible way . . .'

Celeste shuddered again, this time volubly. 'It is the one thing that has haunted your great-father all of his life. The notion that this beast is out there, roaming. A mutant of some kind. Part wolf . . . part . . .' she trailed off, unable to finish her sentence.

'I'm sorry,' said Raphael, half meaning it, for his great-mother looked so stricken at this buried memory. 'I didn't mean to dredge up something so . . .'

'Evil,' she answered with a voice like stone. 'Pure evil.'

After Celeste had retired to bed, Raphael took a drink into the large sitting room on the second floor. A fire burned brightly in the grate, and as he sat cradling his glass in his hands, he stared mesmerised at the flames and the crackling and spitting of the wood beneath them. For the first time since he'd been a child, he felt something other than rebellion pulsing through his veins. He felt fearful and anxious.

The killer had returned, he was sure of it. Raphael just had to make sure he could prove his identity. There must be some mark, some clue that made this boy cub – or whatever he had turned himself into – unique. Raphael wanted to find him, and a part of him wanted to bring him to justice once and for all. But he would be lying to himself if he didn't feel this enemy could be useful in some way.

Outside it was pitch black, the moon, not quite full in the sky. The whole of Nissilum seemed a more sinister place tonight. Somewhere out there was a threat to its entire civilisation.

CHAPTER SIXTEEN

'Who are your family?' I asked Soren, who was using two heavy pans as small weights. I had been trying for the last half hour not to look at his bare torso. It was surprisingly muscley. Sinewy, strong. Soren let out a small gasp as he brought the weights down to the floor. He breathed out heavily, a light film of sweat on his forehead, his dark hair pushed back off his face, but for one inky cowlick. He flashed me a smile.

'Everywhere . . . and nowhere,' he replied annoyingly at last. 'I am a chameleon.'

'Soren.' I shut my eyes in brief annoyance. 'That's not an answer. There's enigmatic and there's downright weird.'

'How about enigmatically weird?' he said, picking up his T-shirt and pulling it over his head.

'Why are you so determined to keep your past a secret?'

I got up from Vanya's kitchen table and walked over to the sink, filling a cup of water. When I turned back, Soren was staring at me. With his tousled hair and white T-shirt clinging to his chest, I had to stop myself from staring back. Instead I held out the cup of water.

'Drink,' I told him.

'I am beginning to realise that you are really quite bossy, Miss Jane,' he said, then took a long gulp.

'I'm serious. Why can't you tell me?'

I watched as he finished his water, placing the empty cup on the table. He finally engaged with me, a more thoughtful look on his face.

'Listen, there are some things you really are better off not knowing,' he said quietly. 'Things that might . . . well, that might give you the wrong idea about me.'

'But that's just it, I have no idea about you. I know that you are trying to help me in some way . . . and I really can't think why you're going to so much trouble, Soren. I mean, I know it's because of Lila. But you hardly mention her . . .' I paused. 'What exactly is she to you?'

'What?' he looked sharply at me for a second. 'I have already told you. Lila and I are meant to be together.'

'Uh huh.' I sighed. This conversation was going round in circles. And many things still didn't seem right.

'OK. Look . . . It is a little more complicated than I

have let on perhaps . . . My past. Who I am . . . If you really knew . . .'

'Tell me.' I stepped forward. 'Just tell me.'

'I can't.' He looked pleadingly at me. 'Just try and trust me . . . Soon . . . you will find out, but then you will have got what you want and it won't matter any more.'

'Soren!' I flapped my arms around, exasperated. 'You have to trust me! I'm not some innocent little girl any more. In the last year and a half I've dated a boy who turned out to be a fallen angel . . . fallen in love with a werewolf who just betrayed me . . .' My voice broke, saying it out loud.

He moved over to me quickly and I felt his arms around me. His long neck nestled into mine.

'It's OK. I am sorry. I know you are strong. I suppose I am just trying to stop any more confusion than is necessary in your life.'

With the solid weight of his arms holding me, I let out a small, inappropriate giggle.

Soren pulled away. 'Now, you find it funny? What is so amusing to you?'

'It's just . . . it couldn't get any more confusing if it tried,' I said, properly laughing now. 'Or more weird, or difficult . . .' I trailed off. 'It's not like another layer of confusion will make any difference.'

I smiled at him. He smiled at me.

'Come. Sit with me.' He drew me over to the bench by the kitchen table, then craned his neck to see that the door was shut.

Soren sat still without speaking for what seemed an eternity before he finally took my hands in his.

'A long time ago, I did something . . . terrible here. Something I can't even think about now, and would not, if it didn't haunt me in my sleep. Because of what I did I was sent away from here. And I have stayed away . . . until now. My only friend on Nissilum has been Vanya . . .' he hesitated, seeing my wrapt expression. 'It is a long story, but needless to say, Vanya and I have a close bond – one that goes back a long way . . . and then there is Lila, of course.'

'Yes,' I said frowning a little, 'there's Lila.'

'Lila is very precious to me. But not in the way I have led you to believe.'

My frown deepened. 'In what way then?'

'She and I were bound together in childhood, as I said. Sharing everything. She looked up to me. I looked after her. But then . . . when she was very young. I . . .' He stopped and I saw that his face was stricken.

'Soren, what is it? I coaxed. 'You can tell me.'

150

'I need to find her. I need to put things right.'

'Put things right?' I moved closer to him.

'Lila is my sister,' he got out finally. His whole body seemed to crumple as he spoke.

Did my heart skip a beat? It certainly felt like it.

'Your sister?' I slowly shook my head. 'Why didn't you tell me that before . . . and then, why are you so keen to break her and Luca up? I don't understand.'

'Because I won't let her marry him,' he answered sadly, 'when he doesn't truly love her.'

'He may grow to love her. He will take care of her.' I forced the words out, though it killed me.

'She is second best.' He said with authority. 'It doesn't matter how dutiful he is. She deserves better. She deserves to be properly, passionately loved.'

'Why do you feel so strongly about this?' I studied him. 'I mean, I understand you want the best for her, but—'

'Because I am the reason her life was ruined in the first place. The reason she was wrenched from her flesh-and-blood family and taken in by strangers.' He turned, his face flushed, towards me. 'I killed them. I killed all of them. Our parents, our brother and my other sister . . . Lila was the only one who survived.'

I drew my hands away, my whole body cold with shock.

'This is a joke . . . right?' All the blood had drained out of my face, I was sure of it. 'You . . . Soren . . . tell me this isn't true.'

'I was young . . . a cub. I didn't know what I was doing. An imbalance of some kind,' he said, avoiding my eyes. 'I was very angry.'

I knew I had unconsciously moved further back from him on the bench. I was trying to take this all in, make sense of it. But in my world, only monsters did that kind of thing. Killers.

'Jesus, Soren,' I breathed. 'This is massive. I should never have come here with you, not knowing you . . . I mean, what kind of idiot am I?'

'Please. Jane. Don't think I don't regret with all my heart what I did that day. I would never hurt you . . .'

I closed my eyes. *Where have I heard that before?*

'I am here to put things right . . . I need to put them right. For my sister. It's the least I can do. I have come back to take care of her.' He paused. 'And the more I know you, know of what happened between you and Luca, I see that it is the only way. Don't you see? This whole ridiculous set of meaningless rules and traditions here. Stopping everyone from doing what they really want to do. From being who they really want to be with.'

'And that's what you want? To spend your life with your sister?'

'I . . . I want to put things right,' he repeated dully.

I was still trying to digest this shocking information, when the door opened and Vanya appeared, stretching.

'There you are,' she said, running her fingers through her hair. 'Huddled together as usual, plotting.'

Was it my imagination or was there an edge to her voice? I wasn't about to get on the wrong side of Vanya. Things had already taken a turn I didn't like.

'Not at all,' I said, getting up, hugging myself a little protectively. 'In fact, we were just talking about me leaving.'

'Jane!' Soren seemed to recover his composure, standing alarmed. Vanya arched an eyebrow.

'Already?' She looked at the two of us suspiciously. 'But you haven't got what you came for yet – either of you.'

'I've changed my mind about that.' I gave Soren a pointed look. 'It's not worth all the trouble.'

'Giving up, are you?' Vanya unscrewed a bottle of something dark and potent-looking. 'How terribly mortal of you.'

'Leave it, Vanya,' Soren warned her. 'Jane knows.'

She stopped what she was doing. 'You told her . . .'

'I told her about what I did. Who Lila really is.'

'Ah.' She looked intently at me, then poured herself a glass of the bottle's contents – and I thought her hand was shaking a little as she did so.

'This is all too complicated,' I said. 'I don't want to get involved. All I wanted was to be with Luca. I thought Soren was helping me because he loved Lila. But he was just using me to infiltrate society here . . . pretending to be something he's not.'

I had no idea where that had come from. Except that I needed to believe it, because I was in a mess that was too deep and shocking.

Vanya opened her mouth to say something, then thought better of it and simply shrugged, settling herself in an armchair near the kitchen fire.

Soren was pacing the stone floor, head bent.

'So I'll just get my stuff.' I paused, looking from Vanya to Soren. 'Someone will have to help me get home . . .' I had a sudden thought that they might refuse, now that I was being uncooperative. Why would they want to help me? Vanya had not exactly had my best interests at heart before. My heart sank. I had been so stupid. Too trusting. Had I not learned anything from Evan?

'Of course,' Soren said, surprising me. 'I understand

why you feel this way. I know what it looks like. I know I lied to you . . . But you would never have agreed to help me if I had told the truth.' He gazed imploringly at me. 'I don't want you to go . . .'

'Well, that's too bad,' I said. 'I want to see my family. They'll be wondering where I am.'

'You've hardly been gone,' Soren said quietly. 'They won't be worried.'

'Well . . . I still want to go home. I need to get away. Just forget about all of this. Get on with my life on Earth.' I started quickly towards the exit, running up the stairs to the front door. I didn't have a coat, but I didn't care, I could do without it.

'Jane?' Soren was at my side, one hand holding the door shut.

'Just let me go, Soren,' I said wearily now. 'You're here, on Nissilum. And you can do what you like. You don't need me any more.'

'I do . . .' he said, his forehead creasing with distress. 'You are not a stranger any more. You're my friend.'

I glanced briefly at him, confused by his meaning, but he took his hand off the door.

'Friends don't lie,' I said righteously and, wasting no time, I wrenched the door open, to meet the crisp night air. As I stepped out on to the cobbled street I thought I

155

saw a figure in the shadows on the other side, but it moved back, indistinct. I squinted in the night and saw a black coat disappearing. For some reason I didn't want Soren to see it too.

'So, thanks,' I said curtly. 'If you'll just help me get back . . .'

'I thought we were friends.' He wasn't moving, 'Please don't go like this.'

I realised I was freezing. If I didn't get home soon I would die of hypothermia.

'Look, I just need time to think.' I had no intention of ever seeing Soren again, but if pretending would speed up my departure, then so be it.

'You haven't got much time . . . If you leave now, then—'

'Fine. I'll find my own way home.' I turned my back on him, not really knowing what I was going to do next. It looked like Soren wasn't going to help me after all. As I started walking I was determined not to look back, to see him standing there. So what if he wasn't there to take me back. Maybe I could find someone else?

I retraced the steps of our walk earlier that day, down the cobbled road, past the quaint little houses, silent, eerie . . . like everyone was already asleep. Then I remembered that this was the vampire quarter.

It was dark, so if habits hadn't died away, they should be circulating soon. I needed to be away from here before that happened.

The sound of my footsteps seemed to echo. I thought of the figure I had seen outside Vanya's house and suddenly felt more afraid.

I stopped in my tracks. There might be one person left who could help me . . . someone I trusted . . . who was on my side. *Had been* on my side.

Dalya.

If I could just find somewhere to sleep tonight, somewhere I could hide out. I could set out to find her in the morning. Dalya would help me. I was almost sure she would.

But the wind picked up and sliced right through me, and though I was trying to stop the panic rising, I could feel my eyes pricking. I was scared and cold and alone. And I wanted to see my mother.

The wind seemed to be getting stronger, great gusts of wind, pushing me forward until my legs, my feet, lost the ability to move of their own volition and were propelled forward by some kind of gathering storm.

A large drop of rain splashed on my forehead. Somewhere back there, Soren was no doubt expecting me to turn and go back. My imagination was running away with me. Was this sudden change in the weather something conjured up by Vanya?

I let out a gasp as I felt hands gripping my arms, so tightly that I couldn't turn back to see who was holding on to me so forcefully. This time there was no stopping the tears, they were streaming down my face, mixing with the rain which was pelting now.

'Please,' I whimpered as I pushed forward, 'I just want to go home. Just let me get home.'

And then I felt him, his face against my soaked hair, and a familiar scent – sweet, woody – and I closed my eyes, relieved and confused at the same time.

'Is that you?' I said. 'Is it really you?'

And then reality seemed to blur and, as the sky above us split with a fork of lightning, I felt his arms encircling me and his breath against my cheek.

And I finally passed out.

CHAPTER SEVENTEEN

'You'd think they would have brought you all the way to the door.' My mother shook her head, about to launch into a disapproving diatribe.

'I told them to drop me off in town,' I said, rubbing at my wet hair with a towel. 'Then the rain just came out of nowhere.'

'Well I know this mountain has its own particular microclimate, but it's odd that we didn't see a drop of rain.' She frowned, pulling at my sweatshirt. 'Didn't you take your coat? I could have sworn you left here yesterday with a coat?'

'Oh, right . . .' I shrugged. 'I must have left it on the coach.' I stopped rubbing with the towel and she whipped it from me.

'A bath for you, I think. And I'm going to have a serious word with this Mr Balzac. Totally irresponsible.'

159

You have no idea, I thought, catching sight of my little sister, dawdling in the kitchen doorway.

'Hey, sis.' I smiled, pleased to see her. So pleased to be home.

'Hey.' She slunk into the room, looking me up and down. 'Why are you wet?'

'Rain?' I said facetiously. 'It has this habit of making you wet . . .'

'But I just got back from town with Dad,' she said. 'It wasn't raining.'

'Yeah it was.' I glared at her, and she raised one cute little eyebrow.

'I'm going to take a bath then.' I stood, ruffling her blonde curls. 'Let's catch up later.'

'Uh-huh.' She nodded, and I sighed as I climbed the steps. Part of me wanted to confide in Dot, but it would just mean more complication, and for absolutely nothing.

Lying in the bath, I tried to go back over what had happened. When I'd arrived home, I opened my eyes and just felt confused. For a few moments I felt so disorientated I had no idea how I'd come to be crouched at the bottom of the track, my hair and clothes sopping wet. And then bits of memory came back. I remembered leaving Soren outside Vanya's house, and that wind, coming from nowhere, pushing me forward.

I had to have got back with somebody's help, but it wasn't Soren who had been there.

As I lay back in the bath, watching the mirror steaming up, the heat was making my head fuzzy. It had to be the heat because a fresh memory was there . . . the touch and the smell of someone I knew very well, someone I never thought would touch me again.

Luca!

I shot up in the bath, and sent water splashing over the sides.

It had been him. He'd brought me home. I groaned; everything had moved so quickly. All the times I had imagined being alone with Luca again, I thought we would talk, I never imagined it would be fleeting like it was.

He'd just wanted to get rid of me. That was the only reason he'd helped me. He wanted to make sure I disappeared. Probably for good.

All there was was the sound of the tap dripping.

Everyone had turned on me. Even the boy I trusted most. I had no choice now but to move forwards with my life. Concentrate on college, my future here in the mortal world. At least I knew for sure now. I told myself it was a good thing. It was the right thing. I didn't belong on

Nissilum. That pack of lies Soren had told me. He was a killer and I couldn't believe a word he said.

The water was getting cold now. I looked down and saw tiny goosebumps on my legs. I was cold.

I was so cold.

CHAPTER EIGHTEEN

In the midst of the crowds I spotted the twins perched on the wall outside college. Ashley, or it could have been Emma, was examining a manicured hand, her skinny legs encased in lace-up heels and legwarmers, were swinging like a little kid's. Emma was craning her neck looking for someone. I watched as her eyes travelled around, finally resting on me.

'Yoo-hoo!' She waved manically.

I raised a hand, giving a quick embarrassed glance at the people next to me.

Ashley jumped off the wall, gathering up her pink rucksack and slinging a tiny little bag with a gold-chain handle over her shoulder and the two of them pushed through milling students towards me.

'We heard a rumour about you,' Emma said, patting me on the hand. 'You're a dark horse.'

'What?' I frowned. 'What rumour?'

'About you . . . and that amazing Art teacher,' supplied Emma. 'Mr Balzac.'

I stiffened. 'What are you talking about? I don't know him.'

'Tell that to the rest of your Art class,' giggled Ashley. 'And you don't even wear make-up! What's your secret?'

'Not that you're not totally gorgeous.' Emma linked her arm through mine. 'But it's not fair. Ash and I spend hours every morning getting ready and not one boy here has noticed us. You're just one of those girls who doesn't need to make an effort, I guess . . .'

'Well, thanks . . . I think.' I couldn't help smiling. 'But for your information, there is nothing whatsoever going on between me and Balzac. In fact' – I gave a not-entirely-fake shudder – 'I find him a little creepy.'

'Are you out of your mind!?' shrieked Ashley. 'He's gorgeous. All dark and smouldering.'

'Right.' I wrinkled my nose. 'I just don't see it.'

'That's funny . . . because someone saw you getting in to his car.' She lifted her cute little chin imperiously. 'Sounds cosy to me.'

'Oh that.' I waved my hand about dismissively. 'I forgot to get my dad to pick me up . . . Balzac and I barely spoke the whole journey. I hate him.'

The last bit slipped out before I could stop it.

'You hate him?' The twins stared, wide-eyed at me. 'Why?'

'I mean, I find him creepy . . . like I said.' Flustered, I pretended to look for something in my bag. Even though I wasn't looking at them I knew the twins were staring at me suspiciously.

'Anyway,' I muttered, 'I think he left suddenly or something . . . That's what I heard. At least . . .'

'Well that's funny,' said Emma, 'because unless he has a twin brother, I've just seen him going into the cafeteria in the basement.'

I looked up sharply. 'He *what*?"

'Yeah. About fifteen minutes ago,' she said, looking with amusement at my pink face. 'Did you two have a falling out?'

'Of course not,' I said as light-heartedly as I could, but inside wondering what on earth Soren thought he was doing.

'Um, I'll catch you two up,' I said, shrugging. 'I need to get to the toilet before my first class.'

'OK,' they said in unison, an identically sly look on both faces.

'I'll see you at lunch maybe?' I gave a lame half-wave and turned in the direction of the toilets. I had no intention of going there. My first class was Art. There was no way I was setting foot in that class now. Maybe not ever.

I started to pick up speed, heading for the college main entrance, weaving in and out of kids who were hanging around killing time till their next class. As I turned to apologise to a couple of boys on skateboards, I crashed headlong into someone else.

'I'm really sorry,' I said, seeing only a checked cowboy shirt in front of me. 'I'm in kind of a hurry.'

'Really,' came the silky answer. 'And where do you have to be so urgently?'

My heart sinking, I lifted my head to meet those black eyes, mocking me.

I closed my eyes. 'Please get out of my way.'

'We need to talk,' he said, sounding less self-assured now. 'Really.'

'I have nothing more to say, Soren,' I hissed, trying not to look too conspicuous. I'd already got people talking here, apparently. I didn't want to get some kind of reputation.

He sighed heavily. 'You arrived home safely I see . . .'

'Obviously,' I said impatiently. 'No thanks to you.'

'You were behaving like a petulant little girl,' he told me. 'You can't just run away when the going gets tough . . .'

166

I opened my mouth in outrage. 'I don't take lectures from killers,' I growled. 'You've got a nerve.'

'I wonder who helped you home?' He arched an eyebrow. 'And you thought he didn't care?'

'You?' I couldn't help myself asking.

'Not me . . . Luca.'

'Luca? Well, if he did, it was just to get rid of me. He doesn't care.' I really didn't want to think about that night. The last time I would ever see Luca.

'Of course he does, you fool. Do you realise what a risk it must have been for him to do that?'

'Oh, I'm sick of thinking about it,' I snapped. 'Sick of thinking how hard it must be for Luca. What about me? What about how hard it is for me?'

I stopped, feeling breathless and angry all over again. All the while Soren just stood, regarding me as though I were a curious exhibit in a museum. I went to push past him but he gripped my arm.

'We have unfinished business,' he pleaded, 'you and I.'

'Well it's not my business any more . . . I don't know about you, but I'm going to get on with my life.' I wrenched his hand away.

'Glad to see you haven't lost any of your backbone, at least.' Seeing the furious expression on my face, his own softened a little. 'I know I can't expect you to believe I have any goodness in me, but killing my family . . . it was not my choice. I was just so . . . angry.'

'What could possibly have made you so angry that you'd take out your entire family?' I shook my head, disdainfully.

He sighed. 'This is not the place . . . Had you stayed in Nissilum I would have been able to explain.'

'Don't bother,' I muttered, as the bell rang.

All at once students were streaming past heading for the surrounding buildings, crowding us. I spotted the twins, arm in arm, heading our way.

'I can't do this now.' I edged away from him. 'I'll see you.'

'In class?'

'Yes . . . no . . . maybe.' I started walking backwards, feeling almost sorry for him as he stood there, looking kind of helpless.

I didn't go to Soren's Art class. I couldn't face it, and I had too much on my mind to concentrate on the subject. Besides, I felt exhausted. Being pushed this way and that. Deep down, I had a feeling that Soren was not a bad, evil person. Though my powers of judgement were not exactly reliable.

There was a café opposite college, usually filled with

students on break, but today it was empty. I found a seat and dumped my bag on the one next to me. I wasn't hungry but I ordered a Danish and a cup of coffee.

Staring out of the window I allowed myself a fantasy, one where time had gone back, to that day he first came into my life. Standing there with his coat that was a little oversized, his long gangly legs, his serenity, his sensitivity. And would I have got him to stay? Could I have stopped his parents from intervening, from deciding his future for him? Maybe if I had just refused to let go, held on to him while Henora told him he was marrying Lila, then he would have chosen me.

But he hadn't chosen me. That was the thing. He had free will and his will chose Lila.

I pushed away the Danish pastry and watched the frothy milk as it began to evaporate in my coffee.

'Hey.' I looked up to see the twins standing over me. Ashley smiled, holding out her hand and gently touching my arm. 'You OK?'

I managed a weak smile in return. 'I'm fine. Just feeling a little off today.'

Ashley lowered herself into the chair opposite me and Emma followed suit.

'It's about him, isn't it?' she said sympathetically. 'You can tell us . . . We'll keep it a secret.'

'Who? Mr Balzac?' I laughed in spite of my miserable mood. 'Believe me. There is nothing going on there.'

'Maybe not on your side . . .' The girls exchanged looks. 'But we saw him watching you when you walked out of school just now . . .'

'It was a look of pure longing,' sighed Emma. 'He looked so sad. Did you reject him?'

'I . . . I . . . No. Not . . . No, I didn't.' I said, embarrassed. 'It's not like that!'

'You're going red, Jane . . .' Ashley leaned in closer. 'Is it the teacher-student thing? Is that why you said no?'

If only it was that simple. I shook my head.

'You've got it wrong . . . Mr Balzac was just talking to me about art . . . he's kind of intense. Passionate about his subject, I guess.'

'Passionate . . . See, there, you said it. He's passionate.'

'Seriously! You two need to grow up,' I said grumpily. 'Maybe if you had boyfriends of your own you wouldn't try and invent romances for other people.' I stopped, already regretting being so harsh.

'Fine.' Looking hurt, Ashley got up, indicating to Emma to do the same. 'But maybe if you were less of a grouch you might actually get a boy to like you, not somebody practically old enough to be your dad.'

I couldn't help a little smile at that.

'What's so funny? God, you are such a bitch, Jane,' whipped Ashley. 'I would have thought you'd appreciate a friend. I mean you don't seem to have any others.'

'I wasn't smiling because . . .' I shook my head. I didn't have the equipment for this kind of thing. I had never actually had a friend, after all. They were right.

'I'm sorry,' I said awkwardly.

'Forget it.' Ashley tugged on Emma's arm. 'Come on. We need to get to class.' She shot me another glowering look before the two of them headed for the café exit.

As the door closed behind them, and I watched them crossing the road, arm in arm, I felt a pang at their closeness. Ashley and Emma might have a simplistic view of the world. They might seem a little shallow sometimes, but they had each other. They would always have that special bond.

I wanted mine back. I wanted it back more than anything. But at any cost?

I paid for my food and trudged back into college, checking my watch. If I was quick, I would make it for the last half of my Art class. As much as I never wanted to see Soren's smug face again, I didn't want to mess up my future. I took a deep breath and headed for the Art block.

* * *

'Today, we're going to do something a little different. I am going to tell you a story.' Soren looked around the room, his expression serious. I waited for him to try and engage me, but his eyes swept swiftly over me. 'And when I have finished telling you this story, I want you to draw what has captured you most about it.'

Students exchanged puzzled looks. Soren leaned back against his desk, waiting until the whispering had died down before he began.

'There was once a good boy. A boy born into a hard-working law-abiding family, who raised him to be good-mannered, considerate and honest. They were emphatic about these qualities and the boy did his best to make them proud. The boy had two sisters and a brother. He was close to his siblings, but in particular to his younger sister, who adored him. This boy would have done anything for her in return. He was very protective of her. The boy lived happily until he was ten years old when something happened to destroy everything he believed in . . .'

Soren paused for a few seconds, seeing that the entire class was enthralled. In spite of myself, I waited for him to continue too.

'On his sixth birthday, a man came to the door and beckoned to the boy to come and sit with him outside in the front garden; he had something to tell him. Curious, but a little nervous, the boy sat with the man on a bench in his garden and the man – who seemed so kind, with his twinkly blue eyes – told him without very much ado that he – this little boy – was his son. The boy was shocked, but at once he knew it was true. There was something about this man that drew the boy to him. He felt safe and he felt that this man was very familiar somehow. As though he knew him.

'But then the boy began thinking about his mother and father, who had been so emphatic about honesty, and that they had lied to him. They had been good to him, but they had lied. And then the boy thought of his sister, and that she wasn't really his sister, and then he felt very alone and scared that he would be taken away from her. And as he listened to the man talk he grew even angrier, because this kind man seemed to be saying that he didn't want the boy for his son . . . that he had only come to ease his guilt. And the boy felt used. He felt that all the adults around him had only thought of themselves and not him, that he wasn't loved and never would be. And once his beloved younger sister found out he wasn't truly her brother, she would hate him, when once she had loved him.

'The man saw that the boy was upset and he himself

was distressed. He told the boy that his mother was still his mother, that she had carried him inside her, and that would not change. He thought this would mollify the boy, but it made everything much worse.

'Because the boy now realised his mother had committed a terrible betrayal, one that was worse than anything. That his own mother was a bad woman. And the boy, thinking of how often she had scolded him for misbehaving, felt a surge of hatred for her. He knew he could never think of her in the same way again. He knew that he no longer loved her, he hated her. He felt a fool believing that his whole family had known all along. All except for his little sister, who was surely too young and who still believed he was her flesh and blood.

'The boy stood and thanked the man for telling him. The man held out his hand. He asked the boy to forgive him, and forgive his mother, and said that he – his true father – meant to pay penance for what he had done.

'The boy tried to smile, but he knew that he could not do as his true father asked. He felt such betrayal and anger and confusion with the world in which he lived, that he didn't know what he would do, but he knew he no longer wanted a relationship with the people who had brought him up.

'As the man walked away from him, the boy stood and

looked around. He looked at the carefully tended flowerbeds, and the grass kept short and moist, and the neatly clipped hedge around his freshly painted house. And as he looked he grew more incensed at all this perfection, which meant nothing any more. And the boy walked towards his father's shed at the side of the house and inside he found his father's axe. He took it back to the house, where he sat at the kitchen table.

'The boy waited two hours before he heard the sound of his parents coming into the house. When his mother walked into the kitchen and saw him sitting there she began to scold him for sitting idle while there were chores to be done around the house. And his father nodded in agreement. And behind his parents, his older brother and sister looked on in a judgemental kind of way. And seeing them there, so self-righteous, the boy stood and just stared coldly at them all; he knew his father would now beat him for his apparent insubordination, but he didn't care, he cared about very little any more. He felt no emotion. As his father advanced towards him, he lifted his axe and he spliced his father's head clean open.'

Soren stopped again, his whole face a grisly grey colour. He swallowed hard, looking straight ahead of him before he went on.

'And stepping over his father's body, he did the same

to his mother. He didn't know where he had the strength to do this, he just seemed to grow bigger and stronger . . . and more like an animal. He *was* an animal. He carried on until all four were dead, lying in their own blood on the floor of the family kitchen.'

I looked around me, to see everyone wide-eyed and shocked. When I came to look at Soren, I saw that his black eyes were shimmering. For the first time I recognised serious emotion in him. And I knew he wanted to finish this story and that he was telling it for my benefit alone.

Soren sighed. 'And then, as this boy stood looking at what he had done, he heard the sound of footsteps, light and innocent, coming up to the door of the house, and he felt the pulse of his heart as though it would burst through his chest – and finally emotion. Not for his dead family, but for the owner of those footsteps. He dropped the axe and he moved quickly to greet her, hoping to get to her before she came in to the kitchen . . . but he was not quick enough and the little girl ran straight into the site of his murder, and she took in her bludgeoned parents and her lifeless siblings, and he saw a look cross her face that would haunt him ever after that. It was first a look of horror and disbelief . . . shock. Then when she turned to him it was a look of pain he hoped never to see again. And then she started to scream. She did not stop. And the boy, knowing that he would be discovered, and with some semblance of self-preservation left, ran from her and into the woods. He ran for days and nights and though all he saw was his sister's face, so twisted in pain, he did not turn back.'

Soren looked up then and his eyes met with mine. So it was true, he had come back for Lila. Not because he wanted to marry her, but because he wanted to protect her . . . He was making up for what he did. I attempted a half-smile, still not quite sure what I felt about this. He was a good storyteller for sure, he made it sound lyrical, moving even . . . but he still did it. He still—

'Is that story actually, like . . . true?' asked a hippyish girl called something like Skylar, sitting at the front.

Soren gave a non-committal shrug. 'Does it matter?'

'Well, it's pretty horrific . . .' She turned back to see what the rest of us thought. 'I mean . . . I'm not sure I want to draw a bunch of dead bodies.'

He smiled tightly. 'Well . . . don't then. Draw what appeals to you about it . . .'

I put my hand up. 'That isn't the end of the story, though, is it? What happened to the boy? And his sister?'

Soren's eyes seemed to bore into me. Whether he was

annoyed or not, I couldn't tell. He looked perfectly composed as he answered.

'You want to hear what happened?' He cleared his throat. 'I don't know if . . .'

'You don't know the end of the story?' I held his gaze.

'Of course I know . . .' he said softly. 'The boy never went back.'

'What happened to the little kid?' asked a boy two desks away from me.

'She was found . . . and raised by another family, though she was so traumatised that she blocked it all out.'

'What is this?' the boy said. 'Is this someone you know?'

The whole class looked questioningly at Soren.

'In a way,' he said mysteriously. 'Someone I used to know. He started a new life for himself. And he tried to forget. He grew up, and he learned to survive without a family . . . But it changed him for ever.'

'What about his real father – didn't he try and find him?' asked Skylar. 'I mean he went to all the trouble of telling him and then he just abandoned him? It's so sad.'

'He saw his father again. Once. In fact his true father set the law on him.'

There was a collective gasp.

'And he was caught . . . and imprisoned, and his real father pleaded leniency . . . if the boy promised to leave the country and never return.' Soren's shoulders seemed to slump a little. 'That's it. That's the story. Make of it what you will.'

There was silence as the class got creative with whatever had captured their imaginations during Soren's story. I veered away from the bloodshed, like pretty much everyone except a couple of metal-heads at the back of the class. I concentrated on what had come into my head. I drew the wood that Soren had run into. A mass of fierce green trees, dark marshy soil, stretching on for ever and, above the wood, a solid round moon, hanging in a starless sky.

It kind of symbolised my life. Just a thick, impenetrable wood that I couldn't get through, no matter how many times I tried.

It was all so sad. And it seemed kind of hopeless. But Soren's story got to me, not just because of the terrible thing he had done, but of what came after. Who was his real father? And why didn't he help his son like any parent would?

I lifted my head and slowly focussed on Soren, standing at the front of the class, head bent, carefully packing books away in his leather bag. No sardonic jokes, no dry remarks, just contemplative silence. I knew he wouldn't tell me what really happened.

And did I want to know?

Students filed out, handing their work over to him, and he stacked it neatly on his desk.

'Thank you,' he told one of the metal-heads, a guy called Rory, who was the last to give him his drawing. Glancing down, I saw Soren grimace, his face tightening a little before giving Rory a wry smile and putting his work on top of the others.

I took my time putting my stuff away, waiting until the last student had filed out before I spoke.

'It sounded really . . . awful,' I said quietly. 'But not all the pieces are in place. And I'm not going to change my mind.'

'I wish I could put all the pieces together for you . . . But I don't think they would make much sense even then.' He smiled at me.

'What are you going to do? Are you going to resign?'

'What?'

'From here? You can't stay on . . . I mean, what would be the point now?'

'I hadn't thought about it.' He rubbed at his temples. 'But perhaps you're right. There is no point.' He directed a look of real sadness at me.

'I'm sorry,' I said awkwardly. 'I just . . . can't.'

'I know.' He picked his bag off the table with one hand and stretched the other out to me. Hesitating for a second I took it, feeling it warm and responsive in my hand. I realised I was going to miss him.

'I'll miss you,' he said, as though reading my mind. Maybe he had? I flushed a little.

'Me too.' And my fingers squeezed his.

He shook his head, a familiar lazy smile crossing his face. 'I want you to remember how important you are. Maybe years from now you will realise . . .' He shut his eyes briefly. 'I was going to say regret . . . But I can see that I would have been dragging you into a whole mess and danger—'

'Danger?' I said slowly. 'What danger?'

He was silent.

'Soren,' I persisted, 'what do you mean, "danger"?'

'Nothing for you to worry about now,' he said then, too casually.

'Are you in danger? Is Luca in danger? What?'

'What do you care? It is no longer any of your concern.' He turned to pick his jacket off the back of his chair. 'You are safe now.'

Safe. Why did that word sound so deadly all of a sudden. I had longed for safety. Back in the bad old days.

'You're good,' I said, shaking my head. 'So manipulative!'

His eyes widened. 'Me?' he said innocently. 'Whatever can you mean?'

'Not going to work. I have my life to get on with . . .'

'My future to think about . . .' he mimicked, his eyes teasing me.

'Was any of that story even true?' I asked, annoyance rising in me.

'You are going to have to start trusting me, Jane,' he said seriously.

'Not any more I don't,' I said, moving towards the door. 'I'll see you around.'

'I hope so,' he said, just loud enough for me to hear as the door swung shut behind me.

Disgruntled, I went to find my bike. It was growing dark and I hurried through the main quadrant to the bike racks at the back of college. Glancing up at the sky I saw the moon, like a delicate rice cracker, waiting to take its night-time place, full in the sky. And I felt a tremor pass through me. A connection. I tried to shake it off. The moon was just the moon. There was no longer anything significant about it.

Yet as I unlocked my bike in the dimming light, I

couldn't help thinking that somewhere, on Nissilum, Luca was in tune with it too. Dangerous, in physical pain, struggling against his destiny.

CHAPTER NINETEEN

'You're very late,' the old man said, getting to his feet, screwing the top back on his bottle and stuffing a bag containing his supper into his pocket. Clumsily he picked up his hat, putting it on as a mark of respect for his visitor.

'I know.' Raphael waved a hand at the old man. 'Please, carry on with your meal . . . I can return tomorrow, I have simply come to . . . be with him.'

The old man grunted, the bunch of keys tied to his wrist jangled loudly. 'Visitors usually come in the day, sir. *She* comes in the day . . . Better in the day.'

'My great-mother?' Raphael nodded, anxious to put the old man at ease. 'Yes, I know. I simply wanted to . . .' He trailed off, unable to find the words to explain.

The old man looked confused, though he seemed to understand the boy's agitation, his need.

'One minute, I will fetch a torch.' Turning his back on Raphael, he shuffled over to the building behind him. Standing at the locked gates, Raphael shifted from foot to foot, half regretting coming out to the Celestial memorial grounds so late at night, putting the old man to such trouble. The old guy had been here as long as he could remember. Day in, day out, guarding over what few resting places there were here. Death was not part of life on Nissilum. Only a few exceptions had their tombs here. Old Quin had little to do each day and had slowly turned more eccentric and unsocialised in his old age. The son of a peasant angel, he had never married or had any children, his only companions were the ghosts of the unfortunate few left rotting in this place.

Raphael was about to call out, tell old Quin he had changed his mind, that he shouldn't bother himself on such a cold night, but then the old man reappeared, grinning, half his teeth missing, a few tufts of blond hair fuzzy on his head.

'Good one here . . . Bright enough.' Quin waved the torch about, smiling. He shook the keys off his wrist, catching them in his palm, then deftly found the one to unlock the main gate.

'Thank you,' Raphael said, 'I won't be long.'

The old man shrugged good-naturedly, turning the

key and unlocking the heavy gate. It creaked back, and Raphael was free to walk inside the grounds.

The old man beckoned to Raphael to follow him, through a narrow alleyway, either side of which stood the old tomb shelters. The boy suppressed a shudder as they walked, turning at the end, where an ornate stone arch heralded the resting place of the Celestial family.

Quin unlocked the heavy stone door in the middle of the arch, coughing and muttering under his breath as he did so. Raphael was increasingly regretting coming here. He had never been before;, had refused to admit that his father no longer existed. Standing out in the damp cold, about to enter a less inviting place, he rubbed his hands together.

As Quin held the door to the tombs open, he turned, grinning, as though he was almost excited at the prospect of a visitor at last. He handed Raphael the torch, nodding in a half-witted kind of way.

'Perhaps you could accompany me . . .' Raphael gestured inside at the pitch black. He hoped the old man would understand, that he wouldn't have to explain.

To his relief, Quin nodded kindly. 'Yes, yes,' he said gruffly, gently pushing Raphael into the building.

'There.' The old man pointed directly in front of them.

Gabriel's tomb was an open stone casket of sorts.

As the two of them approached it, Raphael had the urge to bolt, to run for his life. But he stood his ground.

'Do you come in here much . . . ?' he asked Quin. The hand that was holding the torch trembled a little, casting dancing shadows on the walls.

Quin shook his head furiously. 'Forbidden,' he said. 'Only your eyes, your mother's, your great-mother's eyes, shall see.'

'Oh.' Raphael was now even less inclined to see his father – or the bones that were all that was left of him.

Quin watched him, waiting.

Raphael stepped forward and, even in the cold, he felt a light sweat on his forehead. Swallowing, he forced himself to look down at Gabriel.

Who wasn't there.

Raphael frowned, both relieved and disappointed at the same time. He flashed a look back at the keeper.

'There's nothing there,' he said quietly. 'My father is gone.'

Quin shook his head slowly. 'Mistake,' he said, 'you have made a mistake.'

'Look.' Raphael drew Quin closer to the casket. 'Nothing there.'

Quin peered inside, sticking his lip out, perturbed, then scratching his head.

'You've never seen my father in here?' Raphael stared hard at him. 'Perhaps he never was?'

Quin looked dumbfounded. 'Yes, yes. He was here.' He looked helplessly at the boy. 'Your great-mother . . . she saw to it all.'

An echoing silence passed between them. Raphael struggled with an inexplicable truth.

His great-mother had lied.

An owl hooted. Night-time rodents scuttled around at his feet, but Raphael barely noticed. He felt a mixture of anger, fear and extreme curiosity. As he drew nearer to the back of the palace, he glanced up at the vast bay window where the lights in Celeste's sitting room burned cosily. Raphael let himself through the gate to the garden that lay in front of the servants' entrance. It was quicker to come this way, where he could slip, no questions asked, down the long passage that led to the great hall.

'Sir.' One of the pretty maids bobbed, as he passed her. He smiled briefly, hardly seeing her, and continued on his way. He had a reputation for erratic behaviour, he was aware of that. He was certain that the girl would scurry into the kitchen and report one more incidence of it. Raphael didn't care. He had long since stopped caring what others thought of him. All except for his great-mother, that is. It had always mattered to him what she thought, with her integrity and her kindness. Her lack of guile.

But he must have been wrong about that. Walking through the hall he stopped at the foot of the great staircase. Celeste too had it in her to deceive. Like his father.

Was his whole family steeped in hypocrisy? The door to her sitting room was ajar. As he pushed it further open he saw her seated on her favourite chair, head bent over her needlework. A cello concerto played at just the right volume on the ancient record player – she refused to upgrade to anything else.

She heard him, lifted her head, and a beatific smile lit up her face.

'Raffy.' She put down on her sewing. 'What is the matter, boy?'

'I went to see my father,' he said without preamble. 'I went to the Celestial tombs.'

Her face darkened, but she kept the smile on her face. 'I see.' She clasped her hands together – nervously, he saw.

'I went to talk to him . . . to talk out everything on my mind.' Raphael came to sit next to her. 'And I suppose to get some kind of closure. Acceptance of his death—'

'Raffy,' she tried to interrupt, but he silenced her with a wave of his hand.

'Imagine my surprise when his tomb was empty! Old Quin was taken aback too . . . All very odd.' He stopped talking and his head dropped. He waited for her to speak.

She shifted in her seat. 'Raffy—'

'Where is he' – Raphael raised his head – 'if he's not in his tomb?'

'Darling . . . you know that death here is not as it is in the mortal world.' Celeste rose, picking up her needlework and placing it in a white wicker basket at the side of the sofa. She seemed unable to look at him.

'Yes.' He stared at her back. 'But we gather the bones when our people are gone . . . But my father's are gone. I want to know where.'

Celeste sighed and her usual immaculate posture drooped. She turned and finally met Raphael's eyes, moving cautiously towards him. Finally she sat herself next to him.

'Raphael, I don't know where your father is . . .' She breathed out at last, as though letting go of some burden, all the time watching her great-son.

'What?' Raphael felt his heart skip a beat, or perhaps stop altogether, just for a second. 'But, you said . . . I saw . . .' He stopped; he remembered the last time he had seen Gabriel, half mad, gibbering, while Dorcas wrung her hands next to him. He had been so shrunken and pale, where he had been larger than life, full of vitality. He had just kept repeating the same word: 'sorry'.

'Your father was very weak,' said Celeste. 'And your mother – well, she couldn't cope. She still can't . . . But who knows—'

Raphael shook his head impatiently. 'I don't want to talk about my mother.'

'I was his sole carer. I felt as though I was with him night and day, trying to comfort him, tell him that whatever he had done, it was not worth wasting away over. Your father's valet, Milo, was devoted to him too as you know. Between us we tried to keep him from . . . disappearing. Then one night, Gabriel was in a particularly bad way. His skin was grey, and he shook all over. We knew that there was nothing *physically* wrong with him, we knew that it was his mind, destroying him. Milo went to the physician to fetch a sedative while I stayed with Gabriel, but he was gone for so long . . . and Cadmium – never the most patient of men – was eager for me to accompany him on a state visit on the other side of Nissilum. I felt torn, but the staff assured me they would watch over my son . . . And so I left.'

Celeste paused, her pain visible in her eyes, before going on.

'I was away for a day and a half . . . And when we returned I rushed to his room, hopeful that he would be calm and peaceful. Milo was standing guard outside and when he saw me approach, his whole face seemed to freeze in fear – he told me that Gabriel had gone . . . he had literally wasted away overnight.'

'Yes – I know that he wasted away . . .' Raphael could see how difficult she was finding this explanation, and it made his heart soften towards her, just a little. But he wanted the whole truth, the whole story, however hard it was for his great-mother to tell it.

'I didn't believe him at first and I must say I pushed past him and ran in to see for myself.' She paused, taking a breath. 'And there on the bed was what I took to be him: a collection of bones underneath a blanket.'

'So you saw his bones?' Raphael leaned forward. 'It was true?'

'I couldn't bear to look . . .' A tear slipped down on to her cheek. 'I remember sinking on to the bed and sobbing. Thinking of you, a boy without his father, whose mother had gone . . . I suppose all that had happened over the years since Gabriel first broke down suddenly came upon me, like a great weight crashing down.' She blinked at Raphael through her tears. 'The next thing I remember was waking up with Cadmium at my side on the day of Gabriel's ushering out ceremony.'

'But what about my great-father, my mother, my aunts? Nobody saw for themselves that Gabriel was dead?'

She shook her head. 'Nobody could face it. And then he was taken to the tombs and nobody visited. By that time you were starting to . . .'

'Yes.' Raphael nodded. 'My own "madness" had begun.'

'And when I did finally first visit the tombs – I saw that his was empty, and I just left and never told a soul. I pretended to the family that all was well. Cadmium refused to talk about Gabriel . . . I knew he would never go there. Dear old Quin was practically jubilant at the sight of me. Clearly nobody else had been there. The only one who knew was me . . .'

'And Milo?' Raphael pushed her. 'Milo knew. Did you not try and find him when he went to live with his cousins in the South?'

She stared at me, and I knew. She had no idea where Milo was either.

'They both just disappeared,' she whispered, hoarsely now that her tears were coming thick and fast. 'Just . . . gone.'

'He could still be alive,' said Raphael, trying hard to take it all in. 'Somewhere . . . Gabriel is still alive.'

CHAPTER TWENTY

When I woke up the first thing I saw was the moon through the window. Translucent, shimmering, perfectly round. I looked at my clock, two a.m. I had gone to bed with that moon staring at me, and woken up to it. For months I had barely noticed it and now it seemed to be beckoning to me. All over again.

Careful not to wake my sleeping family, I drew back my quilt and softly crossed the room to the window.

It was a windy night, but milder than usual. I shrugged off the thick cardigan I had worn to bed and forgotten to take off. A tiny draught lifted the fine hair on my arms and outside the black-topped trees swayed rhythmically. The wind must be strong because it was as though the whole of the mountain was whispering. *Just leaves hitting leaves*, I told myself. But something felt different tonight . . . I felt a strange sensation. No, not strange . . .

familiar. I had drifted in and out of sleep, things coming into my head . . . Not exactly a dream, but images. I wanted so badly to see Luca. But all I saw was fleeting. Black eyes. Not green. A thick green forest and the sound of breathing.

And a low wail. Like a wolf's.

I lifted the window latch, pushing it open, feeling the slight nip of the difference in temperature. It felt cool, soothing, gentle fingertips stroking my arm. I shut my eyes, wanting to feel sleepy again.

'Jane.'

My eyes snapped open, met a flash of a face. But was it him? Was I just making him up . . . and those unmistakeable mossy green eyes? I opened my mouth, but as I did so, he disappeared. Breathlessly, I leaned right out of the window, searching on the ground below. I didn't imagine it, I knew. Someone had been there.

'Luca,' I whispered out into the night, 'please. Don't go.'

But I was met only with silence. The yard was deserted, the trees still gently swaying.

I closed the window, defeated, and as I moved away from it, I caught my reflection on the dressing table mirror. My hair was tangled and messy, and dark shadows lined my eyes. I looked terrible, like I hadn't slept for months. All the happiness drained out of me.

I knew I would never sleep now. But I climbed back into bed, pulling the quilt over me, leaning back against the headrest.

Luca had not spoken to me for months, hadn't contacted me through my dreams like he had all that time ago. And now, tonight... Was he trying to tell me something?

Or warn me?

Suddenly my heart was beating fast and adrenaline started to surge. Was Luca in trouble? Hugging my knees, I glanced again at the clock – only ten minutes had passed – and then my eyes fell on my phone. Flipping it open I scrolled through the numbers. I had barely used my phone since I'd got it . . . but I remembered the text from Soren, the creepy one he'd sent on the day I got it. Had I saved the number? Had there even been a number?

No. But the text was still there. Shaking my head, wondering if I was opening up a whole new can of worms, I pressed Reply.

WHERE ARE YOU?

I sent the message and snapped the phone shut. It was the middle of the night, who knows how long I'd have to wait for a reply. Slipping down in the bed I closed my eyes, willing myself to sleep, just as my phone beeped.

WHEREVER YOU WANT ME TO BE

Typical. I rolled my eyes as I texted back.

I THINK I NEED TO GO BACK. THIS ISN'T OVER YET.

I'd hardly sent it before his response flashed back on the screen.

I KNEW YOU'D COME ROUND. LET'S TALK IN THE MORNING.

Infuriating, yet I couldn't help the smile that crept across my face.

OK I tapped back, before turning the light out.

As dubious as my trust in him was, Soren was my ticket back to Nissilum. My only chance.

Weaving my bike in and out through the college students standing around the main gates, I craned my neck to see Ashley and Emma deep in conversation, sitting on the wall.

It was time for a proper apology.

'Hey,' I said, dismounting. The girls looked up from their conversation. Ashley was aiming for cross, which just looked a little comical on her sweet face. Emma went for a half-smile, shrugging her delicate shoulders.

'Listen . . . I know you think I'm rude and weird and . . . stuff,' I began. 'But I'm just a little touchy about boys at the moment.'

The twins glanced quickly at each other.

'About Balzac?' Ashley asked. ''Cause, we wouldn't say anything . . .'

'No . . . It's not him. He's just a teacher taking a special interest in my work . . . It's . . . Well, I broke up with a guy a few months ago. I guess I'm not really over him yet . . . I took it out on you two, I'm sorry.'

They simultaneously crossed their arms over their chests.

'Apology accepted,' they said in unison, before Ashley jumped down off the wall.

'What happened?' she asked, biting her lip. 'Or don't you want to talk about it?'

'No. It's OK. It's a guy I was with for a few months . . . He lived a long way from here. Kind of a long-distance romance.' I sighed. 'I thought he was my soulmate, but his family kind of had other plans and . . . it didn't work out.' I smiled grimly. 'But I still think about him. A lot.'

'We're sorry.' Ashley looked back at Emma, whose doe-eyes focussed on me. 'That must be awful.' She flared her nostrils. 'And what a loser! Dumping someone as pretty as you . . .'

'It's a bit more complicated than that—' I began, but the girls moved to either side of me, linking their arms through mine.

'Who needs boys anyway?' said Emma. 'They just mess with your head.' She gave my arm a little squeeze with hers. 'You need someone older. More mature . . .'

'Maybe you should give Balzac a chance?' said Ashley casually. 'I mean it's obvious he so totally likes you.'

'No.' I shook my head, almost laughing. 'He doesn't. Not like that. Believe me.' But I could see them exchanging looks behind my back.

'If you say so,' Ash replied. 'But you could do a lot worse . . .'

'Maybe.' I wrinkled my nose, just as Soren rounded the south corner of the quad and headed straight in our direction. I tried to stop myself from going red.

'I'm just going to lock my bike,' I told the twins, before they clocked him. 'I'll see you at break?'

'OK. But don't you want to say hello to Mr Balzac first?' said Emma, innocently. 'It seems a little rude . . .'

'He'll survive,' I said, turning off at the path to the cycle racks. 'I'll see you later.'

I had put some extra clothes in my rucksack, together with a toothbrush and all the things I had never thought to take to Nissilum before. I hadn't needed them. I wanted to be more prepared this time. I shoved the key to the bike lock in a zip pocket.

'So,' came a voice behind me, 'what's happened to change your mind?'

I turned and rose up from my crouched position on the ground.

'Hey,' I said. 'Thanks for . . . you know, replying to my message.'

'Not a problem,' he replied. 'What's going on?'

'I just . . . I think Luca was trying to tell me something in my sleep,' I said, 'last night.'

'Really?' Soren nodded. 'I must try that.'

'Try what?'

'Talking to you in your sleep.'

'I thought the connection had been broken,' I went on, ignoring him. 'He hasn't spoken to me for months. I think he is in trouble . . . Or something's wrong.'

'Are you sure it was him?' Soren frowned.

'Who else would it be? I didn't . . . don't have that connection with anyone else. I mean – it has to be him.' I watched Soren's expression turning anxious.

'What? What's the matter?' I asked.

'Nothing,' he put on what looked very much like a fake smile. 'Nothing's wrong.'

'Right. Because if you know something?' I said, lifting

my chin. 'If—'

'Jane. Jane . . . calm down. I am merely absorbing this latest turn in events,' said Soren, giving what he thought was a reassuring smile. 'I am as curious as you are.'

'OK.' I hoisted my rucksack on to my shoulder. 'I told my mother I was spending the night with Ashley and Emma, so—'

'Ashley and Emma?' Soren stroked his chin. 'Those two blonde creatures I saw you walk in with just now?'

'Huge fans of yours,' I said, warningly. 'So, don't knock them.'

'I wasn't going to . . .' He held up a hand in protest. 'They just don't seem like the sort of girls you would be friendly with, that's all.'

'I . . . They're not, I guess . . . But I've never actually had a friend before, so I'll go with it.' I shrugged. 'They're OK. If a little . . .'

'Girly,' he supplied. 'And pink.'

I gave him a light shove. 'Like I said, Soren, for some reason, those girls think the sun shines out of your—'

'Yes, OK,' he said dryly. 'I understand. There is to be no mocking of the girly blonde twins.'

'That's right,' I said imperiously, 'because I need all the friends I can get right now.'

Soren looked at his watch. 'Right, Ms Jonas. I will see

202

you in class later on.' As I walked past, he put a hand gently on my shoulder. 'And I'm glad you have changed your mind. I am sure that this is a sign . . .'

'I don't know what it is. I just have an uneasy feeling,' I said, quietly. 'It's just so out of the blue . . . Luca may not have chosen me, but if he's in trouble, I have to go to him.'

CHAPTER TWENTY-ONE

'I am simply asking how loyal you are,' Raphael said. He took a swig out of the flask in his hands. 'To the Celestial family.'

Lowe stood with his shoulders back. 'I am a patriot,' he told him. 'As you know. I am deeply loyal.'

Raphael nodded. 'And you would do anything I asked of you?'

'Well . . .' Lowe scratched his head. 'Yes. I respect you, Raphael.'

'Why is that?' Raphael put down his flask, looking intently into the younger boy's eyes.

'Because . . . I think you have a backbone,' said Lowe. 'And you despise dishonesty.'

Raphael nodded. 'Are you sure it is not because you are frightened?'

'Frightened?' Lowe looked confused. 'Of course not.

I am not afraid of anything!'

'Perhaps I should have used a better word,' Raphael said. 'Threatened, for example?'

Lowe's face clouded over. He looked confused and even more indignant.

'Raffy,' he said, 'why are you being like this? I would do anything you asked of me.'

'But you don't really know who I am,' Raphael went on mysteriously. He moved closer to the boy, their noses practically touching. 'How can you be sure I am somebody who deserves devotion?'

Lowe was silent, but his body flinched a little.

'Are you . . . feeling unwell,' he asked Raphael cautiously. 'Perhaps I should leave you to rest?'

Raphael laughed, a short bark of a laugh. 'I am not unwell. In fact I am the most lucid I have ever been. I see the world so simply now. And I see it is nothing like what I have been led to believe.' He tugged at Lowe's collar. 'You would do well to take those scales from your eyes, Lowe. Your loyalty is misplaced.'

'I have no idea what you are talking about. I just know that there have been things happening here lately that I don't like – that need to be stopped before they cause harm. That stranger, that black-eyed stranger, for example. Here with the mortal—'

Raphael smiled, though his blue eyes were cold. 'Your enemies lie so much closer to home . . . If you weren't so caught up in the pointless beliefs of your parents, of the state, you might see that. As it is, you enjoy the pain all this deprivation causes others. Even your own brother.'

'I too want to protect Luca.' Lowe spoke passionately, misunderstanding. 'I will do whatever it takes.'

Raphael sighed then, looking as though he wanted to say something more, but he merely shook his head, patting Lowe in a brotherly fashion on his chest.

'I didn't mean . . .' he said at last, before realising the pointlessness of carrying on. 'It doesn't matter. You had best go home now. I have things to attend to.'

Lowe looked relieved.

'Of course,' he said, though nervously. Raphael turned from him, already regretting being so outspoken. Lowe was not stupid, though he was notoriously hot-headed. If suspicion were to start to grow in him, it would not be long before ripples of suspicion would grow within the community.

Minutes after the boy had left, Raphael sat on a stool next to the stalls. The horses, as though detecting impending change, stirred and pawed the ground, though

Raphael barely noticed them.

He drew out of his pocket a sheaf of paperwork that he had managed to obtain from the state offices. His great father, Cadmium, was the only one with authority to retrieve any official paperwork from the files, but Cadmium was still stricken with some kind of malady and had foolishly granted Raphael access to the state records. It seemed as though events were naturally conspiring to enable Raphael to overturn the status quo – starting with the very heart of its political and sociological ethos: the Celestial government.

He unfolded the papers. The first one was his father's death certificate. Raphael's heart seemed to freeze a little as he glanced at the ornately inked facts. His father had died in the presence of his loyal servant Milo.

The document went on to state that Milo was now living in the South, in a location that he chose not to disclose on the document itself. *Why not disclose it?* thought Raphael. Milo did not want any of the family coming to question him too closely. And Cadmium had authorised this.

Raphael leafed through the rest of the paperwork until he came to the one he thought was most important. It concerned the terms of succession should Cadmium cease to rule Nissilum. If he stepped down, it was stated, that if the masses of Nissilum, a quantity of more than fifty percent of the population, were to call for a change of leader, even the removal of the Royal family itself, then an election could be called.

The boy dropped the documents on the stable floor. He loved his great-father, even admired his fierce but fair governance, just as he loved Celeste, and would wish no harm to come to her. But they had lied to him. All the time that they were claiming that he, Raphael, was mentally unstable, they had been lying to him about the true fate of his father.

Why had they not called for a search for him? Why had they let him disappear into the darkness?

What had Gabriel done to be treated like that?

This place, this place – far from being a beacon of morality, had its own share of corruption, of dishonesty. And yet it dared to preach to its people about loyalty, to family and state; about curbing impulses, urges, power; about the importance of marrying, breeding within the various breeds. The boy realised that he had been living under a vast misapprehension over the years. That it was time for the truth to be uncovered.

Time for Nissilum to be set free.

CHAPTER TWENTY-ONE

'This is getting rather boring now, dear.' Vanya folded her exquisite silk dressing gown around her. 'I thought you had resigned yourself to a life of mundane mortality.' She sighed, turning her attention to Soren, who had helped himself to a plate of caviar and toast. 'How did you convince her to come back?'

Soren swallowed a mouthful of food, then brushed his lips with a napkin. 'I did nothing. It was Luca who called her back.'

'Luca?' Vanya drew out a seat, more animated now. 'Tired of his paramour already.' She glanced warily at Soren, who was frowning.

'Leave her out of it, Vanya. She is a separate issue.'

'Whatever.' Vanya waved her hand about dismissively. 'The point is, the boy is still pining for Jane.'

Soren flashed an odd sort of look at me.

'I don't know what he was trying to tell me – it wasn't like before. But I first came to know Luca in my dreams,' I told them. 'It was the way he communicated with me, before we actually met.'

'Was it a dream?'

'That's just it. I felt as though I was awake . . . But then that's how I felt before.' I shook my head, feeling a bit muddled about it all now.

'The wedding is not far off – you must act quickly if you have any chance . . .' Vanya narrowed her eyes thoughtfully. 'Though whether it actually happens or not.'

'What do you mean?' Soren and I spoke together.

'Just that there seems to be something going on at the Celestial Palace.' She needlessly lowered her voice. 'Cadmium appears to be unwell. And the boy – Raphael – has been pacing around in a state of some distress.'

'How do you know?' Soren arched an eyebrow.

'Valdar has been advising Celeste on the renovation of the Great Room and has been privy to some palace gossip.' Vanya nodded at me. 'He says there are whispers in the higher echelons of the Angelic circles. The tension in the palace has been palpable these past couple of weeks. With no fit heir to take over from Cadmium, Celeste is wringing her hands.'

'But what about Evan – I mean, Raphael?' I asked. 'He's the rightful heir, isn't he?'

'Technically, yes. But what sort of a leader would he make? All that ghastly business . . .' She gave a disdainful little shake of her head.

'So what are you saying?' Soren changed tack, thankfully. 'That there will be no wedding because the Celestial family are going through turmoil?'

'Who knows?' She inspected her fingernails. 'That boy has been snooping around in affairs of state, I hear. I don't trust him. Nor, I imagine, does his great-mother.'

'Wedding or not, I have to try and see him,' I said. 'Alone, I think.' I glanced at the two of them apologetically. 'No offence.'

'Don't be ridiculous,' said Vanya. 'You won't get anywhere near him . . . Or if you do, that headstrong brother of his will be on you like a tonne of bricks.'

'But if it was him, last night? He might be expecting me . . .'

'Henora is no doubt watching him like a hawk . . . No, no – you must have some kind of plan. You cannot go storming over to his house. Apart from the fact that you would never find it before a creature of the night got to you first, you will have his entire, vitriolic family to deal with.'

211

'She's right – let me come with you.' Soren looked a little imploringly at me. 'Perhaps Lila is—'

'Be careful,' hissed Vanya, getting up from her seat, clutching at her dressing gown. 'The girl does not know you – you must approach with extreme caution.' She put her hand on his arm. 'Remember what you did.'

Soren closed his eyes, clearly doing just that. He nodded briefly before opening them again.

'No . . . I see that. But I came back here for Lila.' He paused. 'To make amends and to stop this "marriage".' He looked down at the floor. 'It was always my intention to tell her who I am.'

'But you have to somehow get her alone,' I said. 'How do you think Henora will react if she finds out before you have had a chance to win Lila over again? She will see to it that you are locked up before you get the chance. And you will never see Lila again.'

Vanya cleared her throat. 'Jane is right. You both need to choose your moment. Away from the Hunter wolves – or at least the parents. I don't know how you're going to do it, but that is your only chance.'

Soren and I had the same hopeless expression on our faces.

'Tomorrow is the Celestial Parade,' she went on. 'The whole area will be teaming with all manner of pathetic loyalists . . .' Then her eyes widened, and she put an elegant hand to her mouth. 'And the ideal occasion to mingle unnoticed in the crowds.'

'Perfect,' said Soren. 'Jane, you had better borrow something from Vanya. You're going to stand out a mile in jeans and sneakers.'

Vanya visibly perked up, tying the cord of her gown neatly and beckoning to me. 'No time like the present dear – let's get you kitted out.'

'I don't know . . .'

'Don't look so concerned,' she said, with a chuckle. 'We want you to go unnoticed, yet make an engaging impression at the same time.'

'This is serious, Vanya . . .' Soren said darkly. 'Please.'

'Yes, yes.' She sighed. 'I won't let you down.'

Trusting Vanya did not come naturally to me, but I had no choice. I had to take every opportunity to find out the truth. Before all hope was dashed. For good.

It was a beautiful clear, bright day – nearly autumn – and the colours in the trees that lined the long road to the palace were muted orange and fading green; lovely and understated. Walking from Vanya's house, Soren and I fell behind a group of women, taking up the full breadth of the cobbled street. Beyond them stretched the road that Soren and I had walked down what seemed weeks ago, but in fact was just a matter of days.

The women gossiped with each other in excitable hissing tones. I recognised one, smaller than the rest, a thatch of wild bird's-nest hair atop her head. Tilly. I shrank back, sure she would recognise me. Soren looked down at me, frowning.

'I know that witch,' I said, grimacing. 'She caused a scene at the Great Ball . . .'

Soren craned forward to take a better look at her.

'She's a midget,' he said. 'Harmless, I'd bet.'

'Don't be so sure . . . if she rumbles me now then the whole day will be ruined.' I lowered my head, lifting the hood of the cape Vanya had leant me over my head.

'Well, don't do that!' hissed Soren. 'That really will draw attention to yourself.' I sighed and eased the hood off again. Vanya had scraped my hair back into a tight bun; so painfully tight I wondered if she had done it on purpose. And then she had placed the short dark wig, a bob with a blunt fringe, over the top of it.

'Do you want to be instantly recognised?' she'd said, pulling my hair up from my neck and examining it. 'All this hair is rather lovely if you like that sort of messy milkmaid kind of thing. But no good at all, if you want to stay incognito.'

214

'You look good,' Soren told me, taking my arm to slow us down a little. 'Very sophisticated.'

I sniffed. I dreaded to think what I looked like. I'd caught a glimpse of myself after Vanya had spent hours doing make-up. All I saw was heavy black kohl and dark red lipstick.

'I look like a vampire,' I said, trying to keep the disdain out of my voice. 'It's weird.'

'You still have those lovely grey eyes.' He stared straight ahead of him as he spoke, thankfully. I didn't know how to deal with compliments from Soren. He always seemed so intense, yet the next minute he would be smiling facetiously.

'Remember, keep by my side,' he went on in a low voice. 'And try not to engage with anyone – not until it is safe.'

At the thought of seeing Luca again, face to face, I felt a bubble of excitement. I touched Soren's hand.

'What will you do if she is there?' I asked. 'Lila?'

I looked quickly at his profile. His mouth set impassively, deliberately. 'I'm sorry, Soren. I can't imagine what it must feel like . . .'

'Don't pity me. Pity my poor sister.' He squeezed my hand and the touch of his fingers felt good. Reassuring and cool.

There were shouts ahead of us, boisterous. I put my hand to my chest.

'Lowe,' I hissed. 'We need to turn back.'

'Keep calm.' Soren kept his hand on mine. 'You're getting paranoid.'

'I wonder why . . .' I looked furtively around me. We were hemmed in now, clusters of – well, I didn't know what they were. Vampires? Witches? Werewolves?

'I'm seriously beginning to think this was a bad idea,' I muttered. 'What was I thinking?'

'You were thinking that you hadn't given up yet.' Soren leaned in to talk into my ear. 'You get the merest hint of a sign from Luca – that he still feels that bond with you – and you're willing to go back on your refusal to come back here . . . That was what you were thinking.'

'OK.' I sighed. 'The truth is I am nervous . . . I don't want to find Luca and realise it meant nothing after all.'

'Trust in your power,' said Soren, sounding very much like Vanya. 'Look – we're approaching the palace. See the gates?'

I peered through the witches in front of us. The palace was fronted by a large torch – like an Olympic torch – which blazed impressively in front of the main gate. Either side stood lines of people dressed in pale yellow military-like uniforms. Men and women of all ages, standing perfectly still, arms poker-straight by their sides.

'Impressive,' I said, taking in four riders on horses at the far ends of each line. I squinted and my heart leaped into my throat.

'He's there.' I nudged Soren, who followed my gaze.

'He's part of the parade,' I said, my heart sinking back to its regular position. 'It's hopeless.'

'There must be some kind of communal banquet afterwards – there usually is at these events,' Soren said, still staring over at the horses. 'I imagine Luca will be attending that.' He turned to look at me. 'Don't look so anxious, you're a very convincing vampire.'

'Kind of what I'm worried about,' I said, wishing more than ever I could see just how ridiculous I looked.

'Come.' Soren took hold of my hand, pulling me with him through the crowds. In the tight suede boots Vanya had insisted I wear my legs felt constricted. They laced all the way up over my knees. I winced.

'Bring me my sneakers,' I murmured.

'Rubbish, you look rather . . . sexy,' Soren pulled me faster, giving me no time to dwell on the flush that crept over my face.

Eventually he stopped and I realised we were right at the front of the throng looking at the people in yellow – and right in the eyeline of the boys on horseback. A flash of blond hair stood out. Raphael, sitting erect and somewhat haughty-looking, to our right. His eyes seemed to be trained on some point in the distance behind us.

I couldn't quite make out the rest of the horsemen, and allowed my gaze to roam to the left, half dreading, half hoping that I would meet Luca's eyes head on. But the rest of the boys were staring straight ahead too. If it hadn't been for his still floppy brown hair and delicately boned face, I would not have recognised him.

But then, just for the briefest second, I saw his head drop and almost imperceptibly, his eyes catch hold of mine.

CHAPTER TWENTY-TWO

Inwardly, Raphael's mind was whirring and, though the crowds were there in front of him, cheering, happy to be part of this seasonal event, he barely registered them. At any moment, the bugle would sound, and he would take his position in front of the Celestial military. His grandparents were making their way to the balcony, too fragile today to face the people at close proximity. A bubble of anger coursed up through him. All this ridiculous pomp and ceremony. And he, who had been lied to for years, was representing the great and honourable Celestial family.

He cleared his throat, glancing over to the left, where the most skilled riders in this part of Nissilum sat astride their horses, patiently. He allowed a longer glance at Luca, whose handsome face looked sad. The Luca Raphael had known as a boy had been calm and smiling, and it had always irritated him. He realised now he had been envious. Still was.

But lately the wolf-boy seemed to have . . . paled. He was sombre. Unhappy.

Beyond Luca was Lowe. An insouciant look on his face. Now there was a fool. So caught up in machismo, patriotism, that he was blinded to the point.

The point that Nissilum was little better than a prison. More oppressive than the tiny basement room in which Raphael had spent the months after his father's death, half mad with grief, and confusion.

She let me believe, he thought, another surge of anger hitting him.

The bugle sounded, and Raphael moved to stand ahead. His heavy military coat felt hot, suffocating. Symbolic of his life.

He entertained a fantasy in which he drew out the pistol from its holder on his thigh and shot into the crowd, then watched the crowd scatter and panic. As he smiled at the faces in front of him, he imagined the unrest, the frightened horses, the confusion on the faces of all those who trusted in this great majestic family.

The time will come, he thought, his eye falling suddenly on a familiar face at the front of the assembled throng. He nodded, wondering where he had seen her before. There was something about the eyes, exotically made-up . . . She was beautiful indeed; one of Vanya Borgia's cohorts, no doubt . . . The girl seemed uneasy with his attention and simply dropped her head, coyly. That's when he realised.

She was no vampire. She was the mortal girl. She was Jane. And next to her, with a face that looked both too old for his years and youthfully handsome at the same time, was the boy she'd been with the other day.

Remembering, Raphael smiled broadly for the first time.

He didn't know why, but this Soren character seemed charged with the same contempt for this place as did Raphael. He had known it the first time he'd met him – and then again when he'd come knocking on Vanya's door to find him.

With the discovery that his father may not be dead after all, the stranger – and who he could possibly be – had faded a little from his thoughts, but seeing him standing there with Jane, Raphael recalled the book in the library and what he had read. He couldn't prove it but something told him that this boy – man – was connected to this story.

A shout from behind him told Raphael that it was time to begin the procession. He turned to signal to the others that they must follow him.

As the horses trod elegantly towards the crowd, it parted respectfully to let them pass. Leading the way, Raphael was careful not to make eye contact – not until he passed the two of them. He saw Soren's hand reach out subtly to take Jane's.

Raphael dropped his gaze until he had her attention. Her dark eyes regarding him warily.

'Hello, Jane.' He mouthed the words, saw her lips part, confused, and lifted his head back as though he had not seen her.

CHAPTER TWENTY-THREE

'He saw me . . .' I looked up at Soren. 'Raphael recognised me.'

Soren frowned. 'You know him – a born troublemaker. He will forget about it soon enough.' He smiled unconvincingly.

But my hand, still holding his, was trembling a little. My eyes focussed on the boy astride the black horse next to us.

'Don't,' Soren said, as loud as he dared, but Luca had not seen them. I released my hand from his and instead reached out quickly to touch the horse's flank, my head bent, hiding my face.

'Careful,' said Luca, not knowing me. Soren watched me look up at him.

'Jane . . .' Soren pulled me back, stopping me from revealing myself at this moment. And to his obvious relief

I allowed myself to be pulled.

But though Luca continued, directing his horse through the throng, he suddenly stopped, and we both saw him turn, looking back curiously at me before the crowd began chanting, encouraging him forward and on with the procession, forcing him to turn away.

The rest of the people followed the horses, leaving Soren and I standing on the periphery.

'That was close,' breathed Soren. 'You should have kept your head down.'

'How will I ever get near him, talk to him?' My shoulders slumped.

'I told you, there will be time.' Soren dodged a couple of small boys. 'But really, you must learn not to wear every feeling on your face!'

'I can't help that.'

'Personally, I think it's charming.' He smiled. 'But this is a game you are playing. And a game involves strategy. Ergo, you need to be more strategic.'

'Like a game of chess? I never was any good at board games.'

He laughed then, slipping an arm around me.

'Well, thank goodness you have me here to teach you.'

I relaxed. He could feel a little tension easing.

'Now,' he told me cheerfully, 'shall we try and have a

little fun? I think I see Vanya and Valdar over there.'

'Not them,' I shook my head. 'Vanya has this way of . . .'

'Twisting things?' He grinned. 'At seducing you into doing things you would rather not do?'

'Exactly.'

'I know you don't trust her, but really, she is a good ally to have.'

'Hmm. And a dangerous enemy.' I crossed my arms over my chest.

'Listen, Jane. The truth is, you should never trust anyone but yourself . . . Not completely. The trick is to exploit the qualities you find in others – take from them what you need.'

'Well, that's not cynical at all . . .' I gave him a playful shove. 'You have this way of making the most obnoxious traits sound worthwhile.'

'And you have a way of turning every minor problem into a disaster.' He arched an eyebrow. 'Of doubting everyone – and yourself most of all.'

'OK, Dr Freud.' I rolled my eyes. 'Shall we dispense with the amateur psychology and follow the procession?'

Soren crooked his arm, gesturing for me to take it.

'I thought you would never ask.'

CHAPTER TWENTY-FOUR

'A good crowd today.' Raphael dismounted as he addressed Luca. 'Some interesting faces out there.'

Luca nodded, though he did not look at him, concentrating instead on lifting the heavy saddle off his horse.

'You didn't notice?' Raphael probed. 'You didn't see them?'

The tic in Luca's cheek betrayed his tension, but he still did not engage with Raphael. He carried the saddle over to its place at the back of the stable, taking his time. Finally he walked back over to his horse, brushing his hands on trousers.

'What's the matter?' Raphael stood perfectly still. 'Are you nervous about the wedding?' His tone was subtly mocking.

Luca sighed, resting his palms on his horse's flank,

then leaning his forehead against it.

'Not nervous,' he said, though he didn't move, still did not look at Raphael. 'Just . . .'

Raphael pretended not to understand. 'You are unwell?'

'No!' snapped Luca. 'I am not unwell. I am simply haunted by something I cannot have.'

'By "something" you mean Jane?' Raphael spoke softly.

'Yes.' And Raphael saw that the boy's eyes were wet with tears.

'Luca,' he said, unprepared, 'I didn't mean . . .'

'Of course you did. You meant to be provocative. You always have. Even when we were young.' Luca faced him. 'And I never reacted. You were the beloved prince. Beyond reproach. It was meant to be an honour to be your playmate.' Luca's tone was low and he was as angry as Raphael had ever seen him.

'I . . . I was only playing,' Raphael said. 'You knew that, I hope.'

'As you are playing now, I suppose? Playing with other people's lives. As you played with Jane . . .'

'I'm not . . . it is not . . .' began Raphael. 'I mean no harm to you, or to Jane. But, don't you see? This whole mess is symbolic of this wretched place. You are about to marry someone you do not love, you barely know. Allowing your parents to control your happiness – to destroy it.'

Luca said nothing for a few seconds, then sighed heavily.

'There is nothing I can do – or will do – to stop this. I owe my parents this.' Luca spoke eventually. 'They would be devastated.'

Raphael snorted, he couldn't help himself.

'You don't understand. I can make a good life with Lila. She is a sweet girl – a little naïve, but adorable. She just wants to make me happy, fetching me small gifts, making sure I am all right . . .' he trailed off.

'She sounds . . . a little dull,' said Raphael. 'If you will excuse my directness.'

Luca smiled for the first time, but wryly. 'Since when have you ever cared for others' opinions – or their feelings?'

'That's not fair . . .' Raphael remembered his father with a pang.

'I know you are still angry,' Luca said, 'about your father . . .'

'Oh, you don't know. Not nearly . . .'

'But, perhaps life is just simpler if you make the best of it.'

'But you don't have to do this . . . You could make a life with someone you actually love – and who loves you.'

Luca shot him a look. 'I did see her. Underneath all that make-up . . . But she was with that vampire boy – I saw how he looked at her.'

'About him—' Raphael started, but was interrupted.

'The vampires are not concerned with family loyalty. They are a slave to passion. I daresay he can give her what I can't.'

'I think he is taking advantage of her,' said Raphael abruptly. But as Luca looked up, the door to the stables opened.

'You should come and join the party.' Lowe stood, his tone was light, but his eyes regarded the two of them, suspiciously, perhaps even jealously.

'In a minute . . .' Luca looked over at Raphael, who was hiding his irritation well.

'Now. We'll go now.' Raphael said with authority. He slapped his horse on its rump and it whinnied, moving forward to chomp on some hay.

'The party . . .' Luca shut his eyes and for the first time Raphael noticed the shadows undernearth them. He pushed a hand through his hair.

'And I must find Lila. She and her mother will have arrived by now.'

'Indeed, I have seen her.' Lowe said. 'The prettiest girl at the parade.'

Luca and Raphael exchanged a look.

The noise outside the stables was building, even though the crowds were some distance away.

'Shall we go?' Lowe swept his arm out theatrically. 'We can't disappoint the people.'

'Of course we can't,' said Raphael with a hint of sarcasm. 'That would never do.'

CHAPTER TWENTY-FOUR

A small dark-haired girl broke free from a group of girls her age and ran across the palace fields. Picking up her skirt, her heart-shaped face beamed across at me, where I stood watching – with some boredom – a juggling troupe.

I squinted, hoping it was who I thought it was.

'Is it you?' the girl said, arriving swiftly at my feet. 'I thought it was you.'

'Dalya!' I felt a rush of pleasure at seeing at her. 'Is my disguise that bad?'

Dalya's face creased into a broad smile. 'Only to those who are looking,' she said, before looking down at her feet shyly. 'And I have been looking.'

'Really?' I glanced quickly around her, spotting Soren talking animatedly with Vanya some distance away. I pulled at Dalya's arm. 'Come on, let's get out of here for a bit.'

Dalya took my hand and, feeling its warmth, its link to Luca, I held on to it tightly, happy and sad at the same time.

'So,' said Dalya, with the excited innocence of a child, 'what are you doing back here? Is it true that you and the vampire-boy are in love?'

'What?' I stared at Dalya open-mouthed.

'Oh . . . I didn't mean . . . I thought . . .' Dalya faltered, her sweet face troubled now. 'Lowe is telling everybody.'

'Is he?' I set my mouth sternly. 'Well you can tell that troublemaking brother of yours that Soren and I are just friends, and he's not a—' I checked herself. 'He's not my boyfriend.'

'I'm glad then . . .' Dalya blushed. 'I know it's selfish, but I can't bear to think of you with a vampire.' She squirmed a little to express her distaste. 'The vampires at my school are always the sly ones. The ones who sit back and watch the rest of us get into trouble for fooling around. They're always there, staring at you with their creepy white faces. And their mouths are too red.'

I laughed then, glad of Dalya's chatter.

'So, if he's not your boyfriend, what are you doing with him?' the girl persisted.

I hadn't expected to have to answer this, and my face must have betrayed my anxiety because Dalya put a small hand to her mouth, her eyes widening.

'Is it something to do with Luca?'

I sighed. 'Listen, Dalya, it's complicated. I met Soren back home – in the mortal world. It's a long story, but he told me he could come to bring me back to Luca. That he would help me . . .' I trailed off, realising how pathetic and tenuous that sounded.

'I wish I could do magic,' Dalya said, sadly, taking my hand again, 'and have you and Luca reunited and my parents happy at the same time and everything just perfect.' Her small shoulders slumped. 'But I don't know how to make it happen . . .'

I made sure my face did not betray disappointment. I think somehow I imagined that Dalya was going to tell me that Luca was pining for me, that he was willing to give up everything for me. Instead, I smiled uncertainly at her.

'I think he came to me – in my dream,' I said. 'I'm sure of it. It was odd, because he wasn't as clear as he was when we . . . well, when we first met. But I had such a familiar feeling. Maybe I am wrong . . .'

'You're not wrong, but . . .' Dalya twiddled a lock of her hair. 'Please . . . don't be angry . . . but it was me.'

'It was you!' My insides turned over, registering disappointment first, then confusion. 'What made you . . . ?'

She wrung her hands. 'Henora warned me that as I grew older I would develop this ability to speak to people through my dreams. If they're on my mind . . . If I miss them.' She looked up at me through her eyelashes. 'Luca had the same dreams . . .'

'I remember,' I said, smiling at the memory. 'I thought there was something wrong. I thought it was Luca.' I tried not to show the pain that hit me as I spoke, though ever-intuitive, Dalya squeezed my hand tightly.

'There is no danger. Just a bit of sadness. Luca is . . . well he is not the same these days. He is so quiet. He has no sense of humour. He is like a machine with no feelings. He just does everything Henora tells him to do. But his eyes are dead. I just wanted . . .'

'I know.' Seeing her distressed, I gave her a brief hug. 'I want it too. But perhaps we both have to let go of it.' I could hardly believe I was saying this, and not at all sure I believed I could do it, but Dalya was only a kid. With the weight of the world on her shoulders.

'So now you feel you came back here for nothing?'

'No. Not now . . .' I shook my head. Hesitant about telling Dalya the other reason. 'I am glad to see you. So glad.'

But instead of smiling, Dalya's whole body seemed to deflate. I could have sworn I saw tears in those dark eyes.

'Lila is not you . . . She's nice enough. I suppose she's pretty, but she's . . . needy,' Dalya said with some distaste. 'And the way she sucks up to Mother – like a little girl who wants to be loved.'

'Maybe she does?' I knew the truth about poor Lila, and I wished I could tell Dalya, but I couldn't betray Soren like that.

'Well, she can find some other boy to love.' Dalya looked sulky. 'I mean, why does it have to be Luca?'

'Where is Lila?' I asked. 'Is she here, at the parade?'

'She is arriving at any moment, and I must go and join my family, to greet her. So that we can act out the pantomime. All so that Henora is happy.'

'What a mess.' I reached out for Dalya's hand. 'But you mustn't worry . . . Go now. I hope to see you again.'

'I hope so.' Dalya held on to my hand. 'I can still talk to you, in your dreams, if you like?'

'I like.' I hugged her properly then, feeling her slight frame, and the silky softness of her hair where it brushed against my face. I watched her as she walked away, each step she took looked heavy. Like her heart. Like mine. As she disappeared through a group of people standing at the edge of the field. I turned to think, staring out at the acres of field in front of me. The sun had come out and my face underneath the make-up felt hot. I badly wanted to scrub it off. Be myself again. This whole day was pointless.

As I turned back to face the palace, my eye caught a willowy blonde figure, dressed in a white tunic, her hair pulled back prettily.

Lila.

At her side, was an older woman. Must be her mother, Hanni. Her adoptive mother. Suddenly I thought of Soren. I had lost sight of him. Dalya and I had walked so far from the others. If my own dreams were shattered, I could at least help him.

I walked back, the sound of the brass band growing louder. And the closer I got to the palace, to the people, the louder my heart seemed to beat. Alone, I felt vulnerable somehow, as though, unguarded, all manner of danger might come to get me. I picked up my feet until I was practically running.

'There you are.' A strong arm gripped mine, and I gasped, turning with relief to see Soren.

'She's here,' I said breathlessly. 'Lila.'

'I know. I saw her too.' He shrugged. 'I don't know what to do.'

'You. You don't know what to do?' I almost laughed. 'Well you have to try and talk to her . . .'

'What is the likelihood of me getting anywhere near

her?' He gave a humourless laugh. 'She is surrounded.'

I thought for a moment. 'Soren, this might sound a bit out there, but I know someone who's close to me – and also to Lila. In a sense, anyway. If she knew the truth, she would certainly help.'

He looked bemused. 'Who?'

'Luca's sister. Dalya. She and I have an understanding.' I sighed. 'In fact, it was Dalya who came to me the other night, not Luca.' I waved away the question that was about to come from his lips. 'It's OK. I'm OK. But seeing as my own plight is kind of hopeless. I feel I should help you, if I can.'

'Can you trust this girl?'

'As much as I can trust anyone. I trust her like I trust Dot, my sister.' As I said it, I knew I meant it. 'And she knows there is something . . . a little odd about Lila. She was saying so just now.'

'You have been busy.' Soren nodded. 'But I don't know . . . I don't want to frighten Lila.'

'Has it occurred to you that Lila might actually be happy to know she has a brother? A proper flesh-and-blood brother.'

'It has occurred to me that it would distress her to know that her brother killed her entire family,' he said grimly.

I rounded on him. 'But what about the truth? You can't spend the rest of your life pretending.'

'The rest of my life?' He smiled, but it was a forlorn kind of smile.

'Well . . . eternity then.' I reached out and touched his shoulder. It occurred to me for the first time that living for ever wasn't really the dream that mortals longed for. It could be for ever spent sad and regretful. I realised that underneath the cynical humour, Soren was just that.

'What about you? Are you going to spend your life pretending? You don't get long, after all.'

'Way to cheer me up,' I said, dryly. But he had a point.

'Luca is prepared to . . . So there's not a lot I can do about it. Even Dalya can't see him changing his mind. And in a way, it makes me – well, it makes me love him more.'

'Oh, Jane.' Soren gently lifted my chin with his fingertip. 'Luca is a fool.'

The sky above us was growing darker blue, and over at the palace, tall candles glittered magically.

'Time for the palace party,' Soren said, his gaze crisscrossing. On the lookout for Lila, I supposed.

I linked my arm through his. 'Come on. I'm starving,' I said. 'Let's see if the banquet has started.' I pulled him with me. It was true, my stomach ached I was so hungry. But I wanted to find Dalya again. If she was willing to help get Lila on her own then tonight might be Soren's only chance to talk to his sister. And set the record straight.

The musical theme was jazz. Jaunty trumpets played us inside the palace gates. Palace staff stood about with jugs of sparkling liquid, welcoming the hundreds of guests as they streamed through, keen to get their free food and drink, courtesy of the Celestial family.

Groups of people, smiling, bopping to the music, painted a happy carefree picture. I could see that Nissilum was sometimes a happy jubilant place, where its people were content with living under its regime.

Near to the grand entrance, Vanya stood talking to Celeste. They made an odd couple. Vanya tall, willowy and dangerous-looking, waved her elegant hands about expressively, while Celeste stood demurely, nodding in a polite way. If she was uncomfortable, she didn't betray it. I even saw a flicker of a smile at something Vanya was saying. Vanya briefly caught my eye, lifting her chin, a sly smile on her face.

I just hoped Dalya had not been whisked away. I looked around me, my heart flipping over at the sight of the tall, slender boy standing with his brother and a couple of the palace minions. With his hands stuck into his pockets, he was nodding absently at their banter. I felt my insides contract as I watched his eyes travel away from his companions, looking this way and that, and I saw for the first time how thin he had become. He lifted his head and his gaze came to rest on where we stood, Soren and I. I swallowed, wanting to look away, but I couldn't do it. I wanted to pretend he was no more than a stranger, but I didn't take my eyes off him, and then his eyes met mine, and a look of sadness came over his face as he smiled a secret smile.

I smiled back, not wanting the moment to stop, but within seconds Lowe was tugging at his brother's arm and Luca turned from me, his head bent back, listening to what Lowe had to say.

I had it though, I had the sign I needed.

'Luca!' A pretty voice, like a little bell, chimed through the crowds, and it seemed that everyone standing in the palace courtyard turned to watch the girl practically skip through the crowds.

Luca looked up, recognising her, and it looked like his expression changed, and broad smile lit up his face.

'Stay calm,' Soren whispered, as though reading my thoughts. 'It is to be expected.'

I drew myself up, nodding, and noticed the sulky

dark-haired girl traipsing along with her formidable mother.

'Dalya,' I said, grabbing Soren's arm. 'That's Dalya.'

'The child?' Soren frowned. 'I don't think—'

But I didn't wait for him to finish his sentence. Instead, I darted through a group of witches.

'Dalya!' I shouted, half hiding behind a giant of a man; he must have been a werewolf. I saw her turn, her eyes flashing, curiously, to see who had shouted for her. To my relief she saw me and her face brightened. She turned and came towards me.

'Careful, missy,' said the bearded man, jovially. 'Come to see your Uncle Olwen . . .'

'Olwen.' She bobbed politely, a sugar smile on her face. 'I need to fetch a shawl for Mother, I think . . .' And with that she pushed past him, grinning cheekily, as though to excuse her rudeness, and grabbed hold of my arm. I had forgotten how strong she was. But then, she was a little wolf-girl, I kept forgetting about that.

Looking up at Soren, I saw a flicker of amusement on his face.

'Follow us,' I hissed, allowing Dalya to pull me with her, back towards the main entrance.

Oblivious to my companion, Dalya kept going.

'Dalya,' I said, breathlessly, 'steady on.'

Obviously judging that we were at a safe distance from her family, Dalya stopped, her dark hair a little unruly.

Seeing Soren, her brown eyes narrowed.

'Who is this?' She looked sharply at me. 'The vampire-boy?'

'Actually—' began Soren, but I silenced him with a look. We needed Dalya to trust us, we needed to tell her his story.

Her eyes came back to me. 'This whole event is deadly,' she said miserably. Mother is so neurotic, what with the wedding, and Lila is getting on my every nerve. And as for Luca – well, he would be happier at his own funeral.'

'He looks perfectly happy to me,' I said, unable to keep the edge out of my voice.

'Of course he does.' Dalya sighed dramatically. 'Luca behaves the way he thinks he should behave. But I swear, she's enough to—'

'We need your help,' I cut in, changing the subject. 'Soren needs your help.'

Dalya turned imperiously to Soren. 'So that's your name. It's an odd kind of name for a vampire.'

'It is,' he said, glancing quickly at me. 'But my name is not important.'

Dalya crossed her arms over her chest, regarding him suspiciously.

'So what is going on? How can I possibly help you?'

I took her hand. 'Before we tell you, you have to promise to keep this a secret – just for a bit.'

'Of course. Is this about Luca?' She started to look alarmed.

'No. No . . . well, in a way, yes. But there's nothing to be concerned about.' I drew her to me. 'It's about Lila.'

'Lila?' she said, puzzled.

'It's . . .' I hesitated. 'It's about Lila's family . . . her true family.' I looked sideways at Soren.

'Her *true* family.' Dalya echoed. 'I don't understand.'

'I am her brother,' Soren announced abruptly. I glared at him.

'You can't be!' Dalya smiled nervously. 'I've met her brother.'

Before Soren could respond to that I cut in.

'Lila is adopted. She doesn't remember being adopted. But her parents, her brother – they're not her flesh and blood.'

'Does Mother know?' Dalya's face was flushed.

'I don't know, I doubt it.' Soren hugged himself. 'Lila was taken in by a wolf family when she was very young. Four years old.'

243

'But what happened to her real parents? Were you adopted too?'

'OK. So this is the hard bit.' I bit my lip. 'Soren was very young, and very hurt and angry, and . . . he did a terrible thing.'

Dalya shrank back. 'I should get back,' she said. 'Henora will be looking for me.'

'No. Dalya. Wait. Don't be frightened. It was a terrible thing, but it was a long time ago – and there was a reason.'

'What did you do?' She clasped her hands together, gazing at him.

'I . . . I killed our parents and our siblings.' Soren's voice was shaky as he spoke. 'I was six. I found out that my father was not my father, that my upstanding family were not exactly that. They'd lied to me.' He paused. 'I felt very betrayed.'

'So you *killed* them?' She stepped closer to me. 'I mean, how . . . No, I don't want to know.'

I put an arm around her.

'Soren deeply regrets what he did,' I told Dalya, hoping that this was true, that I was doing the right thing. 'And he is concerned for Lila.'

She swallowed, absorbing what she was hearing. 'You believe him,' she said to me. 'And I trust you, so . . .'

'Yes, Dalya. I do believe him. I know he loved his family . . . He loves his sister.' I waited, hoping she would understand.

She was silent for a minute before finally taking a deep breath.

'Jane, I want you and my brother to be together more than anyone,' she said at last. 'But I don't know . . .' She looked very warily at Soren, who was not the most reassuring of presences.

'You know that your brother does not truly love her,' he said suddenly, almost abruptly. 'And I believe she deserves to be loved. She has no family left . . . No childhood companions – but for me.' His voice softened as he went on. 'Imagine your life without your brothers?'

Dalya sucked in her breath. 'Poor Lila.' She sighed heavily. 'She won't sleep in the dark. And she talks all the time about the full moon and how she has to hide herself. She's like a little girl sometimes. She can never be alone.'

I looked at Soren. His face was taut. It must have been painful to hear what Dalya was saying.

'So that's why her family are so keen to marry her off. Because she is not really theirs either . . .' Dalya shook her head. 'Poor Lila. Nobody truly wants her.'

'I do,' Soren said quietly. 'And I will never leave her again.'

'And she needs to know the truth, Dalya,' I said. 'She needs to know she has a brother who loves her.'

'Yes . . . I see.' Dalya looked thoughtful. 'But she might not believe you . . . I mean, she has been lied to herself. And she wouldn't understand.'

'I know. The truth is I don't know if she will believe me. And telling her might cause more harm than good. But it will haunt me for ever if I don't try.' Soren rubbed at his temples anxiously.

'Well Luca must know too.' Dalya's eyes grew big. 'And he can help us.'

'No,' I said quickly. 'Not yet. He will think—'

'He'll think that this is just a ruse to get him back.' Her look seemed to pierce me, as though she thought that too. But then she smiled. 'At first. But he respects you, Jane. That will count for something.'

'Thank you.' I smiled back, glad to have her trust. 'So you understand. We must talk to Lila alone.'

'I must talk to her alone,' Soren corrected me.

'OK.' I shrugged, turning to Dalya. 'So, can you somehow persuade her to meet Soren alone? Tonight?'

Dalya puffed out her cheeks. 'I'll try. But it will be difficult. She is always surrounded.'

We looked imploringly at her.

'Leave it with me,' she said, thinking. Then to Soren: 'Be in the gardens behind the palace kitchens, after the great banquet. I will think of something. But now I must go.' She squeezed my hand.

'Thank you, Dalya. You're a good girl,' I told her.

'Yes, thank you.' Soren took her hand and kissed it.

'Ugh.' She withdrew it, though with a good-natured smile on her face.

CHAPTER TWENTY-FIVE

Down below, the noise was giving Raphael a headache. He ran a hand through his hair, staring at the piles of paperwork in front of him. Stacks of paperwork, recording the history of the Celestial family. Births, marriages, deaths.

Deaths.

His father's 'death' certificate looked up at him, the first on the pile in front of him; underneath it was a scribbled note, difficult to decipher, but written by Milo. It detailed the description of his father when Milo had discovered him. But the detail was in itself vague. It talked of a 'loss of presence', of a 'physical disappearance'. Milo wrote that he felt his master's soul becoming at peace.

Raphael's lip curled. *What about my peace?* he thought. The peace of those he left behind. Heaving a sigh, he felt as close to tears as he'd been in a long time. Emotions swirled: anger, hurt, sorrow. But not peace.

Nissilum was made of a desire for peace. What an irony. What hypocrites his family were.

On the back of Milo's note was a couple of lines on his feelings of loss. And sadness that he must leave the place that had been his home. But there was no mention of where he was going. His father's loyal servant had simply disappeared.

A sound on the staircase brought him out of his thoughts. Quickly he gathered up the papers and hid them underneath the quilt on his bed. He stood, waiting for whoever it was to make themselves known, but it must have been a servant, because the footsteps began treading down the stairs.

The noise was fading, which meant the banquet was about to begin. He was expected at the head of the vast table in the Great Room, to take his seat next to Celeste and Cadmium. Raphael looked into the full-length mirror opposite his bed. He saw a handsome figure. A head of blond curls, his body honed and fit from riding . . . but a little thin, from lack of food. He had barely eaten the past few days. Still, in his Celestial uniform, he looked the part.

As he came out of his room, he glimpsed the figure of an older man at the foot of the stairs. His great-father,

Cadmium. An elusive presence for weeks now. He looked terrible. Gaunt, haunted.

Cadmium nodded, a weak smile on his face.

'Boy.' He stepped forward with the help of a cane. 'Your great-mother is expecting us.'

Raphael held out his arm and together the two of them descended the great staircase. He was shocked at how his great-father was. Stooped and wincing with every step.

'Perhaps you should lie down?' he ventured. 'Celeste and I can host the banquet . . .'

'No!' The old man snapped, his arms shaking. 'We must be dutiful. We have an example to set these people.'

Raphael gritted his teeth, suppressing the bile that rose in his throat. He had a sudden urge to let go of Cadmium's arm, leave him to fall.

'Of course,' he said instead, 'I was only thinking of you.'

'You understand,' said Cadmium, his youthful-looking face at odds with his demeanour, 'you understand what it means to preside over Nissilum? That all selfish concerns must be sacrificed? We are in a position of great privilege. It is unacceptable to abuse it.'

'I understand.' Raphael turned his face away, but not before he saw the critical expression on his great-father's face.

250

'There is to be no repetition of your past behaviour.' Cadmium's tone was icy. 'Pure selfishness.'

Raphael didn't trust himself to respond. A surge of pure hatred hit him. He wanted to confront Cadmium about his father, Gabriel. About the lies that had been told. He felt disgusted and on some level deeply disappointed in his family.

But he knew nothing would be achieved by speaking out.

'Come,' he said, taking another step down, 'they are waiting for us.'

CHAPTER TWENTY-SIX

It had to be the biggest table I'd ever seen. It took up the whole of the Great Room. And seated around it was a motley selection of Nissilum's immortals. The witches shrieking and gossiping, their pinched little faces sharp and animated. And then there were the vampires. Vanya and Valdar alongside of course, but a whole row of similarly elegant and brooding men and women observing everyone else through narrowed eyes. And of course the werewolves. My eyes slid tentatively over to where Henora and Ulfred were sitting. Henora looked disapproving, fiddling nervously with her glass, while Ulfred was helping himself to bread and butter. With a smile I saw Henora reprimand him, slapping his hand away from the basket. Poor Ulfred.

My gaze roamed, searching for the others: Dalya, Luca and Lila, but they weren't here yet.

Behind me I heard Soren sigh heavily.

'Good grief, I am not sure I can endure this . . .' he muttered. 'There are no seats left anyway.'

I looked and saw two places vacant at the end of the table furthest from where Celeste was seated. Raphael and an older man who must have been Cadmium were setting themselves either side of her.

'Quickly,' I said, 'there are two places there.'

Nodding at a pair of striking vampire twin girls next to me, I sat, confident that having touched up my make-up in the palace bathrooms, I was safe from recognition.

'Fabulous eyes,' said one of the twins, gawping at my face. 'Did you do that yourself?'

Her identical sister rolled her eyes. 'That's Vanya Borgia's handiwork, if I'm not mistaken.'

I opened my mouth, thinking they were like an evil version of Emma and Ashley.

'Natalia, Sofi.' Soren greeted them, picking up his napkin to dab at his forehead.

They preened coquettishly at him and I stopped myself from laughing.

'You're Vanya Borgia's guest, aren't you?' One of the twins held out her hand. So thin it was like a twig with nail polish on it. 'My name is Sofi.'

'And I am Natalia,' said her sister. 'You are?'

'Jane,' I whispered.

'I love your look,' Sofi drawled, sniffing elaborately. Alarmed, I turned from her. I had forgotten how vampires can sniff out human blood.

'Vanya has told the vampire community that you are amongst them,' Soren whispered. 'They are under pain of torture to leave you alone.'

I relaxed, but snuck a look back at the twins, who were whispering together, casting intrigued glances in my direction.

So I was safe from their advances – for the time being at least, but I needed to be alert to Lila's entrance, I couldn't afford to be caught up in conversation with Natalia and Sofi.

As if on cue the door opened and Dalya appeared, followed by a robotic-looking Luca, Lila attached to his arm like a blonde limpet.

'Do you think she dyes her hair?' murmured Natalia unsubtly scrutinising Lila. 'It's a little brassy for my taste.'

'Agreed,' replied Sofi. The two of them regarded her like a couple of hawks.

Under the table I felt Soren's thigh knock against mine, and though I couldn't be sure if it had been intentional or not, I felt something stir inside me. But I blocked it out, keeping my eyes trained on the new arrivals taking their places next to Henora and Ulfred.

Luca seemed too preoccupied to notice anything around him and, though I certainly didn't want to draw attention to myself, I would have been lying if I said I wasn't disappointed that he hadn't noticed me. I looked down for a moment at my hands, realising I had clasped them together nervously, not knowing what the night had in store.

The sound of someone clinking metal against glass silenced the chattering in the big room and we all turned our attention to the figure of Raphael at the head of the table.

'Welcome,' he said, nodding around the vast table. 'Welcome all of you to the seasonal palace banquet. On behalf of Mother Celeste and Father Cadmium, I extend full hospitality to you tonight.' He cleared his throat, lifting his chin. 'Presently we will be serving the first in a five-course dinner, followed by music and dancing from the Vampire Jazz Quartet, and further refreshment if you require it.' He smiled for the first time, years of training making it appear genuine and full of warmth. 'This is your night. Enjoy it.'

He picked up his glass and held it aloft, and there was a cheer around the table before he sat back down again. I saw Celeste beam approvingly at him. Cadmium, I noticed, looked a little sour – ill even. He didn't even glance at his great-son.

'He's rather a dish, isn't he?' I heard Natalia tell Sofi. 'For an angel.'

'There just has to be a vampire-angel alliance one day,' said Sofi. 'Why not start now?'

They laughed throatily and, catching my eye, Natalia arched a perfectly plucked eyebrow. 'Unless you want him?'

I shook my head. *Been there, done that*, I thought.

'That's considerate of you,' I told her, 'but I'll pass.'

Beside me I felt Soren's body twitch a little with suppressed laughter.

Hours later, or so it seemed, the final course was cleared away. Soren hadn't eaten a thing. Nor had Natalia and Sofi, who had pushed each plate away as though it were poison. I, on the other hand, had wolfed down practically everything.

I swallowed my last mouthful of pudding and finally put my spoon down. 'I'm stuffed,' I said, forgetting who I was with.

Soren and the twins looked bemused.

'Extraordinary,' said Sofi. 'Eating.'

'*Vive la différence!*' Soren murmured softly, and this

time there was no mistaking the feel of his muscular thigh against mine. I moved my leg, colour creeping into my face.

The twins stared suspiciously at the two of us.

'Are you two . . . together?' said Natalia eventually.

'God, no!' I snorted, a little too emphatically.

'Why thank you, miss,' Soren muttered feigning hurt, but he shook his head at the twins. 'We're friends,' he told the twins. 'Is this a problem for you?'

'If there's one thing I can detect from a thousand miles away it is mutual attraction between a male and a female.' Sofi sniffed. 'I am never wrong.'

'Yes, you are—' I began, but the sound of chairs being scraped back drew all of our attention somewhere else. I realised that Dalya was on her feet, one hand holding on to Lila's. She was staring beseechingly at Soren and I.

I darted quickly around the back of the dark twins towards her, but stopped at the sight of her mouthing: *In an hour I will come and find you.*

I nodded, turning back again. Sofi and Natalia were practically draped over Soren.

'Soren?' I eyed him. 'Can I have a word with you?'

Soren's relief was visible. He removed Sofi's hand from his arm, politely, and smiled at both girls.

'Another time, ladies,' he told them. 'My friend—'

'Oh, yes.' Natalia drawled. 'Your *friend*.' Her mouth twisted in a lascivious grin. 'But if you should get bored of your little grey-eyed "friend", we'll be mingling in the ballroom.'

She reluctantly let go of him, casting me a look at the same time.

'A narrow escape,' he whispered, slipping his arm around my waist.

I ignored the tingle it sent up my back.

'Dalya will come and find us when the time is right.' I shuffled out of his grip. 'We should go and lose ourselves in the music.'

'I thought you'd never ask,' he said, lightly touching the base of my spine.

I rolled my eyes and realised we were once again trapped behind the vampire twins. They seemed to be everywhere I looked.

'Wonderful,' said Natalia, 'we four will make such good-looking dance companions.'

'Talia?' Sofi's tone was scolding. 'Be nice to Jane. You know how protective Vanya is about her pets.'

Somehow we had lost Soren. I looked behind me, seeing that he was trapped behind Dalya's Uncle Olwen.

'So.' Sofi moved closely to me as we walked. 'How is it that you come to be here? We have heard the rumours but I never thought I would see the day that the Borgias were consorting with mortals. Vanya must be very fond of your companion.'

'I won't be here long,' I told her a little lamely, as somebody brushed past me. I was too busy trying to squeeze through the crowds with Natalia and Sofi to look and see who it was, but his voice at my side made every hair on my body stand on end.

'I am not sure I feel like dancing,' Luca was saying, a little ahead of me, but close enough for me to touch him if I wanted to, to lean in and inhale him.

'Nonsense.' Henora looked at the mass of people eager to get to where the band was playing. 'You need to find that bonny girl of yours and make it your business to dance.'

'Yes, Mother,' said Luca through clearly gritted teeth.

'The sooner the two of you are married, the sooner I don't need to worry about you,' Henora muttered, tucking a grey tendril of hair behind her pointed little ear.

Luca didn't answer, but he turned and I saw his profile, his cheekbone, more pronounced than ever. He looked so despondent, tired . . . resigned. Knowing I was being foolish, I fell back from the vampire twins and reaching out, not knowing if he would feel it, I touched his hand.

And as if by instinct his hand quickly closed around

mine. He didn't look back, but I felt the pressure of his fingers as he held on to me, and a longed-for feeling of warmth and safety flooded through me.

I held my breath, and then he released his hold and moved through the doorway. As he got there, he turned and his eyes found mine; his was a look of happiness clouded by great sadness.

And then he was gone.

I came out into the hall, to my left was the grand staircase, to my right was the door to the kitchens. I remembered what had happened there before, with Vanya and Luca and realised it wasn't so unlikely that tonight it would happen again.

I shut my eyes. I didn't know what was going to happen. No point in inventing catastrophe when it hadn't happened yet.

'I thought I'd lost you.' Soren appeared beside me. He craned his neck in the direction of the ballroom, where the Vampire Jazz Quartet were in full swing. 'I suppose it would be remiss of me not to ask you to dance.'

I smiled at the look on his face. Pure dread.

'You know, I don't really feel like dancing either,' I said truthfully.

'Come on,' he said, holding out his hand, 'let's explore this place, while no one is looking.'

'I don't know . . .' I shook my head, remembering exploring with Luca. I felt disloyal, somehow.

'Quick,' he said, a glint of mischief in his eyes, 'before Celeste and Cadmium decide to retire for the night.' He pulled me with him, towards the staircase and, though I tried not to, I couldn't help myself from looking into the ballroom. Looking for him.

And there, with Henora looking on with a doting expression on her face, was Luca, Lila in his arms. She had her head resting on his shoulder as they danced to a slow, sensual number from the band. I couldn't see his face, but I didn't want to. I couldn't bear to see his happiness. I quickly looked away, hurrying after Soren as he headed upstairs.

Avoiding the faces in the portraits we passed as we climbed, I wondered why Soren was so interested in exploring the palace.

'Soren!' I hissed as we arrived at the first floor. 'What if we are discovered?'

'We hide,' he said, impishly, 'Or we just pretend we are lost.'

I tugged at my wig. 'Can't we just go and sit outside or something? Wait for Dalya to find us?' I tugged at his arm. 'You do remember what you have to do tonight?'

He turned, serious now. 'I remember. If you haven't

'noticed, I am trying hard to distract myself.'

'Oh . . . OK.' I felt bad now and dropped my hand. I looked around me, seeing a long carpeted corridor that seemed to lead somewhere. 'But let's try and not get caught. It's going to look a bit odd.'

He gave me a look with his black eyes. 'Very well,' he said, 'but anyone would think you don't want to be alone with me.'

I am sure I turned crimson. 'Don't be silly.' I gestured at the corridor. 'Come on. Let's see what is down that hall.'

Soren turned the handle of the first door we passed and it opened on to an exquisite room: wood-panelled walls and wall-to-wall glass cupboards containing ancient-looking books.

'Impressive,' Soren said sincerely.

'Imagine all these books.' I stepped closer, peering through the glass of one of the cupboards. 'They must be worth a fortune.'

The lights were off and only a sliver of moonlight cut a streak across the room. It was eerie, but magical.

'I bet you were one of those children whose nose was constantly inside a book – escaping from reality,' said Soren by my side.

I turned, smiling a little. 'You know me so well.'

'I'd like to have known you as a child,' he said then, his voice hushed and low. 'I bet you were a sweet and serious girl.'

I shrugged more nonchalantly than I felt. Suddenly the room felt full of tension. I knew I was avoiding Soren's eyes. It was as though Soren, like Luca, recognised me. I caught my breath, as I felt the touch of his fingertips brush mine. Felt a frisson of electricity.

'Jane,' he whispered.

Confusion. I was not here for Soren. I didn't love Soren. Yet it was Soren who had been my companion, my friend, these past weeks. And then I remembered Luca, with Lila in his arms, and hurt anger made my guilt evaporate.

Finally I turned to him, and we stared at each other, our eyes locked. My heart was racing.

He drew me towards him, and I allowed myself to be drawn, and then he leaned back against the door, pulling me into his arms.

Pressed back against the dark wood panelling I felt his lips brush my cheek. No longer cold, but warm and full, gently touching my skin. I felt myself breathe out, not wanting to feel anything, but feeling everything all at once, my head resting on his chest. I could hear his heartbeat and mine, loud and fierce . . .

'I never thought I would feel like this for a mortal,' he whispered softly into my hair, and I felt the softness of his mouth as it tenderly kissed my neck. I shivered, hot suddenly, and instinctively my back arched.

'I don't want this,' I managed to say, my voice husky and strained. 'This isn't right.'

But as his arms moved to circle my waist, I didn't push him away. Because, despite the words I had just spoken, I did want this. I hated myself for wanting it, but it was consuming me. It was all there was. Right then, in that moment, it was all I wanted.

Finally he drew back and took my face in his hands, his eyes glinting in the darkness, the sharp line of his cheekbones cutting a hard but beautiful shape. And his mouth, wide and perfect, moved closer to mine, taking my breath away.

He put one finger on my lips, and with his other hand he stroked my face.

'It's OK,' he said. 'I'm sorry. It was a mistake, but I couldn't help myself.'

'I . . .' I struggled with relief, and intense disappointment.

'*Shhh.*' He pressed his finger more firmly against my mouth.

And then he was moving away from me, gently opening the door, he disappeared through it, leaving me wide-eyed and disbelieving.

I was left alone, with the sound of my fiercely beating heart.

And the taste of betrayal in my mouth.

CHAPTER TWENTY-SEVEN

'I'm proud of you,' Celeste told him. 'You're a credit to the family – and a worthy heir.'

Raphael summoned a pleased smile, though he had hated every minute of the evening so far. The weight of what he knew sat heavily on him, and he could barely bring himself to look at either of his grandparents. He wondered when, if, he could escape. But an exhausted-looking Cadmium seemed to put pay to that plan.

'Dear, you should rest.' Celeste took her husband's arm, concerned. 'Let me help you upstairs.'

Cadmium didn't protest. With irritation, Raphael saw the relief on his face.

'You will be happy to preside over the rest of the evening?' She smiled winningly at Raphael, patting his arm. 'Good boy.'

Raphael watched them climb the grand staircase, then

disappear out of sight, before he turned on his heel. For tonight he would have to play the part, but his thoughts were more galvanised than ever. He wanted to find out where Milo had disappeared to – if he was still alive. Once he had found him, he would discover what had really happened to his father. And why this web of lies had been laid to cover up the truth.

Standing nodding at the hordes streaming in and out of the great room and into the hall, he recognised Jane, saw her look around anxiously, then move quickly across the hall to the door that led through to the kitchens.

'What is she up to?' he murmured to himself. As he sidestepped the over-excitable Tilly, he was thwarted by a pair of rangy vampire girls, their identical bodies clad in skin-tight black leather dresses. Their faces he saw were identical too. Vampire twins. In spite of his curiosity about Jane, Raphael was stopped in his tracks.

'Haven't you grown?' said one, holding out a skinny arm. 'I remember you as a little cherub of a boy . . .' Her lavish lips parted to reveal pearly white teeth. 'But you wouldn't remember us . . .'

'I'm sorry,' he said politely, 'I don't recall you . . . I can't think why.'

The girls both tittered. 'Charming,' said the other twin.

'Would you care to dance?'

'I really . . . There is something I need to do . . .' he began, before both beauties moved to hem him in.

'Do it later,' one of them purred. 'Surely it can wait a while . . .'

Raphael opened his mouth to protest, but they were clearly having none of it. They quite forcefully diverted him, like a pair of supermodel bodyguards, into the music room. On stage, two women dressed in black silk catsuits were bent over a cello and a double bass, accompanied by a quiffed teddy-boy on drums as a suave, black-eyed and incredibly tall man in a classic suit sung into a microphone.

The music changed from moody jazz to a jauntier swing-style number. Beside him, one of the vampire twins was tapping her foot, her slender arms waving.

'Perfect,' she said, nodding to her sister. 'Ready?'

Swiftly they took one of each of his arms and began a mesmerising dance. Raphael had never been much of a dancer, but these girls were working some magic because he had never felt more assured on the dancefloor.

For the moment, all thoughts of betrayal were gone from his head.

CHAPTER TWENTY-EIGHT

Eventually, I crept, dazed, across the corridor and down the stairs. After the quiet of upstairs, the noise coming at me seemed deafening.

'Luca, Luca, Luca,' I whispered to myself, feeling that if I said his name enough times I could wipe out what had happened only minutes before. I had no idea where Soren had got to and, though I didn't particularly want to find him, I knew that Dalya would be looking for us, expecting Soren to reveal who he was to his sister.

A man in a silver tuxedo slunk past me, holding a circular tray of glasses aloft. He glanced briefly at me as he went, frowning. For a paranoid second I wondered if my dark bob had slipped, that what had happened with Soren was obvious.

But silver tux didn't linger, and I was left alone, still working out what to do.

'There you are.' Dalya appeared in front of me, a little out of breath, her hands on her hips. 'Mother is talking about going home soon. Hanni has already left with a headache. If Soren is going to tell Lila, he needs to do it now.' She peered up at me, a tiny crease in her forehead. 'You look odd.'

'Do I?' I waved my hand. 'Well, this is all a little odd, isn't it?' I heard my laugh, false and tinkling. Dalya's eyes lingered on me a little longer than necessary.

'OK,' she said slowly. 'We really need to find him . . .'

'Good. OK. Yes.' I stammered, catching sight of a familiar figure at the end of the hall. 'I think I see him. Over there.'

Dalya followed the direction of my gaze, then took off, darting in and out of stray guests.

I watched as she grabbed at his jacket with all the impulsiveness of a child, then whispered into his ear. I saw him look up and across at me. I sighed, and walked over to join them.

'You two stay here and I will fetch Lila,' Dalya instructed us. 'Don't move.'

'Are you sure?' I shook my head, reluctantly turning to Soren. His eyes swept over me, unreadable.

'Leave it with me. I'll tell her it is good luck to sit out in the palace gardens,' she said. 'Lila believes in all that superstitious rubbish.'

I really didn't want to be alone with Soren.

'I need to freshen up,' I told him. 'I'll meet you out there in a bit.'

Not waiting for either of them to speak, I ran for the bathroom at the back of the stairs, collapsing into a cubicle, my head in my hands.

'Compose yourself,' I whispered. But so many thoughts were rushing round my head. Being here, the music, kissing Soren. I sniffed, more loudly than I realised.

'Hello?' An unpleasantly familiar voice came from the other side of the door. 'Who's crying in there?'

I held my breath, trying to keep silent. But I hadn't locked the door behind me and one elegant foot was inching it open.

'You?' Natalia stood there, eyeing me warily. 'What the devil is the matter with you?' She bent, scrutinising my face, then quickly straightened up again. 'Lover's tiff is it?'

'I don't know what you mean!' I subtly checked that my bob had not dropped forward. I was literally itching to take it off. 'I don't have a lover.'

I expected to see a smug smile appear on her face, but instead she seemed to relax.

'Thank Lucifer for that. I've had it up to here with the

vulgar displays of affection going on out there. I mean, I adore Vanya, but quite honestly she should know better at her age. She and Valdar – they should have more decorum. It's unseemly, is what it is.'

'Oh,' I said, getting to my feet. 'Well, I guess they must be in love . . .'

'And as for the other two!' She tossed her hair back. 'That wolf-boy and the insipid blonde. All over him like the pox, she is.'

'Oh,' I repeated, feeling nauseous. 'How awful. But you danced with Raphael?'

She snorted, then stood and pouted into the mirror, checking her wide red mouth. 'Not a flicker from him, my dear! That boy is a cold fish, if you ask me. Perfectly charming, I suppose, but one just knows when a man is uninterested . . .' She whirled around to face me. 'So it seems that Sofi, you and I are the party wallflowers,' she sighed. 'Nobody loves us. We should have a little party of our own.'

'I need to be somewhere,' I said quickly. 'But I'll come and find you if—'

'Of course,' she cut in, and I glimpsed a tiny chink of loneliness, of humanity underneath the make-up. 'Another time.'

Leaving her examining her face in the bathroom

mirror, I went to face the music.

The corridor was dark, just a crack of light under a door ahead of me. Not wanting to draw attention to myself, I didn't bother trying to find a light switch, treading slowly and carefully ahead. I could hear the bustle of activity going on in the kitchens and realised I would have to think of a pretty good excuse as to why I was walking through here. How had Soren managed it?

Suddenly the door in front of me burst open, flooding the corridor with light. A girl dressed in a waitressing outfit and carrying a huge silver platter of cake frowned at the sight of me. When she saw my eye-make up, and the skin-tight velvet, she looked wary.

'Can I help you, Miss?' she asked, stopping.

'I need some air,' I said, making my voice a little haughty and authoritative. And a little quiet-time.' I smiled conspiratorially at her. 'All these people are giving me such a headache.'

She drew in a breath, still holding the platter perfectly still.

'Well you're not the first to come through here for a little peace and quiet, Miss,' she said. 'Quite a little procession we've had this evening.'

'Really?' I said casually. 'I was hoping the kitchen

gardens might be empty.'

'Some lovers' tiff going on out there . . .' She sniffed.

'Oh well, I will just take a minute,' I said, pointing in the direction of the kitchen. 'Through here?'

The waitress nodded, watching me closely as I passed by her. If she thought I was a vampire then I didn't blame her.

'Thank you so much,' I drawled, sweeping on. I had to admit, a small part of me was quite enjoying pretending to be a vampire. In different circumstances this evening would have been fun.

The door to the gardens was a little ajar and, peeping through the glass, I could see that Soren and Lila were face to face. I quietly opened the door, stepping out into the cool night air. There was no sign of Luca, thank goodness. But it was only a matter of time before he came back here and found his betrothed with Soren. I needed to stay, but was careful to stand in the shadows next to a pleasant-smelling rose bush. A little noise behind me made me turn round.

'It's me,' Dalya whispered as she slipped through the door. 'I was hanging about in the kitchens, just in case, and I saw you come through.' She hid herself next to me, allowing herself a quick peek at the pair standing at the edge of the gardens.

'Why are you saying this to me?' Lila's voice, confused and breathy, rang out. Without thinking I put my head out to look. She had her head in her hands. In front of her, Soren moved to take hold of her, but she shrank away from him. Passing by, one of the palace cats paused in its night-time forage to gaze curiously up at the pair of them.

'Lila.' Soren's voice was uncharacteristically gentle. I saw his hands flop down by his sides, his face a picture of anxiety. 'Believe me, I didn't want to tell you, but I owe you the truth. In your heart perhaps you have always felt—'

'I want my mother.' Lila's tone turned sulky. 'She is not far away you know, she will be wondering where I am.' She turned in our direction and I moved quickly back, pulling Dalya with me.

'Oh, this was not such a good idea.' Dalya said, rubbing at her arm where a thorn had scratched it. 'Soren is only scaring her.'

I thought for a moment. 'Perhaps . . . perhaps if you went and spoke to her . . .' I said hesitantly. 'Perhaps she would believe what Soren is saying if you backed him up?'

'You think so?' Dalya was reluctant. 'It might make her even more agitated.'

'Well we have to do something – time is running out,' I whispered. But as I spoke the sound of footsteps tramping through grass halted me. 'Now, Dalya. You have to stop her.'

As Lila came closer, I stepped out in front of her, attempting a reassuring smile.

'Lila!' I said. 'It *is* Lila, isn't it?'

'Who are you?' Lila glanced behind her to see Soren following.

'What do all of you people want with me?'

'Dalya,' I hissed, willing her to show herself. And finally she moved from behind me to embrace Lila.

'It's OK, Lila,' Dalya said soothingly. 'Soren is telling you the truth . . . I'm sorry. But you have nothing to fear, I promise.'

Lila looked from me to Dalya, her eyes wide.

'He is really my brother? I don't remember him. I don't remember anything . . .' She paused, a pained expression on her face. 'But that is odd, isn't it? I don't remember anything before I was five . . .' She shook her head. 'Though I dream sometimes.'

'What do you dream of?' Soren asked behind her.

'Nightmares.' Lila stared down at the ground, her lips trembling a little. 'I dream about a day when I was all alone . . . in a house in a wood. And there was a mess on the floor.' She looked up. 'A horrible mess of blood – and people.'

Soren's intake of breath was audible. All of us were silent, giving Lila time to recall events she had blocked out of her mind for so long.

'I do remember a boy. He was there in . . . in the kitchen. And then he ran away. He left me there with all the mess.'

'Lila, that boy was me. I was scared. I had done such a terrible thing to our mother and father . . .'

Lila had paled, her pretty face clouded with pain.

'Dear angels in heaven,' she whispered. 'My mother . . .'

The rest of us stood uncomfortably witnessing her pain.

Lila held out a hand and Soren gripped it. I saw then the tenderness in his eyes as he supported her.

'Why have you come back now?' she asked him. 'All this time . . . I had learned to forget. I had almost succeeded, but for those awful dreams . . .'

Dalya fidgeted a little on the spot. Behind us all the kitchen staff were still clattering dishes, oblivious to what was going on in the garden.

'What dreams?' Soren asked softly.

'Night after night,' she sighed. 'I was playing in a

strange garden with other children, and I was happy. And there was a boy who looked after me. In my dream we were so close . . .' She looked around at all of us. 'But when I told Hanni about the dream she said it meant nothing. That dreams weren't reality. That I should forget about them. But they made me feel so sad. The boy made me feel so sad.'

'That boy is me,' repeated Soren. 'Lila, I know it's confusing. And your mother – your adopted mother – she didn't want you to be upset, that's why she kept it from you.'

'Saul?' she said abruptly. 'I remember that name.' She frowned. 'But that isn't your name. It isn't you.'

'It was my name . . .' he answered her patiently. 'A long time ago. Lila . . . I am so sorry.'

'I wondered where you had gone, but then they came for me and I forgot.' She looked suddenly very confused. 'But how can I be sure it is you?'

'I suppose you can't,' he told her. 'You just have to believe me.'

'I am getting married to such a lovely boy.' Lila said distractedly, confused. She looked eagerly round at at all of us. 'I must tell Luca that my brother has come.'

'I don't think—' Dalya started.

'No. I must tell him. He will be so pleased.'

I wouldn't count on it, I thought, as Dalya made furious eye contact with Soren.

'I would like to spend some time with you first,' Soren said lightly. 'Get to know you again . . . You'd like that, wouldn't you?'

But Lila was uncertain, veering between believing him and uncertainty.

'Just a little time.' He held on to her hand. 'Just the two of us.'

Behind us I heard arguing in the kitchen – a male voice, and that of an older woman. As long as they were involved in some debate there was less chance of anyone noticing us, I thought.

'For goodness sake,' muttered Dalya, 'she doesn't understand. She hasn't actually grasped what Soren has told her.' She looked up at me, aghast. 'I mean he killed her whole family?'

'Who did?'

Dalya jumped – and, turning, we saw him. Standing there, looking anxious and angry all at once.

'Luca . . .' I said, my breath catching in my throat. He looked questioningly at me, then at the others: his sister, Lila and Soren.

'Who are you?' he said to him, quietly furious. 'And what are you doing with Lila?'

'Luca . . . this is not . . . this is complicated. Soren was just trying to explain to Lila.'

'Explain what?' He pushed his hair back off his face. 'And what is he to you, Jane? What are you doing here with him?' He looked and sounded disappointed, or that's how it seemed in the dim light.

'Soren is Lila's brother, Luca!' Dalya was firm. 'You need to know—'

'Go back inside,' he told her. 'I don't know what you're doing here. But this boy is a vampire.' He stopped, and I could practically see his heart beating in his chest, the muscles in his arms straining against his jacket. Dalya stepped back, alarmed, and Soren pulled Lila protectively towards him.

Luca stepped forward, his breath coming thick and fast now. I heard the tear of his clothing as his body grew inside it.

'Luca?' Lila looked confused. 'Sweetest, what is the matter?'

He didn't answer, but his head dropped, then reared again, and I saw his jaw snap.

'You'd better run,' I told Soren. 'Really. Run!'

Soren's eyes narrowed for a minute and it looked like he was going to stand his ground. It occurred to me that as a werewolf himself, he could – if he chose – play Luca at his own game. But with a quick look at me, he tightened his hold on the clueless Lila.

'Luca,' I pleaded, not daring to touch his expanding body, 'this is not what you think . . .'

'I don't know what you've become, Jane. I don't know what he has done to you. But you don't belong here.' Luca's voice was deep, harsh, though he wouldn't look at me.

'It isn't fair, brother.' Dalya defended me, but at the sight of her brother's changing body, she stepped away, and her words faded amidst the guttural growl coming from his throat.

'We'd better get out of here,' she said. And then, with a howl of pain, Luca pushed off after the disappearing Soren and Lila running with the speed of a panther.

'Soren, stop!' I screamed. 'Please, stop.'

At the sound of my voice Soren stopped, still holding on to Lila. Luca, no longer a boy, prowled in front of the two of them.

'This has all gone wrong,' sobbed Dalya beside me. 'What was I thinking? If Henora finds out . . .'

'She won't,' I said, though my own anxiety was palpable. Lila was nearly hysterical at the sight of her fiancée, wailing like a little girl. Soren, trying to stop her from bolting, looked helpless for the first time since I'd met him. And behind us, a small crowd of kitchen staff had gathered to watch.

'Oh, God,' I murmured, remembering how tenuous my disguise was. I edged further towards the three of them: Soren, Lila and Luca.

'Where are you going?' Dalya tried to pull me back.

'I'm going to talk to your brother,' I told her, knowing that was the only way to diffuse the situation. *If* he would listen to me.

I was behind him now, saw the strange transformation of his slender, boyish body now bulked out and trembling aggressively. How could I speak to an animal? I just kept thinking about the time I'd seen him change before. And how he had summoned the strength to change back.

'Luca.' I kept my voice low. 'Please, trust me. Soren is not going to harm Lila. He just wants to talk to her . . . He is her brother. It's the truth.'

The strange sound coming from him quietened almost imperceptibly and he turned very slightly. Hopefully, I edged forward.

'Will you just hear what he has to say? Then I promise you he will go . . . and Lila will stay. I'll make sure of it.'

I held my breath until I saw his body relax, the muscles

lose tension, and his form very slowly returning to boy-shaped.

Lila was still shaking, and her wide eyes were still trained on Luca. Soren shot me a look of relief – perhaps gratitude. I couldn't be sure.

'All right. I'm listening.' Luca's voice when he spoke was breathless and strained. I wanted to reach out and touch him, but this wasn't the time.

I had to let Soren explain.

Don't be arrogant, I willed. *Please, Soren, be humble for once in your life.*

'It's . . . it's a long story. And when I've finished, you may want to try and kill me again,' Soren said slowly. 'But . . . please don't.'

I moved to stand next to Luca and looked sideways at his expression. His normally pale face was flushed.

'Go on,' he said.

As Soren started to speak, I watched Luca's face return to its regular pallor. I couldn't face hearing the story again . . . I turned to see Dalya, shooing the kitchen staff back inside.

'What in heaven's name is going on out here?' I heard the cook scold. 'You, young lady, should be with your family, dancing, not listening to a couple of boys spatting.'

I crossed over, linking my arm through Dalya's. 'Come

on,' I said. 'Let's go.' Ignoring the curious looks, I half dragged her through the kitchen, down the corridor and into the Great Hall, firmly shutting the door behind me.

'What a mess!' I breathed, leaning against it. I felt exhausted.

Dalya looked at me, trying to smile. 'I know it didn't work out very well, but it was the right thing to do to tell her.'

'I hope he'll be OK . . .' I gazed into the distance.

'Soren?'

'No . . . Luca.' I sighed, putting an arm around her. 'This is all so hard for him.'

'You always think of him,' she said. 'More than yourself. You must still love him a lot.'

I shut my eyes, not knowing how to answer. My feelings hadn't changed. If anything they had only grown stronger. I took a deep breath.

'I care about him,' I said. 'That won't change.'

'Henora is going to be very angry.' Dalya smoothed her dress out absently, her little face tense and serious.

'She'll be angry if she sees me,' I said grimly. 'I think it's time I went home.'

'Not yet,' pleaded Dalya. 'Don't leave me here alone.'

'OK.' I smiled. 'I'll stay until we know Luca is all right.'

CHAPTER TWENTY-NINE

'Something is going on in the gardens.' Celeste appeared at Raphael's side, her words almost dying amidst the sounds of the band.

'Oh?' Raphael shrugged. 'It is probably just a scuffle amongst the staff. Too much grape juice I imagine.'

She shook her head. 'No, dear. Cook is very worked up. She says there are two boys out there, in a very serious discussion.' She looked warily about her before lowering her voice. 'One of the boys is Luca.'

'Luca? That doesn't sound like him . . .' Raphael was interested. 'And who is the other boy?'

'No one really knows. Cook says she thinks it is an acquaintance of Vanya Borgia . . .' Celeste sighed. 'I was having such a civilised discussion with her earlier. I do hope she's not up to her old tricks.'

The Vampire Jazz Quartert finished the number, and

paused to tune their instruments leaving the hubbub created by the room full of people.

To Celeste's obvious dismay, Henora was approaching, an irritated look on her face.

'Say nothing of it,' his great-mother whispered to him.

'Celeste.' Henora nodded. 'Lovely banquet.' She left a respectable few seconds before she added, 'I don't suppose you have seen that son of mine anywhere about?'

'Lowe?' Raphael shook his head, quite enjoying her discomfort. 'I'm afraid not. Have you checked the stables?'

'Not Lowe.' She failed to keep the edge out of her voice. 'Luca?'

'I – I'm sure he's somewhere with that lovely young fiancée of his.' Celeste said nervously. Raphael didn't come to her aid. Contrary to appearances, she wasn't that unfamiliar with dishonesty, he thought. Let her fumble.

He held out his hand to Henora, who took it, uncomfortably.

'Why don't we have a look?' he said smoothly. 'He can't be far.'

Ignoring the alarmed expression on his great-mother's face, he led Luca's mother to the door.

As they walked through into the Great Room, an almighty commotion met them.

'What the . . . ?' Henora started forward. 'Luca? What is going on?'

Raphael took in the boy, his shirt and jacket torn, and his face a picture of stress. He appeared to be in a world of his own, oblivious to onlookers. Behind him stood Lila, dazed, clutching the hand of the vampire-boy, Soren. And there, huddled into the corner together, stood Jane Jonas and Luca's sister Dalya.

CHAPTER THIRTY

'Luca.' Henora's tone was deep with fury. She clasped her hands together trying to maintain some decorum. 'Explain to me exactly what is going on.'

Luca seemed to come back to the present then. He pushed a shaking hand through his hair and I saw the familiar tic that appeared in his cheek whenever he was distressed. I held my breath, waiting for him to speak. But he was hesitating and his eyes darted between Lila and Soren. Lila was sobbing quietly and unhelpfully, and I saw Soren's arm slip protectively around her. He looked calm enough, only his black eyes, shimmering slightly, gave him away.

'Well?' Henora lifted her chin, imperious and judgemental. 'Speak!'

Yes, speak, I willed him. *Tell her the truth*.

But Luca turned to Raphael, who was observing

all of us suspiciously.

'This person should be removed from the palace,' said Luca. 'He has come here to cause trouble – for reasons that are unclear to me . . .' He paused, as though carefully thinking through his next words. 'He has fed Lila a dangerous pack of lies; cruel, inexplicable lies. He means to cause a rift between us. And he has dragged others into the mess.'

As he spoke the word 'others' his eyes came to rest on me. Following his gaze, Henora looked disdainfully at me.

'And who are you?' she snapped. 'Get back to the rest of your . . . kind.' As she took me in, I waited for her eyes to widen in recognition.

'Dear heavens, it is you!' She glared at me, moving closer. 'I thought you were long gone from our lives.'

From somewhere behind her I heard Tilly's cackle, and I cringed. God only knew what I must look like. Black make-up all over my face. Hair scraped back.

'Mother,' Luca intervened, 'leave her.'

'Don't defend her!' she snarled. 'She is clearly in league with this . . . this vampire!' She pointed at Soren, then turned to Raphael, who looked frozen to the spot. 'Raphael, remove these people. I implore you.'

I wanted nothing more than to be at home. With my

family. Without this ridiculous make-up. But the injustice of the situation made me stand my ground. I had long since blown my chances with Luca and his family anyway.

Raphael cleared his throat, nodding over at two of the palace guards, who had entered the hall with a troubled Celeste.

'Take the boy' – he gestured at Soren – 'take him to the cell in the palace basement.' He was calm, authoritative, with not a hint of emotion. I waited for him to order the same for me, but he only stood back to allow the two men to get to Soren.

'I'm sorry,' said Soren to his sister. 'But I spoke the truth, Lila. Remember that.'

'Enough!' roared Henora. 'You have caused enough harm. Please be silent.'

Luca watched as Soren was led away and then his eyes found mine. This time there could be no mistaking his look.

Disappointment.

But my heart had grown numb. I could see no way out of this. Who would believe Soren's story? I pushed away my own nagging doubts and looked down at the floor. I tried to concentrate on how exactly I was going to get out of here now.

A cold hand took hold of my arm and for a moment it seemed like I was going where Soren was going. But as I lifted my head, it was Vanya's face I saw.

'What happened?' she whispered, turning her back on the others and focussing on me. 'Soren didn't . . . he didn't tell the girl, did he?'

I nodded. 'It seemed like a good idea at the time.'

'The hell it was!' She rolled her eyes. And somehow just the sight of her indignation was comforting. She whirled round, sending even Henora skittering to stand behind Luca. 'Just for the record, Soren is not a liar,' she hissed. 'But clearly he is out of his mind – he'd have to be to expect any of you to actually use your imaginations for once.' She put one hand on her hip, her skirts swaying a little in her agitation.

'Spare us your display,' Henora said, though she still hid in her son's shadow. 'I don't care what you and your . . . despicable cohorts get up to in private. But you will not infect my innocent son and daughter-in-law with your poison.'

Something snapped, and I saw with a mixture of fear and admiration, the gleaming white fangs visible through Vanya's perfect red lips.

'Poison?' She reeled back, her hips swaying in a snake-like movement. 'You are delusional. It is you who harbours the poison. You' – she stabbed the air – 'maliciously depriving your children of happiness.'

'How dare you!' Henora finally bolted forward. 'I have endured you – up until now – for the sake of peace on Nissilum. But your flagrant abuse of the law – it's gone too far.'

'Not far enough!' Vanya snarled and in a flash she was right up against Henora, her tongue running itself threateningly over her lips.

'Vanya!' Luca growled, but after his recent turning, he was clearly too weak to do anything more than lurch forward a little.

'Vanya, stop it!' said Raphael a little wearily. But when I looked at his face, I saw a kind of wonder there. Like he was a spectator enjoying entertainment at a brawl.

With a narrowing of her eyes, Vanya obediently stepped back from Henora, closing her mouth in a petulant pout.

'Yes, stop it, you ridiculous woman,' Henora added unnecessarily, though it was clear she was shaken.

'Oh, don't speak.' Vanya covered her ears theatrically. 'It's like the whine of a tiny little dog.'

I bit my lip. Despite the hideousness of the situation, or maybe because of it, I felt a real sense of absurdity. Catching Raphael's eye, I suspected he was feeling the same way. I immediately switched my gaze forward.

'Ladies,' he said finally, 'as entertaining as this is, there is a celebration here today. We should be mingling harmoniously with each other.'

Was it me, or was there a touch of derision in his tone?

'Raphael, forgive me, but I have known you since you were a small boy,' said Henora haughtily. 'I do not appreciate being made to look like a source of comedy or being preached to by a . . . a child.' She couldn't help herself glaring at him.

Celeste, who had been hovering meekly at some distance, flapped her dainty hands about.

'Of course you don't. Raphael, please have more respect for your elders.' She smiled a wavery smile, expecting her great-son to demur.

'Respect?' He threw his head back and laughed heartily.

All of us stared in astonishment.

'Raphael,' Celeste said in a fearful whisper, 'please . . . behave.'

But his laughter seemed to chime like a deafening bell around the Great Room.

'Dear, oh dear,' Celeste murmured in distress. I once again felt the seriousness of the situation.

Was no one in control here?

'That's enough.' A low but authoritative voice spoke out.

As though reading my thoughts, Luca released himself from Lila's grip and stepped forward, until he was squarely in the middle of his mother and the still-smarting Vanya.

'There is no need for this.' Luca eyed the two women, then cast his glance around the rest of us. It skimmed over me, unreadable, and I lowered my gaze.

'The boy has been taken away,' he told his mother. 'And that is the end of it. Please, can we not all just get on with the evening?'

'Don't be naïve,' Henora snapped. 'Don't you realise that your . . . friend' – she spoke the word as though spitting out acid, and though I still had my eyes to the ground, I knew she was looking at me – 'that your friend means to come between you and your happiness? She has exhorted the boy to aid her. Spreading lies about Lila.'

Somehow I found my voice, aware that all eyes were on me now. 'Believe me, Henora, I have never wanted anything but happiness for Luca. That has never changed.' I swallowed, locking eyes with him. 'And Soren is not trying to do anything but rebuild a relationship with his sister.'

'As I said,' Henora snapped, 'lies.'

'Mother,' Luca began calmly, 'there is no harm done. There is a lot to take in . . . I need to make up my own mind about Soren.' He looked apologetically at me when he added, 'I need more than a story to convince me.'

'I will decide who is lying and who is not,' said Raphael. 'And as for spoiling Luca's happiness . . .' He paused, and at once there was silence as he stared hard at Henora. 'Perhaps you should look a little closer to home on that score.'

'How dare you!' She paled, her body trembling. 'I demand you fetch my husband!' She pointed rudely at a serving boy loitering nervously at the door to the Great Room. 'You! Go and fetch Ulfred.'

With a subservient nod, the boy fled through the doorway.

'Lost your celebrated manners now, haven't you?' Vanya told her dryly. 'I always thought you were an ill-disguised fishwife, and here is the proof.' She lifted her chin, looking as though there was an unpleasant smell beneath her nose.

Luca made no move to come to his mother's defence, instead he looked as though he were frozen to the spot. I saw him looking at her, though, and it was not a look of love. It was a look of embarrassment – shame even. As my eyes wandered over to Dalya, she too appeared aghast, though she was rubbing half-heartedly at Lila's arm in a gesture of comfort.

Was Henora showing her true colours at last?

'Mother, please . . .' Luca tried to take her arm but she shoved it away impatiently.

'I have never been more humiliated,' she growled. 'We're all going home. As soon as Ulfred gets here. We will be leaving.'

'Excellent,' purred Vanya. 'You are rather spoiling the atmosphere around here.'

'Vanya!' I couldn't help myself. 'Just – leave it . . .'

Luca flashed me a look which could have been gratitude.

She sighed melodramatically. 'If that's what you want, darling. You've been through quite enough tonight, I imagine. I have no wish to make things worse.'

I shrugged. 'It's not me we should worry about – it's poor Lila. She doesn't deserve any of this.'

'No.' Luca looked at me softly, a half-smile on his lips. 'Well said.'

And just for a bit, everyone else melted away as something familiar passed between us.

'Pah!' Clearly irritated that I had spoken out, Henora pushed rudely past me. Luca frowned, opening his mouth to speak, but shut it again quickly. With his eyes, he tried to signal an apology to me. I smiled quickly, before looking away.

Luca then followed his mother, and Dalya and Lila trailed behind them.

'I'm sorry,' Dalya whispered as she passed by me, but I shook my head.

I hoped it wasn't the last I'd see of her, but I had a sinking feeling.

I badly wanted to go home. To see my wonderfully normal parents and my wonderfully normal, if slightly annoying, little sister. But I couldn't leave Soren to face this on his own. I stood, rubbing at my make-up, my disguise in tatters, and soon it was just Vanya and I – and Raphael at some distance – standing in the Great Room. Celeste had disappeared along with the others.

Vanya heaved another sigh. Glancing at me, she turned her attention to Raphael.

'I am not leaving without seeing Soren,' she told him haughtily. 'I assure you I will not allow him to be punished because of some misplaced allegiance you palace folk have with the werewolves. I will personally act as his defence attorney.'

He raised an eyebrow. 'That is your choice. I am all in favour of a fair trial. Believe it or not, honesty is important to me. I mean to sort the lies from the truth, just as you do.'

He turned on his heel and began to walk away, but as he reached the foot of the great staircase, he hesitated before turning back to us.

'And for the record, I have no allegiance to anyone in particular. And no truck with outmoded law and order. You'll realise that soon enough.'

Without stopping for a response, he turned back quickly and began his ascent up the staircase.

Watching until he was out of sight, Vanya pressed her lips together, a determined look on her face.

'Well, well, well,' she said softly. 'Perhaps, Jane, all is not lost after all.'

CHAPTER THIRTY-ONE

'Your mother is in her bed,' Ulfred told him. 'She is not herself.' Concern etched his face, as he scratched at his beard in agitation.

'Father, I regret what happened today,' Luca told him, looking down at the torn clothes he was still wearing. 'It was such a strange . . . unexpected event.'

Ulfred nodded. 'And what of this boy's story,' he said carefully. 'He told you he had killed his entire family but for Lila?'

'That's what he said.' Luca sighed, remembering the terrible tale Soren had told him. Outlandish, impossible. 'But it cannot be true. It simply can't . . . nobody behaves that way on Nissilum. There has never been a murder, certainly not so terrible. We would know of it, wouldn't we?'

Ulfred drew in his breath sharply, and Luca

watched him, curious.

'Father . . . what is it?' He frowned.

'I am just tired, boy.' Ulfred leaned against the wall in the kitchen, where they were standing. 'It has been a long evening.'

'It's not her fault, you know,' Luca said abruptly.

'I know . . . She just wants the best for you.' Ulfred smiled reassuringly at him, misunderstanding.

'Not Henora,' Luca uncharacteristically snapped. 'Jane. It is not Jane's fault.'

Ulfred's smile faded. 'It is better that you don't speak of her, son,' he said gravely. 'She is the root of all this trouble.'

Luca bristled at this injustice. There had been a moment, back in the palace gardens, when he had to admit he had suspected Soren's story had been concocted with Jane's help, to somehow stop his marriage going ahead. But quickly Jane had shown her true colours. And they had been the same shimmering, pure colours he had been drawn to – what seemed a lifetime ago. Jane was modest, selfless . . . and grown up. The great irony was that his mother hadn't thought her a fit partner for him for the simple reason that she was a mortal. The truth was that there could never be a more perfect girl for him.

But what of Soren's story? It seemed so far-fetched.

And for all the world the boy looked nothing like any wolf he knew. But what then was Soren's motive in making the story up? Luca sighed, overwhelmed by conflicting feelings and a little angry with himself; did he not want to see the real truth, because of all the upset and unhappiness it would cause his family? In particular, his mother. Was he too scared to confront it?

He couldn't see a way out of this mess. And now, more than ever, he realised he needed to protect Lila. Jane was right. She didn't deserve this. Any of it.

After Ulfred had made his own way to bed, Luca looked in on Dalya, who lay on her bedroom floor, her nose in a book. She looked up at the sound of his footsteps and he made his way over to sit on her messy bed.

She put her book face down on the carpet in front of her.

'I don't want to talk to you,' she said sulkily. 'I hate this family.'

'No you don't.' He spoke gently. 'It was an awful evening, and emotions ran a bit high, but—'

'You're an idiot,' she interrupted him crisply. 'But if you want to ruin your life, it's up to you.'

Luca sighed, angling his head to see the cover of her book.

'*Persuasion?*' he said, his tone just slightly teasing. 'Isn't Jane Austen a little old for you?'

'Actually, it's really quite appropriate,' she said dryly. 'Perhaps you ought to read it, Luca? It might open your eyes to the truth of things.'

He was silent, recalling the central theme of the mortal novel: selfless, pure and noble love.

Dalya huffed audibly. 'I thought better of you – all those books you used to read, the stories you told me . . . I thought you believed in love, Luca.' She shook her head. 'You have changed, brother.'

He was silenced – something in what she had just said pierced him. He realised he had barely noticed how much he had altered over the past few months . . . until now.

'Maybe I just grew up,' he said after a while. 'I had to grow up one day. I'm sorry you feel left behind.'

'How is this being grown up?' she retorted. 'Marrying someone you don't love.' She said the last with a passionate flush in her cheeks.

'Dalya,' he warned her, 'Lila is in this house, remember?'

'Yes,' she sighed, exasperated. 'How could I forget? I am the one who keeps her company. Remember?'

Luca smiled, nodding. He understood her frustration – and her sentiments. He'd had them too, even more

302

strongly. Finding, meeting his soulmate had been everything to him. But now . . .

'Life gets complicated,' was all he could think of to say.

'No. People complicate it.' She stared hard at him.

'And what about you – when the time comes for you to marry. Will you go against Henora's wishes and marry outside of the breed?'

She opened her mouth, hesitating, then: 'I'm not getting married – it's nothing but a repressive institution designed to restrict imagination and passion.'

In spite of his sadness, Luca burst out laughing. Dalya picked up her book and threw it at his head.

'You dare laugh at me,' she hissed. 'But I am the only one now who has passion. Who dares to believe.'

Luca stopped laughing. He saw his little sister's face, the tears clouding her eyes, her elfin face troubled and sad. He reached out and grasped her hand.

'I have to do this . . .' he whispered hoarsely, holding on tight. 'It doesn't mean the ache in my heart will go away. Or that I have stopped believing in love.'

And as he said it, he felt the weight of his own emotion and his eyes pricking. He felt his sadness washing over him like a giant wave. And he held on to Dalya's hand for comfort now, even though she obviously despised him.

But she didn't let go. She saw his sadness and he knew that her tender heart had made her anger ebb away, leaving only a look of pity on her face.

'Well,' she said finally, 'I want to finish my chapter. I'm at a really good bit . . .' She released her hand, but gently, and Luca got up from her bed.

'You are not my enemy, are you, Dalya?' he asked her. He knew his words were pathetic. He felt lost.

'Never your enemy,' she said, picking up *Persuasion*. 'I want only your happiness.' All of a sudden her little face looked wise beyond its years, humbling him.

'Thank you,' he said. 'Goodnight, little sister.'

CHAPTER THIRTY-TWO

It was very late. With Soren gone, I couldn't get home, and Vanya had disappeared to find Valdar, presumably to concoct a plan to help Soren. I had not been invited along, just left to wander around the palace.

Reaching one of the palace's bathrooms, the first thing I did was take off the wig and shake my hair out. Despite hours spent underneath the fake hair, it wasn't so bad, if a little messy. I ran my fingers through it until it looked more or less respectable. Then I scrubbed off the horrendous smudged make-up. A few of the kitchen staff came in and out, but I was beyond caring about the odd looks. After what had happened, it didn't seem to matter any more.

My clothes were at Vanya's. I had no choice but to stay in the vampish ensemble I'd been wearing all night. The effect was considerably less glamorous than when I had started out this afternoon. *Was it really only this afternoon?* I thought.

I made my way to the Great Room where the last of the guests were sitting around at table, supping grape juice, or whatever it was, helping themselves to the slabs of cheese and oatey-looking biscuits laid out on the table. I even saw the band, the Vampire Jazz Quartet, deep in conversation at one end of the room.

As I walked in, all eyes immediately alighted on me, and I saw faces leaning into each other whispering. I found a seat apart from everyone and settled myself on it, concentrating my gaze on the tablecloth. When I did allow myself to look up, I was relieved to see that the occupants of the room had lost interest.

All except one.

I looked up, and my heart sank at the sight of Lowe standing at the entrance to the room. Thankfully he had made himself absent while all the drama had been going on in the hall, but seeing him, lounging – insouciant and mocking – in the doorway, brought back memories of another time, another palace party, and another me. I swallowed my food and tried to set my face in an unfazed expression.

'You?' he drawled, coming towards me. 'My goodness. You had me fooled I must say . . .' He pulled up a chair next to me and I couldn't stop myself from shrinking away.

'I am not interested in anything you have to say,' I said, lifting my chin. 'I'll be gone soon.'

He regarded me, a weirdly peaceful look on his face.

'Not yet, I don't think. Raphael may want a few . . . words with you first.'

I rolled my eyes. 'Well I have nothing to say to him, either.'

'Oh, but you are now implicated in a serious contravention of the law.' His self-assured tone sent a surge of irritation through me.

I inhaled, to stop myself from reacting in the way he wanted.

'Go away,' I said blankly.

'But this is important, this is not just between you and Luca . . .' He put his cracker back on the table. 'Who is Soren? Where did he come from? Nobody knows him. Lila – well, Lila is confused. She is gibbering something about a brother, but' – Lowe looked about us, before leaning even closer, his tone confidential – 'Lila is a sweet, innocent girl. I just wonder what exactly *his* motivation is?' He raised an eyebrow, indicating that I should explain.

I shrugged. 'Nothing that you should concern

yourself with,' I told him. 'Really. It is none of your business, Lowe.'

He sat back. 'You've developed a bit of a backbone, haven't you? Or perhaps you have just exposed your true character?' He grimaced. 'You're still trouble. And you will harm our family . . . And that boy being held downstairs – he is trouble too.'

'So what do you want?'

Lowe frowned. 'I want him thrown out of Nissilum. But mostly I want you gone. We don't want the likes of you on Nissilum.'

'We?' I said boldly. 'Perhaps it is just you?'

'We don't accept mortals infecting our society with their loose morality,' he replied coldly.

'We have a word for people like you in my world,' I told him, shaking my head.

'I'm assuming it isn't complimentary . . . ' He eyed me. 'Have it your way, then. But one way or another you will not get what you want. You're a miserable, doomed mortal. One day you will die, and you will deserve to . . . All of you do. You have no proper society. No real authority. You all do exactly as you wish, and damn the consequences.' He slammed his palm down on the table, jolting me, and making everyone else in the room look over in our direction. Ignoring them, Lowe got up, pushing back his shoulders arrogantly.

'You're wrong about that,' I whispered.

'They'll be asking for you soon,' he told me. 'If I were you, I'd get my story straight. The Celestials don't look kindly on subterfuge.'

With a last look around the room, Lowe walked out of it, leaving me the subject, yet again, of unearthly intrigue.

CHAPTER THIRTY-THREE

Though the expression on his face was one of fierce authority, appropriate to his status, Raphael felt curiously excited. He had lain awake all night, eyes wide open, running through the bizarre events of the night before.

But were they bizarre?

For as soon as Luca had come in and told them all of Soren's revelation, an important part of the puzzle had fitted into place. If Soren was to be believed, then he could indeed be Saul, the renegade cub who had committed that infamous crime, documented by the palace, all those years ago. Soren's connection with the vampires was the one jarring fact; given the bad blood that lay between the vampires and the werewolves – throughout entire mythology – how had Vanya and her lot come to be his family?

Raphael was wired as he walked the cellar corridors,

impatient to get to the prisoner. He had got very little out of Jane Jonas, who had been protective of Soren when he'd talked to her last night – refusing to deny or confirm anything. The girl had got tougher, Raphael had observed. No longer the fresh-faced, trusting creature she had been when he first knew her.

The guard outside Soren's cell was slumped on his chair half asleep. As Raphael approached, he cleared his throat to announce his arrival.

The guard jerked awake, fumbling, embarrassed, with his hat, and getting to his feet.

'Sir?' He nodded, the keys at his waist jangling. 'Good morning, Your Celestial Highness.'

Raphael nodded back curtly, his eyes on the grid on the door.

'One moment . . .' The guard shuffled to the grid, opening it to take a view of the prisoner inside.

'Wake up, boy,' he said gruffly. 'Make yourself ready for your visitor.' There was the sound of shuffling and coughing, and the guard motioned to Raphael to go in.

As he entered the cell he saw the large dark shadows underneath the boys eyes which, like his hair, glistened black. Soren was gazing at him, but without emotion. Raphael took a chair from its place against a wall and drew it up in front of the boy.

They exchanged a look of hostility then, but of some understanding too.

'Who are you?' Raphael said without preamble.

'Interesting question.' Soren had the beginnings of a small smile on his face. 'Interesting that *you* should ask it.'

'What does that mean? Are we going to be talking in riddles? Is this another part of the game?'

'It's not a game,' said Soren. 'I assure you of that.'

'So . . . answer my question. Tell me the truth. What was that display all about yesterday?'

'The truth needed to be heard.' Soren sat forward and bent his head over clasped hands. 'This whole place – is like a perfect rosy apple, but deep inside there is a rotten core. You are all delusional.'

Not all of us, thought Raphael, but he said nothing, waiting for Soren to continue.

'I spent a long time hiding the truth from myself – growing cold-hearted, but then something happened. I came back here to see Vanya Borgia—'

'Vanya is a friend of yours?'

'An old friend.' Soren gave him a wry smile. 'It was Vanya who showed me true friendship many years ago. After' – Soren hesitated – 'after I did what I did.'

'Tell me,' Raphael said calmly, 'what . . . exactly . . . did you do?'

'If I tell you, then that's it.' Soren sat back, crossing his arms over his chest. 'You would be hard pressed to find a punishment severe enough to fit my crime. It is simply unacceptable. Why do you think I ran away, hid myself from everyone for so many years?'

There was a tense silence. Outside the cell, the two of them heard the guard snoring lightly. It would have been a comical moment, if either boy felt in the least bit humorous.

'What if I told you there would be no punishment?' Raphael looked hard at Soren. 'That in return for your help, this whole thing would be forgotten?'

The other boy frowned. 'I don't want it forgotten,' he said. 'And in what way would I "help"? I don't understand.'

'I believe you share my opinion of Nissilum – the rules, the rigidity of its traditions. And now that the cracks are beginning to show, I realise it is all an utter sham. Even my own family—'

'Are corrupt?' Soren's expression was at once lit up by a wry smile.

'You find it funny?'

'No – no, not funny . . . just terribly predictable. Of

313

course they are corrupt.' He shook his head. 'My family were certainly corrupt – or at least my parents were. My mother committed a sin – and then she covered it up. When I found out, I—'

'What did she do?'

'She was unfaithful to my father . . . became pregnant. With me.'

Raphael's eyes widened. 'Indeed, that is unusual. You wolves are such sticklers for fidelity. You pride yourselves on it.'

Soren answered with a wan smile.

'How old were you when you discovered this?' Raphael asked.

'Ten. And I never would have . . . had a stranger not told me.' Soren sat up, looking more animated. 'Just walked into my life, and then out again, leaving me to deal with it. My real father—'

'So you have come back here to find the family you have left – and that is all?'

'Is that so hard to believe?' Soren stared at him. 'That I should want to find the sister I grew up with. My closest companion.'

Raphael shrugged. 'I suppose not. But you realise that what you did has not been made public. Deliberately. Why would Henora believe you? Why would Lila?' He hesitated. 'I wonder why you were simply sent away . . .'

'Because the Celestials have no idea how to deal with the kind of crime I committed,' Soren said. 'It is not in their remit.'

'Indeed not.' Raphael sighed. 'I need to think about this. Perhaps there is a way we can be of help to each other.'

Soren raised an eyebrow. 'You mean to leave me here.'

'I need to look as though I am dealing with you . . . There are certain troublesome factions who bay for blood, as it were. I need to attend to a few things,' Raphael told him. 'But you are safer here, for the time being.'

Soren shrugged. 'I have to trust you. I have no choice.'

'No, you don't.' Raphael got to his feet. 'But I appreciate your honesty.'

He left the cell, turning things over in his mind. He didn't know what to make of Soren, but something told him, there was more to the boy's story than he was letting on.

CHAPTER THIRTY-FOUR

I had changed back into my own clothes, but in every other way I didn't feel myself.

I sat on the bed in Vanya's room, wondering how, if, I would get home. Soren was still at the palace, and the only other person who could help me was holed up with his parents. Not that he would help me. I was mixed up with Soren now – the enemy – as far as Luca was concerned.

I also didn't want to leave until I knew what would happen to Soren. Vanya had gone back to the palace this morning, but Soren had sent her home again.

'Apparently I am surplus to requirements,' she'd told me as I sat waiting for her in her dark kitchen basement. 'Raphael tells me that Soren doesn't need anyone's help, that he won't be punished. I can't say I find that terribly reassuring. Raphael is not exactly known for his consistency . . .' For the first time I saw Vanya looking something less than coolly beautiful. She looked wiped out.

I fell back on the bed, and as my head hit the pillow I felt tiredness overwhelming me and my eyelids closing. Faces, voices flashed inside my head. Lila, confused and child-like; Soren's pain and unexpected vulnerability; and Luca. Still standing his ground. His was the last face I saw, those green eyes, that look of softness when he realised my intentions were good. And then his face faded and sleep came.

'Jane, wake up.' Vanya was shaking the bedclothes, her face a picture of anxiety. 'There is something going on out there . . .'

I sat up blearily, the sound of shouting ending my peace. Vanya was at the window, craning her head to see what was happening.

'So, who is it?' I rubbed at my eyes, putting my legs out and on to the ground.

'What a ghastly noise!' she muttered, then turned to me. 'There seems to be some kind of protest going on . . . I am sure that's the wolf-boy's brother out there. I forget his name . . .' She wrinkled her nose, thinking.

'Lowe?' Suddenly I was alert, jumping up and joining

317

her where she stood. Down below, Lowe and a couple of his werewolf friends I vaguely recognised appeared to be rousing the gathering crowds.

'We need to cleanse Nissilum of this creature . . . and of the mortal girl in our midst,' he spat out nastily. 'She has wrangled her way into this world to seduce my brother, despite the fact that he is about to be married!' She is the real poison.' He cast a glance up at Vanya's house, and she and I ducked away from the window and out of his view.

There was shocked murmuring from the observers gathered around him, faces frowning. Lowe was garnering support.

'Idiot boy.' Vanya sighed. 'It's always the young who are destructive . . . So full of misguided vitriol. Such a pity. Youth is indeed wasted on them.'

'The Celestial monarchy are too soft on criminals. Let's hope that the heir to the Celestial kingdom will come down harder on these renegades in our society!' Lowe shouted. 'If justice were done, Soren Balzac would have been banished from Nissilum by now. The mortal girl needs to be taught a lesson she will never forget.'

The crowd muttered and cheered, carried away by Lowe's oratory.

'The devil save us from the likes of Lowe,' whispered

Vanya. 'Little ignoramus. Blindly unaware that he is the real liability on Nissilum.'

I nodded. Lowe's answer to everything was aggression. He was threatened by anything he didn't understand. As young and stupid as he appeared, though, his venom scared me. I had no idea he hated me that much.

'How tedious! We now have to stay holed up inside until that wretched boy gets bored and shuffles home for his dinner,' Vanya said, in a bored tone. She turned to me. 'On reflection, my dear, aren't you glad you no longer have to face being part of the wolf-boy's family? I mean, it's not just the brother, is it? It's that carping mother of his too.' She shuddered. 'Unbearable.'

'Luca and Dalya are different,' I said firmly. 'Lowe is a nasty piece of work.'

'You can say that again. What annoys me is that we, the vampires, are always branded as the evil, untrustworthy ones. When we are simply direct.'

I smiled at her. 'You certainly are.'

'It's a virtue, darling, not a vice.'

The sound of the crowd was growing faint and, peeping out, I saw it had drifted away from Lowe – who was still standing, an impassioned look on his face, hands on his hips.

'Nobody wants to join his revolution after all,' I said,

relieved. 'But I have a feeling Lowe won't give up easily.' I looked at Vanya. 'What will happen to Soren?'

Vanya barely hid her concern. 'I'll make sure nothing does,' she said firmly. 'I don't care who I have to fight to get him released.'

I looked at her curiously. 'How do you know Soren?' I asked. 'I mean, it's all a bit vague.'

A flicker of something passed over her face. 'Oh, we just ran in the same circles for a while,' she said – which was even more vague as far as I was concerned.

'How?' I frowned. 'I mean, he ran away . . . I don't—'.

'Don't pry,' she said abruptly and a little severely. 'You might regret it if you do.'

'OK.' I carried on looking at her profile. 'But I won't judge. I don't live on Nissilum. I'm used to mortal frailty.'

She turned slowly to face me, and relaxed a little.

'I can't go into it . . . I am not willing to open that particular "can of worms".' She annunciated the phrase almost comically – a way of distracting me, I knew.

'So . . . how did Raphael seem? Was he angry?' I said after a pause, changing the subject.

'See, that's the rather odd thing.' Vanya sat down on my bed. 'Raphael seemed to be almost enjoying the whole thing. I do hope that doesn't mean he is having another breakdown – that doesn't bode well for anyone.'

I shuddered. My memory of Raphael in his mortal form – as Evan – was of someone capable of chilling twists of mood. Volatile.

'He allowed me to see him last night,' she went on. 'He was almost charming. It was all very odd. I asked him if I could be allowed to defend Soren – in the spirit of fair justice – and he laughed. He said that there was no such thing on Nissilum, but that Soren could be in a position to redeem himself.'

'What does that mean?'

'No idea. Some kind of trade-off perhaps.' Her face paled a little, but regained its colour almost instantaneously.

'If Luca brings charges against him, then there has to be some kind of trial.' I thought of how the justice system worked in the mortal world. But this wasn't my world. Things worked in a very different way.

'If Luca was going to do that, he would have done it by now. I wonder if Henora is so embarrassed by the whole thing that she has silenced him.'

'I doubt that. She thinks Soren and I are co-conspirators. She'll want us out.'

'Well. maybe now what Henora wants won't count for much. She has shown herself to be somewhat unhinged.' Vanya looked unusually anxious though.

'Perhaps things are going to change at last.' I looked at her. 'Lowe is a hot-headed fool – but in a weird kind of way he is kicking up the dust. Forcing people to notice what is going on.'

'Pah – he is barking up the wrong tree altogether. That boy has the "constitution" so ingrained in him, he would die defending it. This twisted sense of superior morality!'

'But something is going on now, isn't it?' I looked at her. 'Raphael is ascending as ruler of Nissilum. The establishment is changing.'

But what would this mean for Luca? Would it bring us together at last? Or would it wrench us finally apart?

After Vanya had left me alone, I sat staring out through the window at the perfect blue sky, and in the distance – treetops, harking back to another time and place for me and for Luca. Nothing stays the same. But sometimes change is a good thing. It was time to move on.

CHAPTER THIRTY-FIVE

Night was coming again. Raphael lay in his darkened bedroom, where he had been for many hours, unable to do anything but stare at the shapes caused by the dim light in the room. Down below, deep underneath the palace, Soren was still incarcerated and Raphael was not ready to speak to him again, or let him go.

He was still going over the words, trying to focus on what it was about him that seemed familiar.

Soren had risked severe punishment to speak out to Luca. He didn't want sympathy . . . But he did want something. He was searching for something.

Noises were coming from downstairs, the servants going about their business. Celeste had not come to him – not even to find out what he had done with Soren. Perhaps she sensed that the net was closing in on her and she was ashamed of her own dishonesty

– she couldn't face him.

At this last thought Raphael sat up abruptly. The mirror opposite the bed showed him to be unkempt – his curls in disarray, his clothes creased and dirty from the night before. He stood quickly, removing his shirt and trousers. He would bathe and then start preparations. What had been a seed of a revolution in his head was now about to become a reality. But he needed to create some fervour, even if it meant lying about his intent.

It was late, but the palace horses were always ready for a bit of exercise. Approaching the stables, he heard them moving about restlessly inside. Saddling up his own, he rode as quietly as he could, past the bemused-looking guards and then more quickly across the fields, heading for Henora and Ulfred's home on the outskirts of the Celestial Quarter.

Lila and Dalya were together in Dalya's bedroom. Luca was not one for eavesdropping, but he couldn't help himself from lingering at the sound of their voices; Lila's high and still a little hysterical, Dalya's calm, but serious.

'I'm frightened,' said Lila, 'and confused . . . I do remember my brother, but Henora says I don't . . . She said that what Saul— what Soren did was try and confuse me. Maybe she's right? Maybe I just wanted to . . .'

'But why would you?' Dalya sighed. 'Why would you think you remembered something as big as that? It doesn't make sense.'

Luca heard her lower her voice then and he strained to listen.

'Mother is terrified of anything getting in the way of your marriage to Luca,' she said. 'It has made her a little intense. Not herself.'

'What do you think, Dalya?' Lila asked. 'Is it just a wicked story?'

There was a silence and Luca found he was holding his breath.

'No. I know it to be true. I have no proof. But I have the word of someone I trust.' She gave a small laugh. 'Who is like a sister to me . . . But who I am sure I will never see again.'

'That pale girl with the grey eyes?' Lila said. 'Who is she?'

'Oh. Just . . . someone.'

Luca shut his eyes. *Just someone.*

'Are we still holding the engagement ball?' Lila asked innocently. 'I have had my dress especially made.'

'I don't know, Lila,' Dalya said kindly. 'I don't know what's going to happen now.'

Luca moved away from the bedroom door, treading

backwards, away from them. His sister meant the world to him and he knew she wasn't fanciful by nature. If Dalya truly believed Soren had been telling the truth, then he owed it to her and to Lila to find out for himself.

He could hear Lila talking again, light-hearted this time, playful, Dalya gently humouring her, and he smiled sadly.

He couldn't just leave Lila. Promises had been made. Albeit to Lila's parents from Henora and Ulfred. But his family's duty was his duty. Nothing had been instilled in him more. And Lila was vulnerable. He couldn't let her down – could he?

Jane didn't need him. She had her family, her strength, her courage. And she would soon find a replacement. He hoped for her sake it would be a mortal boy, who could offer her straightforward love.

He reached the top of the stairs and began climbing down. Lowe was at the base, struggling into a coat, one foot inside a riding boot.

'Lowe?' Luca reached him. 'Where are you going in such a hurry? It's late. You were up half the night . . .'

Lowe pulled his other boot on. 'I am not sleepy, I'm going for a ride.'

'Now?' Luca's eyes darted to the living room, where Henora and Ulfred were. 'Seems a bit odd.'

'Lowe shrugged. 'You're a fine one to speak of odd.'

Luca eyed his brother suspiciously. 'You are up to something . . . sneaking about. You were up at the crack of dawn this morning too. You, who never rise until midday.'

'Somebody needs to do something,' said Lowe darkly. 'Stop this.'

'Stop what?' Luca stepped closer to him, anxiously.

But Lowe was not forthcoming. He secured his coat, slapping his chest in a gesture of machismo. It would have been amusing in other circumstances. But not tonight.

'If I were you, I would concentrate on comforting your fiancée,' Lowe told him condescendingly. 'From what I gather you were hardly the hero last night. Mother said you stood like a meek little lamb, and it was left to her to deal with the situation.'

Luca sighed, shaking his head. 'One day you will learn that rushing recklessly into matters that you don't fully understand is not the adult thing to do.'

'So I should just stand about mewling, allowing all manner of low-life and mortal interlopers into my life?' Lowe pulled on his coat, buttoning it up to his neck. 'I don't think so. Unlike you, brother. I will not allow myself to be disrespected. I have pride. Raphael has asked me to help him, and I have a feeling that the vampire-boy will be receiving his due punishment tonight.'

Luca opened his mouth, trying to find the real meaning in Lowe's little speech, but he couldn't find the words to respond. He stood back, even opening the door for Lowe.

'Just be careful,' he said. 'Sometimes your trust is misplaced.'

With a derisive snort, Lowe pushed past him out into the night, heading for the stables.

As he shut the door after him, Luca leaned back against it, an uneasy feeling creeping over him. He glanced upstairs where the girls were, and then at the door to the room where his parents were talking.

His brother was right. He was too passive. Minutes passed as Luca turned ideas over in his head. Then moving quietly, he gathered his boots and a jacket, and an old deer-stalker style hat of his father's, then, deftly opening the door so that it made no sound, he crept silently out the door.

CHAPTER THIRTY-SIX

As Raphael knew he would, Lowe cantered eagerly towards him, his hair swept back by the wind.

'Is there trouble with Soren?' asked Lowe, panting a little from some hard riding.

'Soren is locked up in his cell,' said Raphael. 'I need you to round up the stable boys, have them ready for my instruction.'

Lowe's eyes widened. His excitement was visible. 'Is it the vampires? Have they staged some sort of revolt on his behalf? We will be glad to put them in their place. It's about time.'

Raphael nodded. He didn't contradict the boy. He needed him to cause trouble, to create unrest.

'Fetch the stable boys, then meet me at the palace cellars. We need to raid the armoury.'

'You mean to fight?' A shadow of doubt crossed Lowe's

face. 'This is serious.'

Again Raphael nodded. 'Just meet me there in an hour,' he told him.

Lowe looked slightly hesitant for a second, but he pulled on his horse's reins. 'Of course. I won't let you down.'

Of course you won't, thought Raphael. And as Lowe rode away, he kicked his heels into his mare and began the journey back to the palace.

Loosely tying his horse, Raphael ran through the palace kitchens. It was late and all the staff were in bed. The stable boys would be grumpy and reluctant to get up, he thought. But they all shared Lowe's ridiculous vigilante spirit. At the hint of a threat to the palace, they would come out in arms to defend it. To defend the Celestial family.

But Raphael wasn't interested in the Celestial family – only that as a member of it, he had power.

To expose a palace secret in the midst of chaos.

He found some paper without the palace emblem on it, and hurried up the great staircase to his room. There he took out the sheaf of documents relating to his father's disappearance, together with another set of documents relating to the infamous wolf cub killer, and tucked them both deep into his pockets.

To his satisfaction, he heard the thunder of hooves outside and the sound of Lowe shouting something indistinct but vitriolic out into the night.

Raphael ran further up the stairs, to the floor where Celeste and Cadmium slept. His breath was coming thick and fast and adrenaline coursed through him.

He reached the door to their vast chamber and put his fist to it and banged as hard he could.

'Celeste!' he shouted, banging harder. 'Cadmium!'

Then he waited, agitated, for his great-mother to come to the door.

Eventually she appeared, her usually calm face distressed.

'What is it, Raffy?' she said, taking in his wild eyes and breathlessness. 'What in heaven is the matter?'

'There is revolution outside the palace,' he said. 'The wolf-boy, Lowe, has enlisted the stable boys and means to upturn the Celestial ruling.' He spoke theatrically, seeing Celeste's mouth open in shock.

'You must stay in here. Lock the door and don't unlock it until I say so.' He watched her face, waiting for some protest, but she merely nodded obediently, casting a look behind her.

'Cadmium is asleep – it would be unwise to move him

in any case,' she told Raphael. 'He must not be aware of what is going on. This is unprecedented!'

'I will alert the palace servants to stay on their guard. And send some up to secure your room.' He had no intention of doing such a thing, but if it meant his great parents were in their chamber, feeling safe – if oblivious – then so much the better.

'Don't put yourself at risk, will you, Raffy?' she said. 'Please take care.' With a worried smile she closed the door on him.

Raphael descended the stairs, taking two at a time, and to his annoyance bumped into one of the footmen, adjusting one of the portraits on the wall that flanked the steps.

'Your Highness.' The footman half bowed, but when he lifted his head his anxious expression was clear. 'There is a great deal of noise in the palace grounds – shouting and bawling. Do I need to call the palace security?'

Raphael shook his head. 'Just some high jinks from the stable boys.' He smiled. 'I believe one is soon to be a father – they have celebrated with a little too much grape juice.'

The footmen didn't look convinced. 'Are you sure you don't want me to—'

'No, no . . .' Raphael lowered his voice, practically

pushing the footman down the last few stairs to the hall. 'Nothing at all to worry about. Go to bed and sleep – it will all be but a memory in the morning.'

He watched the man go, realising he had only a short amount of time in which to carry out his most important task.

He winced at the sight of the carefully protected books in their glass cupboards. A childhood of respecting literature, both academic and for pleasure, made what he was about to do seem all the more barbaric.

First he opened a window, then he locked the library door from the inside. Then he turned out the lights. Thinking for a moment, he unlocked one of the cupboards, took out a book, and then re-locked the cupboard and pocketed the key. He opened the book at the page he had flagged the last time.

Raphael stood for a moment, taking a deep breath, taking one last look at perfection, then he took the stone he had collected from the kitchen gardens, and he smashed the glass in the cupboard before him, sending shards everywhere. He kept his eyes shut and one arm across his face, but a small splinter embedded itself in his cheek nonetheless. Refusing to feel the pain, he turned to the other cupboard and again attacked it. He didn't stop until all the glass had been smashed and the carpets were covered in shards.

He stopped. There was no sound from inside the palace. He waited, expecting to hear heavy footsteps, but nobody came. Exhaling with relief, he took the documents out of his pocket and spread them across the table. There in the moonlight, they exposed a connection, and lent themselves a significance that it would be difficult to overlook.

Finally, Raphael moved quickly to the open window, and carefully, stealthily he climbed out.

CHAPTER THIRTY-SEVEN

'It's been long enough.' Vanya paced her kitchen, glaring at Valdar, who was casually turning the pages of a newspaper. She directed her gaze at me, sitting anxiously at the table.

'I need to get home,' I said, aware that I sounded pathetic. And unhelpful.

'Yes. Yes I know that,' she snapped. 'Unfortunately I have not got the connection with you. You'll have to wait for Soren—' She stopped, looking a little frantic, for a second. 'And who knows what they have done with him.'

'So what do you suggest?' I asked her, stifling a yawn.

'We need to go and get him.' She marched to the cupboard just outside the kitchen and drew out a white hooded cape.

'Now?' Valdar lowered his paper. 'They won't let you see him now.'

'Oh, Raphael will, if I harangue him sufficiently.' She buttoned her cape at the neck and her dark hair spilled out, making her look like a devilish snow queen. 'Jane, get your . . . hood thing, and let's go.'

I rose robotically. I really didn't want to show my face at the palace again, but it seemed I had no choice. I glanced behind me, to see my hoodie lying crumpled on a leather armchair by the fireplace.

'Don't sulk, darling,' she said briskly. 'Do you want to get home or not?'

I nodded. 'But perhaps I should stay here and wait for you to come back with Soren . . .' I caught Valdar's eye and he smiled hungrily at me.

'Or maybe I should come along for support,' I said quickly, pushing my arms through the hoodie's sleeves.

'Good girl.' She ruffled Valdar's hair. 'I won't be long, sweetest.'

Valdar shrugged. 'I'd put a wager on it that you come back with your tails between your legs.'

'Well you know what they say,' she quipped, 'nothing ventured, nothing gained.'

Valdar picked up his paper again, shaking his head.

'Right.' Vanya drew some impossibly elegant white kid gloves on. 'Time to straighten this mess out, once and for all.'

Luca pulled on his horse's reins as the sound of breaking glass startled him.

'All right boy . . .' he stroked the horse's ears, dismounting. He was outside the Celestial Palace gates, on his way to finding his brother.

'What have you done?' he wondered, feeling breathless with alarm. He saw light by the side of the palace, and then saw – he thought he saw – a black jacketed figure there, running in the other direction.

'Lowe!' he shouted, then ran to the guard's box. The man on duty had dropped off to sleep.

'Hey!' He pushed at the man's arm, watching him slowly come to.

The guard grunted. 'Clear off,' he said, having assured himself that Luca was nobody important.

'Did you not hear that?' Luca asked him.

'Hmm.' The guard looked bemused. 'Hear what?'

'The . . .' Luca stopped. If Lowe was responsible, as idiotic as he was, better not drag the palace security in to the matter. 'Nothing,' he finished, stepping away. 'Nothing to worry about.'

The guard shook his head, frowning. He waved Luca away.

'Fed up of you young fools running around the palace

shouting,' he said. 'Some of us are trying to sleep.'

Luca forced a smile. 'Of course.' He walked back to his horse, wondering what was going on. The whole place was silent now. As he put his foot in the stirrup, he felt his unease growing. Where was his brother?

Something felt wrong.

CHAPTER THIRTY-EIGHT

We virtually ran down the cobbled street. The palace was a ten-minute walk away if I remembered right. I struggled to keep up with Vanya, who moved as though she was being propelled by jet force.

'If you weren't with me, of course, I would be there in a second,' she said, gripping hold of my arm. 'But as lovely as you are, you are simply to heavy for me to carry there.'

I pulled on her arm as best I could, since I had lost control of bodily movement. 'Vanya! Ten more minutes won't make much difference. Slow down.'

Flashing me an irritated look, Vanya reluctantly slowed her pace.

At that moment, the almost deafening sound of hooves hit us.

'What the . . . ?' Vanya shrunk back as four horsemen

appeared at the end of the street.

My heart rate increased. The rider in front looked suspiciously familiar.

'There!' he shouted, one hand holding on to the reins, the other pointing aggressively at Vanya and I. He thundered towards us, and I let out a small shriek, darting out of the horse's way.

His horse whinnying, Lowe smiled maliciously at the two of us and he pulled brutally on the reins to bring his the animal to an abrupt halt.

'Good grief,' Vanya said, regarding him distastefully. 'Shouldn't you be tucked up in bed, child?'

He snorted. 'You think you are above the law, you vampire crone,' he told her. 'Well I am here, under orders from the heir to the Celestial throne, to arrest the mortal.' He shot a look at me.

'Really,' Vanya sighed wearily. 'I wish to the devil you would get a female companion of your own, wolf-boy. Perhaps then you would not vent your adolescent hormones on innocent people.'

'Hush.' He put a finger to his lips, and I drew in my breath. Lowe had some guts, I'd give him that.

'I beg your pardon.' Vanya's nostrils flared, and I felt her tense beside me. 'How dare you speak to me like that!'

'I have authority to do what I like,' he said, hardly showing a trace of fear but for a subtle tremor in his hand as he held on to the reins. 'Celestial authority.'

My stomach dropped. 'What's happened? Has something happened at the palace?'

'It's time to cleanse Nissilum. Finally.'

'You haven't thought this through, have you, dear?' Vanya sighed. She looked around us. 'I mean, what exactly do you think you're going to do – a handful of stable lads?'

He shrugged. 'I will stop you. You were going to see that despicable vampire-boy, no doubt.' He chuckled nastily. 'I think Raphael has plans for him – may even have disposed of him already.'

'No!' Vanya and I said together.

I watched as Vanya's skin seemed to tighten and her pale face took on a translucent, shimmering quality; her lips blood red.

Blood red.

There was fear in Lowe's eyes as he took her in. Her eyes, blacker than coal, seemed to gleam, and he put his hand up to cover his own eyes.

'Vanya . . .' I whispered, not daring to touch her. 'Don't.'

'Don't look at me,' she hissed, 'if you want to stay safe.'

I moved away obediently.

341

And then there it was, the snap of her jaw, and her teeth, sharp and deadly.

'I told you,' she said, sounding guttural, 'you haven't thought this through . . .' She took a step closer to Lowe's horse, which reared away, panicked. His hands were holding on tightly, but he had no control over the animal now.

'You see, it takes enormous self-control not to sink my teeth into your miserable flesh on a daily basis,' Vanya snarled. 'It is a measure, I think, of my respect for Nissilum' – she took hold of the horse's snout in one hand – 'that I don't give in to what I am bound to be for ever.'

Even in the darkness Lowe's fear was unmistakeable. He swallowed, watching as Vanya took her hand away from the horse. At some distance, his companions were already turning their horses around in alarm.

'Next time you want to stage a rebellion, enrol the help of the big boys,' she said. She closed her lips and I saw her face return to normal, the gleam in her eyes disappearing.

'It will happen,' he said, headstrong to the last. 'Your days are numbered and you know it.'

'Oh shut up and get off your horse,' she said wearily. 'My companion and I need to be somewhere, now.'

He made no move to dismount.

'I said, get off your horse, boy!' she roared, and he scrambled off, standing, resentfully by while she climbed up.

'Come,' she said, holding out her hand to me. 'We haven't got much time.'

CHAPTER THIRTY-NINE

The palace was awake. Slipping through by the kitchen entrance, Raphael heard the sounds of footsteps running up the great staircase.

He hesitated. He needed to find his way up to his great-parents' room. But he couldn't be seen. The kitchen corridor was dark, silent. But how long before it was full of ruffled servants?

Quickly, he darted to the door leading into the hall. Looking around it, he saw with relief that it was deserted.

Soren was still locked away underneath the palace. Safe. He would deal with him later. No one could get to the boy without Raphael's authority.

He ran up the stairs, and headlong into a servant carrying some small brown bottles.

'Your Highness,' she said nervously, 'we have been looking for you . . .'

'What has happened?' he said, his face a picture of concern. 'It's the middle of the night.'

'Oh, there has been a break-in, master . . .' she stammered, clutching her bottles. I have just been to administer calm remedy to the Great Mother – she is very distressed.'

'Who . . . where have they broken into?'

'Into the library, sir, ' she went on. 'There is glass everywhere, master. A terrible sight.'

'Nobody has taken anything?' He eyed her. 'Is there anything strange?'

'I – I am not sure. The house butler is in there now. Are you well, sir ?' she pointed at the tiny cut on his cheek.

'Yes, thank you,' he said dismissively, pushing past her and on up the stairs. He glanced up the next flight to the floor where his great-parents were. But he had no time. He needed to get to the library.

Luca saw the lights go on, one by one in the palace. He frowned. There was no sign of his brother, or of Raphael. He had searched everywhere around the palace: the stables, the fields. He dropped to his knees, rubbing at his scalp anxiously. There was a throbbing in his head, a low deep throbbing that matched the beat of his heart. Shutting his eyes, he willed the thud to go away, but it persisted, and behind it a picture was forming. She was forming, as though thousands of tiny pixels were rushing together, making up her silky dark curls, and her eyes, grey like pretty slate.

Why had Jane come back so forcefully into his head? For months now, he had managed to keep the strength of his feelings for her at bay, replacing her with other things – his family, Lila. The right thing.

He somehow imagined that Jane had gone home . . . But it seemed she was still here. He could feel her presence, together with another, fiercer presence. The thud in his head reduced to a hum now – like a radio that continues to buzz after it has been turned off.

Luca lifted his head – the lights were still on. He saw shadows moving behind the windows. Was she in there somewhere? He bit his lip, thinking, and a moment later realised he had bitten so hard he had drawn blood. He could taste it, sweet and somehow a relief. A release of something.

No, Jane was not in the palace. But she could be somewhere locked up in the grounds . . . Underneath the palace, where prisoners were kept.

Luca got to his feet. The likelihood of him gaining access to the palace cellar was slim. Impossible, in fact. But he knew he had to try.

Turning the collar of his coat up, he glanced over at the trees where his horse was tethered. The animal would be all right for a while.

Luca approached the same guard he had spoken to earlier. As he hoped, the man was asleep. Luca peered into the box where he sat, looking up to the side where he found what he wanted: a large bunch of keys hanging on a hook. Reaching inside, he carefully unhooked them. Checking the guard was still snoring, he unlocked the palace gates as quietly as he could.

CHAPTER FORTY

As Raphael entered the library, he was careful to register shock on his face.

'What on earth . . . !' He scanned the room. 'How could anyone have got in here?' Then his gaze went across to the open window. 'Somebody left a window open.' He looked sternly at Sion, the chief butler, who held two shards of glass – one in each hand.

'I will find out who it was and they will be punished,' Sion said earnestly. He added the pieces of glass, one on top of the other, to a growing pile of shards on the floor.

Soren studied the table. The opened book, the documents, they were still there. He pointed at them.

'It seems they were after something . . .'

Sion frowned. 'I did see, yes . . . Your Highness.'

'This will need to be reported to the state police,' Raphael said authoritatively. 'Whoever broke in here was

348

looking for some kind of' – he turned the book around, pretending to read the open page for the first time – 'information, or – what's this?' He picked up the book. 'My father's death certificate and the reported case of the killer cub?'

'Master?' Sion came forward, peeling off the gloves he had been wearing. His brow creased as he took in what was there on the table, then looked up at Raphael. 'I know it was not made public knowledge, but I recall that terrible tragedy when I was a junior footman – people at the palace talk . . .' He shook his head. 'The boy cub was banished by – well, by your father, in fact, master. Gabriel ordered him to leave Nissilum. We all thought it was rather strange under the circumstances. That kind of massacre . . .' He trailed off, realising he had spoken out of turn.

But Raphael was pleased that Sion had been so forthcoming. Sion had provoked the very discussion he wanted. Except that he wanted it to be in front of his great-parents. He wanted Celeste and Cadmium to stop hiding the truth. A public confrontation would give them no choice.

It was unkind perhaps . . . But the alternative, to overthrow his family would be worse. And he wanted answers, not a battle.

Sion handed him a large plastic wallet with a zip.

'Perhaps this would be useful?' he said tentatively.

'You will be my witness,' Raphael told the man seriously. 'For this to be investigated, there needs to be a witness.'

'Of course.' Sion nodded.

'Witness to what?' A soft feminine voice spoke behind Raphael.

Celeste trod unsteadily into the room, seeing the glass still splintered on the floor. She inhaled a sharp breath, putting her hand on the door frame to support herself.

'We have had an intruder.' Raphael felt a lurch of compassion for her, whatever she had done. But his anger was still there. 'It seems they were looking for something . . .'

Celeste looked ashen. 'What in heaven . . . ?' Her eyes had alighted on Gabriel's death certificate. 'But this document has been stolen from the state files!' She moved forward, looking stronger. Raphael saw her glance quickly at the book, colour finally creeping into her cheeks. She looked up at him with fear, or shame visible in her expression.

'What I'm wondering is why they have left all of this out – for all to see?' he said, watching her carefully. 'What is the significance?'

Sion moved uneasily towards the door, clearly

sensing a family crisis and not wanting to be witness to that also. With a furtive look at Raphael, he disappeared out into the hall landing.

'Celeste,' Raphael said softly, now that they were alone, 'before this becomes public knowledge, before all this is sifted over and examined by those you have put in power to legislate, before that, perhaps you can tell me what this all means?'

'I . . .' She lifted a hand to her cheek, touching her flushed skin. 'I suppose I knew this would all come to light, eventually . . . I just didn't know how to tell you.'

'Well. The time has come.' He sighed, pulling out a chair for her. 'So tell me.'

CHAPTER FORTY-ONE

Vanya pulled Lowe's horse to a stop, right by a tree, where another horse was tethered. We were outside the palace.

On the ground I rubbed at my thighs, which were aching from the ride. Looking up, I saw the palace lights blazing.

'That's odd,' I said. 'It's late . . .' I looked at Vanya, who was a dramatic vision in her white cape. 'Something has happened.'

Vanya regarded the palace. 'Good. They will be too busy to notice us breaking out Soren.'

'The guards will notice. Unless you do that thing where you hypnotise them . . .'

'Glam them?' She grimaced. 'I'd rather not. I'm out of practise, and it is exhausting.' She thought for a moment. 'But a little persuasion might be in order.'

She took a pair of gloves out of her pockets, silky and white, and pulled them on up to her elbows.

'Intimidation chic,' I said, half smiling.

'I believe one should always look one's best – however unsavoury the task,' she said, looking me up and down. 'A philosophy you might want to adopt yourself, darling . . . No offence.'

'None taken.' I zipped up my hoodie. 'So, we need to get past him first.' I pointed at the man sitting in his little booth outside the palace, suspiciously slumped in his seat.

Vanya and I exchanged a look.

'Conveniently asleep,' she said, clasping her hands together. 'This might be a little easier than I thought.'

But as we approached the gates, we saw that they were already unlocked, swinging a little in the breeze.

I frowned. 'What's going on? Do you think Lowe got here first?'

'I can't think how, but we'd better hurry.' Vanya pulled her cape around her, pushing the gate open wider. 'I don't like the look of this.'

Luca gave the iron door one more push, but it was most definitely locked up and unrelenting. He pressed his forehead against its coldness. That thud was still

353

there in his head. The pictures more muddled and confusing now.

He turned and fell to his knees, leaning back against the door.

Voices – he heard voices. They weren't in his head, they were real. But Luca felt as though all the strength had been drained from him. He should move, but . . .

'I can't see how we will get to him.' A female voice . . . Luca's heart skipped a small beat as he recognised it.

'Leave that to me . . .' An older, also unmistakeable voice.

'Vanya?' Luca tried to get to his feet, but he couldn't move.

'Well.' Vanya rounded the corner and saw him first. 'You're the last person I expected to find here.' She stopped, turning slightly to her companion, who moved out from her shadow.

'Luca?' Jane stepped closer to him. 'What's happened? What are you doing here?'

They eyed each other. She was back to her normal self. No make-up, her dark hair curling messily over her shoulders. She looked beautiful. He tried not to stare at her, but he couldn't help himself.

'Have you seen the palace?' he asked hoarsely. 'Lights

on at this hour. There is some trouble brewing. I can't find my brother . . .'

'Last seen in the Celestial village,' Vanya told him, snippily. 'We relieved him of his . . . mode of transport.'

'What have you done to him?' Luca tried to stand again, but still his muscles were not obeying him. He saw Jane watching him, her eyes wide with concern.

'Nothing! That boy is pure poison,' Vanya shot back. 'Really, I know he's your flesh and blood, but he's a nasty piece of work.

Luca didn't bother to defend his brother. He could well imagine Lowe's behaviour. Relishing it, too.

'It doesn't make sense,' he said. 'Why would Raphael want to go against the Nissilum code?'

'Oh, I'm not remotely surprised about that.' Vanya brushed a stray lock of hair off her face. 'Once that boy officially ascends to the Celestial seat, I am sure he will reverse many of the state rulings. He has a great deal of anger issues.'

Jane bit her lip, and Luca could see she was trying not to smile at Vanya's turn of phrase. It was then, close up that he noticed the exhaustion in her face, in her grey-velvet eyes.

He just wanted to kiss those shadows away.

'Anyway. I'd love to stand around chatting, but I

need to get Soren out of that hellish little cell.' Vanya took a deep breath and advanced towards the iron door.

'Good luck with that,' Luca said flatly. 'That door is indestructible.'

'Have you tried knocking?' Vanya told him patronisingly. 'It is customary to knock if you want to be let inside.'

Luca rolled his eyes and, as he did so, he caught Jane's impish smile.

'I have been banging at that door for a good ten minutes . . .' He trailed off.

'Move,' Vanya ordered. 'Let me try.'

Luca obligingly got to his feet.

'Are you OK?' Jane asked softly.

Before he could reply, Vanya's voice peeled out shrilly.

'I demand you open this door immediately,' she said, banging hard on it.

Almost at once there was the sound of a key turning in the lock, and then the door creaked open, to reveal a young guard, rudely awoken by the looks of it.

'I'm sorry, madam, I have orders only to let the Celestial family in,' he said, nervously, as Vanya was glaring at him, her shoulders pulled back.

'Now listen to me, young man,' Vanya stuck one hand in the door jamb, ensuring that if the guard shut the door, it would be at the cost of her fingers, and woe betide him then. 'There is trouble at the palace – as we speak, there is quite a commotion going on. I have spoken to Raphael and he needs all the men he can get over there. He sent me personally to deliver this information.' She sniffed. 'He would have called, but there is no signal down in the cellars, as you must be aware.'

Her bluff was impressive, Luca thought, awed by Vanya's nerve.

The guard scratched his head, looking unsure.

'I don't know . . . I have a prisoner down in a cell. He needs constant surveillance. The master was very firm about that.'

'Which is exactly what we are doing here,' Vanya told him, before altering her tone to something a lot more gracious. 'The three of us.' She jerked her head back to indicate Luca and Jane. 'We will watch the prisoner.'

But the man looked thoroughly unconvinced – and with an exasperated sigh, Vanya glanced quickly behind her before her arm snapped out and her long fingers closed around the guard's throat.

Luca was appalled. He stood frozen to the spot.

'Now, listen to me . . .' Vanya leaned into the man, and Luca saw his eyes widen in what looked like shock, then lock in position, his mouth hanging open slack.

Her hand stayed where it was, her nails digging into his flesh and a glazed helpless look replaced the shock on his face. She released her hand and the glammed guard swayed a little. Then looking down at the keys in his hand, he opened the door wider, motioning for the three of them to go through.

'Thank you,' said Vanya, patting his chest. 'Now run along. Your prisoner will be safe with us.'

The guard moved passively past her, pausing only to say, 'He's dangerous, my lady. You'd best not provoke him.'

'Yes, I'm sure. Off you go.' She stared at him until he was safely outside, then gestured to Luca and Jane to follow her.

Only Vanya Borgia would be able to achieve the impossible, Luca thought.

'He is still here . . . that's the main thing. Raphael hasn't decided to inflict some sadistic punishment on him.' Vanya marched ahead, Luca and me in her wake.

'So it's true,' Luca asked. 'He really did that to his family? Why have I never heard of this . . . massacre? A wolf cub committing such a crime? It just seems strange that my family don't know about it.'

Vanya slowed in front of him. 'Well it was hushed up, of course,' she said quickly.

'Why "of course"?'

Vanya jangled the keys in her hand, stopping outside the cell door.

'Because of the disgrace,' she said. She was about to put the key in the lock but hesitated, turning to Luca, her face deadly serious. 'An angel fathering a wolf child? Not exactly something the family would want broadcast to the nation.'

'What?'

'His father is – was – an angel, darling. Mixing blood like that . . .' She shuddered melodramatically. 'Can you imagine the scandal.'

Luca turned to me and I saw the same shock I was feeling in his eyes.

'Gabriel,' I breathed. '*Gabriel* is Soren's father?'

CHAPTER FORTY-TWO

Celeste wrung her hands. 'Cadmium must not find out that I have told you,' she told Raphael. 'It would kill him.'

Raphael lowered his head, he didn't trust himself to look at her. He felt sick.

'I don't really care any more what Cadmium thinks,' he said in a low and threatening voice.

'Don't say that, dear. He did what he thought was best.'

'He watched my father tear himself apart,' Raphael snarled. 'Yet again, because of the laws of Nissilum. His own son, he made him pay for his involvement with that mortal girl.' He snapped back at her. 'We are not a good and forgiving family, we have no compassion. We are rotten.' He stood and paced the library, the glass breaking under his feet. 'And Soren lives to haunt me.'

'I dreaded the day he would return,' Celeste's voice shook. 'That night after the parade . . . I felt sick to my stomach.'

'He returned because he means to reclaim what he thinks is his – the kingdom,' said Raphael. 'It seems obvious to me.'

'I don't think he would do that,' she said meekly. 'Surely not?'

'How naïve are you, great-mother? You really think he came back to be reunited with Lila? Lila was just a convenient way to worm his way back into society – befriending the mortal girl, helping her, then convincing her to help him. All along he had his eye on the main prize.'

'Oh dear.' Celeste looked as thought she was about to faint. 'Is the boy still under lock and key?'

'Thankfully, yes. To think I nearly thought of releasing him. I entertained an idea that we could be allies . . . I had big plans you see.'

She said nothing, just looked questioningly at him.

'What did Cadmium do with him?' he said. 'Where is Gabriel?'

Celeste looked as though she were about say something vague, but hesitated, drawing in her breath, then: 'Gabriel is in the mortal world, Raffy . . . Your great-father sent

361

him there with Milo to take care of him. I have no idea where he is.'

'He's alive?'

'I don't know.' She looked down at her hands. 'I wish I knew.'

'You could go and find him. But your loyalty to Cadmium is greater,' Raphael said sarcastically. 'How noble!'

'What are you going to do now?'

'I'm going to make sure that Soren never sees his sister again, for one thing. And as for his share of the kingdom . . .' He shook his head. 'He will die before he has that.'

Noise from outside drew their attention to the hallway, where Sion was arguing with a young man Raphael recognised – the guard he had left watching Soren's cell. He frowned, moving quickly to interrupt them.

'What is this?' he asked. 'Has Soren escaped?'

'No sir . . .' the young man bowed awkwardly. 'The lady sent me over . . . She said you needed my help.'

'Lady? Who?'

'A lady with black hair and the blackest most bewitching eyes . . . She was very certain that you needed me here . . .'

'Heaven above!' Something snapped in Raphael's head

and a rush of adrenaline shot through his veins. 'Fool! I told you not to leave your watch, on any account!' He stepped up to the guard, glaring at him, his fists clenched. He turned his glare on to Sion, who looked alarmed. 'Round up all male servants – and if you see Lowe, the wolf-boy, tell him I want everyone armed.'

'Raphael?' gasped Celeste behind him. 'You cannot use force. We are a peaceful people.'

'To hell with you and your "peace",' he snarled as he marched angrily down the hall landing. 'To hell with *you*.'

CHAPTER FORTY-THREE

'Oh, darling, you look awful.' Vanya rushed towards Soren, who did indeed look awful.

'I'm fine,' he said, though he looked shattered. 'I've endured worse.'

She knelt by him, tenderly, and I glanced at Luca, who was regarding Soren, closely examining his face.

'It's true then,' he said, as Vanya cooed and fussed over the boy. 'You really did that?'

'It was a long time ago.' Soren's eyes found mine and I felt myself squirming a little, remembering what had happened between us in the palace library. We hadn't spoken since, and with the warmth of Luca's body next to me, I felt a little sick. I looked away, hoping that my cheeks weren't burning.

'You don't look . . . you don't look like a wolf . . .' Luca said suspiciously. 'Not like any wolf I've seen. I could have sworn—'

'Well, appearances can be deceptive,' Vanya interrupted, a distinct edge to her voice. 'Don't dwell on petty details.'

But it was true. Soren's black eyes, his complexion . . . Pure vampire. I looked at Vanya and then back at Soren.

I suddenly remembered the canvas in Paris. The dark-haired woman. It was *Vanya*.

'You're *Vanya's* son!' I breathed. 'I can't believe I did not see it before . . .'

'Jane—' Vanya began soothingly.

'No . . .' Luca edged closer to me. 'Jane's right, Vanya. And now that I see you, so protective, so fierce in your defence – just like my own mother. Soren is your son.'

There was a heavy, shocked silence. I don't know why but I felt horribly betrayed. As though Vanya and Soren had been in on a joke behind my back.

'I don't know what you are up to,' said Luca, and his hand brushed against mine, so close that I wanted to grab hold of it, 'but how do I know that this whole story isn't false? You have seized on a conveniently buried murder to somehow cause trouble here? The two of you.'

'You don't know what you're talking about!' Vanya stood defiant.

'Vanya, don't.' Soren put his hand on her arm.

'You want the truth? Then, yes, Soren is my child . . . But he was brought up as a wolf cub. He was raised by a family who were paid by his true father to keep silent about his birth parents. Myself . . . and Gabriel.'

'This has got to be a joke!' I said, and felt Luca's hand tighten on mine. 'How? How did . . . ?'

Soren was grim-faced. 'I loved Lila like I was truly her brother. I missed her when she was no longer there. And I felt so – broken up by what she saw.'

'You fed on your family didn't you? You didn't kill them as a wolf would have done. You fed on them, and then you left them to bleed to death.' Luca was aghast.

'Lila wasn't the real reason you wanted to help me . . .' I eyed him. 'Are you planning to claim your right to power? If Gabriel is your father, you would be entitled—'

'No – I don't care about that! Lila is the only reason I am here, Jane. That, and you—'

'Stop!' I put my hands over my ears, frightened of what he would say. Looking quickly at Luca, I shook my head. 'I need to get out of here . . .' I breathed. 'It's all too much.'

'Jane!' Luca held on to me, concerned. 'Don't go.'

'I just need some air,' I said, dropping my hand. 'Let me be. Just for a moment. Let me be.'

I ran. I didn't want to leave Luca, but I felt suffocated by the whole situation. And ashamed. I regretted that moment in the library with Soren – more than anything now. While I was gone, Soren would no doubt tell Luca what had happened. He had been about to, I was sure of it.

The door to the basement was open, and with relief I burst out into the palace courtyard, running as fast as I could for the gates.

But before I could get there, an arm hooked itself roughly around my neck, dragging me backwards, and my heart nearly jumped up through my throat.

'It's over.' A voice whispered, dark and guttural, in my ear as I struggled. 'Nowhere to run to now.'

I stopped my futile wriggling and my attacker released his hold, just a little.

'Lowe,' I said, 'I am going home. You don't need to do this.'

He turned me round roughly to face him. 'I'm going to make sure you never come back,' he said nastily. 'I won't be content until I know you are gone for good.'

I looked into his brown eyes. Unlike his brother's, they were steely and aggressive. It occurred to me that he wanted to kill me. Looking down at his body I saw the familiar chilling signs I had been dreading.

Lowe was about to turn.

Should I scream? Who would hear me? Would Luca? I swallowed. Lowe seemed to be battling with what was happening to him. He even leaned on me for support, putting the full weight of his body on me. I nearly collapsed then, but I saw a chink of hope. I stood back, and Lowe staggered forward, the jacket on his back tearing, an angry growl coming from him as he bent in pain.

Seizing my chance, I ran. Faster than I had ever run before, slipping through the gates and out into the acres of black night in front of the palace. My heart was beating so fast I thought it would explode, and I needed to think fast. I had to go where Lowe wouldn't find me. But not knowing the layout of the palace grounds, I was stabbing in the dark.

The piercing roar coming from the courtyard hardened my resolve, and sharpened my wits.

And adrenaline sent me running for my life.

CHAPTER FORTY-FOUR

Raphael was thwarted on his way to the cellars by the sight of a lone wolf roaming the courtyard. He shrunk back a little, unused to this animal display, but the wolf appeared to be gazing at him, imploringly, and he frowned, waving the beast away, horrified.

With a final look at him, the wolf roared, pawing at the hard ground, before moving stealthily out of the courtyard – to Raphael's relief.

'How in heaven did he get in?' he muttered, though he couldn't pause to think about that now. Seeing the wolf bounding out into the darkness, he turned to continue on to the cellars. Cursing, he saw the outside door wide open. As he clattered down the stone steps, he was met with silence.

The door to Soren's cell was wide open. The cell was empty.

Raphael shut his eyes, his lip curling. In his hand he clutched a crossbow. Violently he kicked at the door.

Glancing down at the floor he saw something. A white feather. He frowned, picking it up curiously, turning it over in his hand. A memory came back to him. His parents, Gabriel and Dorcas laughing. Dorcas had dressed him as a fictional angel with white feather wings . . . He had only been about five. He remembered the look on his father's face. Amused, loving. He remembered his own enjoyment. He swallowed. Memories such as this he had pushed away for so long. His heart had become so hard, so cynical. All innocence lost.

One of his headaches was coming on, pulsing at the back of his head. He sat down on the hard wooden bench inside the cell, leaning back against the wall, too defeated to move from the time being. Alone in the cold basement, he saw suddenly the pointlessness of going after his half-brother. And he had a sudden and lucid epiphany.

Had he not engineered this whole situation himself? Planted the right evidence – to bring all this to a head? He had not expected to hear that Gabriel had fathered a child outside of his marriage to his mother, Dorcas. But it made more sense that Dorcas had run away, unable to face the Celestial family. Now that he was adapting to the information, a tiny part of him felt intrigued that he had a half-brother. In his heart Raphael knew that, for all his outrage at the dishonesty his great-parents had shown, they had done it to protect him from the truth. And who was he to stand on such moral highground, when he would deny his flesh and blood the same chances that he had had?

He no longer cared if his position was threatened here at the palace. The only thing he cared about was being reunited with the man who had been dealt the harshest sentence of all.

His father, Gabriel.

CHAPTER FORTY-FIVE

I felt my way through the bushes, sharp thorns pricking at my hands. Out of nowhere, it had started to rain hard. Rubbing at the drops on my cheeks, I knew my only hope of getting home was to find Dalya, but it was so late and I had run straight into the woods behind the palace – the opposite direction to where she and Luca lived. And then I had run out of steam, just stopped and slid to my knees where I hoped I would be hidden, undiscovered, until daylight . . . But after an hour or so the sounds of people had me up and on the move again.

'Soren!' I heard someone shout – a throaty female voice. 'Don't waste your time. She is long gone by now.'

Vanya and Soren? Where was Luca? Had they done something to him?

I shut my eyes in the darkness, and my breath came thick and heavy. But the voice was fading. Opening my eyes again, I peered through some leaves and saw Vanya's white cape as she disappeared in pursuit of Soren.

I had thought Vanya was on my side. I had actually thought she and Soren were my friends. But they were keeping things from me. All these lies.

As I started walking again, I felt a sharp pain in my ankle. I must have knocked it and not felt it. All that adrenaline masking the pain. I winced as an agonising twinge hit me again, and tried to take the weight off one foot, limping a little, slowly this time, and then there above me, a small patch of sky through the trees.

As I pushed forward, I heard voices – far away, and shouting but there all the same. Who knew who they belonged to? Raphael and his crew? Lowe?

Panicking, I turned as quickly as I could in the other direction, lamely kicking away the raspy thorns, before something, flying through the trees ahead, stopped me in my tracks.

A crossbow quivered in the trunk of the tree to my left, and then my breath seemed to stop. Putting my hand to my mouth, I stared wide-eyed at the weapon, swallowing back fear.

'There's someone there.'

A voice, familiar somehow, came through the dark. I shut my eyes trying to place it.

'Over there somewhere.'

The voice was closer now. I stepped back, drawing some foliage in front of my face. I was shaking.

As I watched, two figures moved into my line of vision. One I didn't recognise walked over to the arrow in the tree and plucked it. He turned to his companion, whose back was to me now.

'No need to waste a good piece of weaponry.' The boy with the arrow spoke.

'Indeed not.' His companion, taller, dark-haired, took the weapon from him, sticking it in a holder on his back. In one hand I saw he carried a crossbow. But my attention was drawn to something else now.

Lowe?

I pushed myself back and met with a tree. I sank to my knees as noiselessly as possible. The beating of my heart seemed impossibly loud to me.

'She is somewhere out here.'

Lowe's voice was crisp now, imperious. Dangerous.

Wrapping my arms about my body, I crouched hidden, listening.

'She is not our target . . .' the other boy was saying. 'Raphael said—'

'Raphael is taking care of the vampire,' growled Lowe. 'I want the girl.'

Even through the bushes I saw the other boy frown.

'The girl? What crime has the girl committed? She is no one.'

'She is poison. She flaunted herself here with Soren. She was just using him. And while she's still here, she will have her sights on Luca. To take him from his wife, from his family. You saw her—'

'Lowe!' The boy's voice was steady, humouring. 'This is madness. What harm can the mortal girl do? Luca is perfectly safe and happily engaged. Why would he go to her?'

Lowe was silent, kicking at the undergrowth with his boot.

I was aware of exhaustion taking me over, but I couldn't afford to give in to it.

Nonetheless I pushed one leg, which threatened to cramp, out from underneath me, rustling the leaves as I did so.

The boys' heads both jerked in my direction.

'Who's there?'

Lowe stepped roughly, closer to where I was. He couldn't yet see me. I held my breath, a light sweat covering my body.

'It is no one.' The boy took hold of Lowe's arm, gently pulling him back. 'Just the wind.'

From my position I could see Lowe glowering straight at me. But he couldn't see me. His eyes didn't find mine.

'Come,' said the boy, still holding on to him, his eyes wary. 'You are weary, Lowe. Let me take you back to the palace.'

'Don't patronise me.' Lowe hissed. 'I meant what I said, you know.'

'I know.' The boy's voice was soft, coaxing . . . He stopped, and all three of us saw another body approaching through the trees. As the moon moved to become visible above us, the newcomer's inky-black hair was unmistakeable.

Soren. I hated him, but I couldn't deny the relief I felt seeing him.

'Well, well.' He stopped, putting his hands in his pockets.

Lowe's face twisted with hostility.

'You?' he said icily. 'You are not a werewolf. I have never heard of you. Nobody has. Lila doesn't know who you are either – whatever fantasies you have fed her.'

He drew an arrow from its case on his back and stepped boldly in front of Soren, who looked utterly unfazed.

Soren ignored the crossbow. 'But since you are so desperate to know . . .'

Both boys straightened defensively.

'I . . . I am whoever I want to be.' Soren went on just loudly enough for me to hear.

Lowe was gripping his crossbow, his body was rigid, tense. He glanced quickly at his companion. From where I was positioned I could see he was afraid.

'I don't understand.'

'It doesn't matter whose blood runs through me,' Soren went on. 'Unlike you, I don't allow my ancestry to dictate who I am.' He paused, watching their incomprehension. 'And neither does Raphael. Somebody you admire, I think?'

'What are you talking about? You're insane!' Lowe snorted. His friend, however, looked shocked as he stared hard at Soren.

'No need to be afraid,' Soren continued calmly. 'Raphael may have grown tired of the angelic philosophy, but he seems to quite like you.'

'Don't speak of him. You are nothing. A fool. A fantasist.'

Soren smiled broadly in answer, infuriating Lowe even further.

'Jane used you.' Lowe lifted his chin defiantly. 'To get to my brother.'

'Is that so?' asked Soren.

'She just can't take no for an answer. Hanging around

here, trying to make him jealous and regret his decision.'

The smile stayed fixed on Soren's face. It was starting to bug me, God knew what effect it was having on Lowe.

'She's the only person on Nissilum whose agenda is pure,' Soren said. He couldn't see me, didn't know I was hiding . . . I held my breath. Had I misjudged him?

'But what's your game?' Lowe insisted. 'Lila has never met you before in her life.'

'Don't speak of her again,' Soren told him icily. 'Lila deserves better than to have you as part of her family. I would not have believed what a poisonous little fool you were until I witnessed your malice with my own eyes. But now that I have seen it, I know for sure she is better off with me.'

'Nonsense! She and my brother are in love,' snarled Lowe.

'Oh, grow up!' Soren finally snapped. 'Stop meddling in the happiness of others. It is not Lila that Luca loves. There is nothing you can do about that.'

Lowe was silenced, but I saw his hand tighten on his crossbow.

Slowly I eased myself up on to my feet. My breath was coming more evenly now. There was a good chance Lowe would aim his weapon at me if he saw me, but Soren's presence emboldened me. When I was upright, I leaned carefully up against the tree behind me.

'I will do what it takes to protect my family.' Lowe said weakly, anxious to have the last word.

Soren sighed, and I watched as his eyes roamed about him, until finally he settled on me.

'Jane?'

I moved forward, keeping my eyes on the crossbow still in Lowe's hand. His face was set angrily.

'Lucky for you that your little lapdog is here to protect you,' he said nastily.

'I don't need protection,' I said. 'And I am trying to get home.' I glared at him. 'So, you will get what you want . . . Please, stop your whining about it!'

Lowe's eyes widened.

'And finally we see the real girl,' he said smoothly. 'Not so nice, are you?' He shook his head. 'If my brother could see you now!'

The snap of a twig startled us all.

'I can see her perfectly well,' came a voice behind Soren and I felt my heart crash to the ground. Luca, soaking wet from the rain, walked past Soren and towards his brother. 'It's you who disgusts me right now.'

'Me?' Lowe snarled. 'All the games she has played, and it is I who disgusts you?'

'You have always been impetuous,' Luca said, his eyes

flickering briefly over to me as he spoke. 'But you have grown malicious. Clumsy . . .' His voice trailed off. I knew it pained him to talk that way. About his own flesh and blood.

Watching his tall, almost too skinny body, his hair a little wild from the rain, I wanted to walk up to him and put my arms around him. I wanted to look into his sad green eyes, the eyes that had looked at me with love, only months before.

But he turned away from me, refusing to catch my eye. He now faced Soren.

'I appreciate you taking care of Jane,' I heard him say, 'but there is no need any longer.'

I saw Soren's eyes, black as coal, flashing in something like confusion, though I couldn't read his response properly.

'I don't think she wants to leave, Luca,' he said. 'She hasn't got what she came for.'

I winced, cursing Soren's directness. I wanted to explain, but I had run out of words. It seemed I had nothing left in me to convince Luca. I didn't want to convince him. I wanted him to come to me of his own accord.

But Luca didn't respond to Soren's words.

'Brother, this boy is dangerous,' Lowe cut in. 'A demon.'

'Lowe, be quiet.' Luca spoke with authority.

'I'm going.' I said. 'I'm going home.'

'Jane,' Soren said, 'don't be foolish. Let me help you.'

'I told you,' Luca said, silencing him with his tone, 'she no longer needs your help.' Taking his eyes off Soren, he settled them on me. 'She's got me.'

'Luca?' I didn't dare read any meaning into what he had said. 'Go and find Lila. She needs you more than I do.'

He shook his head. 'I know now that Soren was telling the truth. Lila was there the day he murdered her family . . . And she has spent the last twelve years in a state of denial.'

'But I thought you didn't believe him?' I said. 'What changed your mind?'

'Because Henora and Ulfred have just had a monumental argument. In fact the reason I did not get here sooner was because Henora stormed out into the night in tears. Ulfred told her she had to tell me the truth.' He hesitated. 'That she and Hanni both knew about Lila's family . . . But Henora couldn't bring herself to spoil everything by telling her about Soren . . . Saul.'

Lowe looked like a petulant child about to stamp his foot.

'I think you should go to Lila,' Luca said quietly to

Soren. 'She is waiting for you at my home.'

As Lowe started to protest, Luca cut him short with a wave of his hand. 'Keep out of it, brother. I'm warning you.'

Scowling, Lowe shoved his crossbow into his companion's hands and they stomped after Soren. Soon all three boys had disappeared out of the woods.

Luca moved through the undergrowth towards me until he stood inches away. Lifting his hand, he touched my cheek gently, tracing up and down it as he used to and I leaned my head against his hand like a cat.

'I'm so sorry,' he whispered. 'You've been through too much.'

'It's been . . . an adventure,' I said, managing a smile. 'My mother would call it "character building".'

'She's a wise woman, your mother,' he said, a hint of sadness in his voice. 'How I wish I could run from all this and—'

'But you can't.' I said, enjoying being able to examine his face at such close proximity. Taking in his soft green eyes.

He hesitated before speaking. 'Everything I thought I believed in has proved a little flimsy.' He moved closer and took hold of my hands. 'The only thing that has stood firm – like a rock in troubled waters – is you.'

CHAPTER FORTY-SIX

Raphael's horse was waiting for him, patiently. Stroking the animal's soft coat, he lay his head against it.

'I'm tired,' he said out loud, 'but it's not over yet . . . Not for me.' He lifted his head, looking around the sweet-smelling stable. He would saddle up the horse and go for one last ride. Dawn was breaking, the Celestial grounds were beautiful at this time. The last time.

'Running away?' A voice in the stable doorway cut into his thoughts.

He turned. 'He's free,' he told her. 'Soren. He is free to do as he likes.'

Vanya stepped inside, her nose quivering a little disdainfully at the smell of horse and hay.

'He has no wish to take your place,' she said. 'He has spent a long time in the wilderness. Searching for his family.'

'Well he killed them,' he said. 'He has no family. My father—'

'Your father is long gone.' Vanya's tone softened. 'It's time you learned to live with that, don't you think?'

'I am going to find him. I am going to the mortal world. He is there somewhere.'

She took a breath. 'Raphael, your father chose another way. You need to be your own man – stop living in his shadow. It is not right that he abandoned you. But you can be a better man.'

'I have nothing left here,' he said flatly. 'And what do you know of my father? You don't understand.'

'More than you imagine.' Still wearing her white cape, she drew it around her. 'He didn't even acknowledge Soren as his son . . . not properly.'

Raphael studied her. 'What is Soren to you?' he asked. 'Or do you thrive on picking up waifs and strays?'

She was silent, though her face gave away some feeling.

He stepped closer. 'Or are you part of this terrible secret too.'

And then in her eyes he saw tears – though she was struggling not to give into emotion, there were tears.

'He is my son too,' she said hoarsely. 'There. Now you have it. The full gruesomeness of your half-brother's heritage. A vampire and an angel all in one.'

'Gabriel,' he breathed, falling against the stable wall, making his horse whinny in concern. 'Oh, Gabriel!'

'Soren doesn't want any of what you have. Why would he?' she said again. 'He is a free spirit, and he could not be bound by the suffocating rules that come with that position. All he wanted was to see the girl.' She sighed. 'I admit, he drew Jane into his plans. Before he knew it, he was involved in some other game . . .'

He is a better man than I, thought Raphael. *He would make a better king.*

'He did a good thing,' he said seriously. 'A noble thing. Jane and Luca deserve to have happiness together. True happiness.'

'I must go . . . I left Soren on his way to see Lila. But then he will be gone from Nissilum too, and he wants to take her with him. He knows he is not welcome here. And I would like to say goodbye. I may never see him again.' Vanya turned to leave.

'No,' Raphael said firmly. 'He should stay. With Lila. It is their home.'

Vanya stopped, her shoulders relaxing, before turning back.

'Thank you,' she said, with a grateful smile. 'That's . . . gracious of you.'

He shrugged, then dug his hand into his pocket and drew out the white feather.

'Here,' he held it out to her. 'This is for you.'

CHAPTER FORTY-SEVEN

The sun was shining brilliantly as the three of us threaded our way through the tall trees. It seemed like a million years since I had been here last. When we reached the Water Path, I turned to Dalya and drew her close, hugging her tight.

'Goodbye, sweet Dalya,' I said, my voice muffled, buried in her hair. 'I hope I see you soon.'

Dalya pulled away. 'But I am so happy.' She beamed. 'And I will visit you.'

Before I could make sense of this, Luca cut in.

'Remember what I said,' he told her a little gruffly as he stood and watched the two of us. 'Look after Henora and Ulfred – and try not to provoke Lowe.'

She grimaced. 'I can't bear to even look at him,' she said. 'He has behaved like a fool.'

'Maybe he will grow up a little now that I . . .' He

didn't finish his sentence.

She shrugged. 'Henora will be fussing over him now. She won't admit it, but she is remorseful for everything she put you through. She and Ulfred had words.'

She was talking as though Luca no longer existed. I glanced at him bemused.

'She meant well.' Luca moved forward and embraced his sister. Watching the girl's arms clinging to him, I felt a lump form in my throat. It was as if they were saying a proper goodbye. I turned away, pretending to focus on a clump of ferns growing by the water.

When I turned back, Dalya had disappeared – as if by magic.

'Dalya doesn't care for goodbyes,' said Luca.

'But you'll be back again in no time, unfortunately.' I sighed, knowing this was the way it had to be.

Luca was staring at me intently. 'I am the happiest I have ever been,' he said. 'I feel as though every bit of pain has been worth it for this – this second chance.' He reached out and took hold of my arms, almost forcefully pulling me close to him.

I caught my breath, pushing my fingers through his, lifting my chin as he dropped his so that our mouths were centimetres apart.

'I never stopped loving you, surely you must know

that,' he said. 'I love you, more than anything in this world or yours.'

'That's a lot of love,' I said, seeing the creases at the corners of his eyes as he smiled.

'Yet it still seems inadequate,' he said softly, taking my face in his hands and kissing me; a long, soft and tender kiss.

Eventually I pulled away. 'What will happen now here?'

He shrugged. 'I don't know. Raphael has a lot to take in. If Soren stays, then everyone will know that there is a half-vampire half-angel boy who has been denied by the Celestial family.'

'Imagine, a vampire ruling Nissilum!' I said, shaking my head. 'It's going to change everything.'

Luca took me in his arms and held me, and I exulted in his familiar smell, burying my head in his chest, and feeling the tension finally seep out of my body.

'It doesn't matter to me,' he said, stroking my hair back, 'because I won't be here.'

I lifted my head, pulling gently away. 'You won't?'

'No.' He lifted my chin with his fingertip. 'I will be with you.'

I let out a small incredulous gasp. 'Really! You want to come and live on mortal Earth?'

'I want to live wherever you are.' He kissed me fiercely then, and I finally gave in to all the feelings I had suppressed for months, kissing him back hungrily and passionately.

'For the rest of our lives . . . However long that is . . . For the rest of our lives.'

DARK HEART FOREVER

When Jane Jonas develops a friendship with an enigmatic stranger in town, it's exciting, it's new, and Jane wants him more than she's ever wanted anybody – until her mystery dream boy gets in the way.

Now Jane is caught between two worlds: one familiar, but tinged with romance and excitement; the other dark and dangerous, where angels, werewolves, and an irresistible stranger are trying to seduce her …

TWO LOVES, ONE DEADLY CHOICE.

DARK HEART FOREVER

LEE MONROE

Sisters Red

'The wolf opened its long jaws,
rows of teeth stretching for her.
A thought locked itself in
Scarlett's mind: I am the only
one left to fight, so now, I must
kill you ...'

An action-packed, paranormal
thriller in a gritty urban setting,
with a charming love story and
unexpected twist that leaves you
wanting more!

If you've got a thirst for
fiction, join up now

bookswithbite.co.uk

Packed with sneak peeks, book trailers, exclusive
competitions and downloads, **bookswithbite.co.u**
is the new place on the web to get your fix of
great fiction.

Sign up to the newsletter at
www.bookswithbite.co.uk
for the latest news on your favourite authors,
to receive exclusive extra content and the
opportunity to enter special
members-only competitions.